"*Layers* is so much more than a story; it's an *experience*. No book has ever affected me as deeply as Gennie Lynne's. *Layers* will forever be a personal favorite and one that I will read time and time again. Guaranteed."
Erica Mimran Sherlock,
author of *Through Quick and Quinn*

"Just when you think you know the storyline, Gennie surprises you with another beautifully written layer that you never see coming. *Layers* is the book you won't want to put down and one that will continually pull at your heart strings long after you put it down."
Dequindre Jernigan,
author of *Love Through the Storm* and *Still Love Remained: The Choice*

Noted Themes From Readers

"No matter what path we choose to take, God's plans for our life will still be completed." K, 37 years old
Bank Branch Manager

"God doesn't make bad things happen, but He uses them for good." H, 18 year old high school senior

"God's timing is impeccable, and we need to trust Him and allow Him to work things out." G, 18 year old high school senior

"Redemption, grace, and healing"
T, 66 years old Retired High School Counselor

Content Warnings listed on page 297

Layers

The Glass Factor Series

Gennie Lynne

STARLIGHT CLIMBER
Publishing

You may contact us at theglassfactor@yahoo.com.

IG @gennie_lynne_author
YouTube @TheGlassFactor

Identifiers:
ISBN: 979-8-9926522-0-8 (Paperback)
ISBN: 979-8-9926522-1-5 (Hardcover)
ISBN: 979-8-9926522-2-2 (ePub)
Library of Congress Control Number: 2025907196

Cover design by Gennie Lynne
Published in the United States of America

Dedicated to my family.

Your constant encouragement, ideas, and support keep me fueled.

  Love you more.

"For now we see through a glass darkly;
but then face to face:
now I know in part;
but then shall I know even as I am known.
       1 Corinthians 13:12 KJV

If this book saves but one life, prayers have been answered.

Dear Reader,

Please know that I have prayed for you long before you held this book in your hands. I have constantly prayed that God would steer you towards this story, and it would touch you in some way. Prayers for healing, understanding, and forgiveness. Prayers for you and how it will allow you to look at others in your life along with yourself.

When the story began in my head, I knew I wanted symbolism throughout the entire story, including the town's name. I wanted to write a story that would approach the lost issue of giving each other grace. I've always thought if we could all be transparent with each other, how much more would we understand each other? What is more transparent than glass?

When I discovered there was an unincorporated community at Glass, Texas, I was thrilled! My family and I took a long weekend to visit the area and fell in love with the beauty of it all. I knew that was the perfect setting for my book and, hopefully, more to come.

Welcome to Glass, Texas. I hope you enjoy the journey as much as I have enjoyed creating it for you.

Gennie Lynne

Layers

Prologue Annie

First Week of August
Twenty-Eight Years Ago

*A*nnie, *you will always have choices no matter what situation you find yourself in. It won't be easy, and there won't always be an obvious answer, but always make sure your decision is worth it. No matter what you choose, the result of other possibilities could haunt you long afterward, so weigh all your options carefully.*

Grandpa's words of wisdom flashed through Annie's mind as the front windows of the old house rattled when she slammed the door behind her. One last reminder to her parents of how unfair they were being yet again. She was determined to choose a better life for her own children one day. What if her parents had made different choices in the beginning? How different would her life be?

When Annie reached her chevy truck, she quickly checked her hair in the side mirror. The sweltering Texas morning was already causing wisps to frizz at the sides of her face. Her chestnut-brown eyes stared back at her. When she was mad, their darkness intensified.

Wiping away her smeared mascara, she reminded herself to stop furrowing her brow. She did not want a wrinkle to form between them. She swiped her hair back over her shoulder and made sure all her orange butterfly clips were still in place. Her mousy brown hair had lightened up quite a bit from all the chlorine in the pool this summer. Her tanned skin was the darkest it had ever been in her brief life. Spending every free afternoon at the town pool had been worth it. That her crush worked there was an added bonus.

Annie heard the front door swing open. Prepared for a verbal assault, she turned to face it, only to see her four-year-old brother waving goodbye. She longed to whisk her two younger brothers away and find a job somewhere that would enable her to take care of all of them. But she knew there was no way that could ever happen.

"I'll see you in the mornin', Tater Tot!" She blew him a kiss. Tate caught it in the air and slapped his own forehead in the same spot she always kissed him good night. She told him it was his love spot right next to his brain.

She heard her mom yell at him to shut the door. Apparently, he was letting all the cool air out, so Annie waved him back inside. Her anger washed back over her. *Why do they care what I do? They never care about anything else.* They had already lived their lives as far as Annie was concerned.

Her dad, smelling like a sewer, popped a beer as soon as he walked in from working under people's houses all day. They knew not to address him until he had at least three beers, and the third was usually drunk in the shower.

Her mom wasted her day away sleeping in and watching soap operas. Annie couldn't remember the last time she had seen her mom smile. All the chores were saved for Annie and her little brothers for the weekend. Her mom yelled commands from her spot on the couch, and the three of them were trained to obey or else face the consequences.

Annie typically fixed cereal for both breakfast and supper for herself and her brothers while her parents splurged on frozen meals. The house felt suffocating, and she was tired of being cooped up with them. *They are always trying to ruin my life.*

Annie drew in a deep breath to get her mind on her plans for the evening. She had just celebrated her sixteenth birthday and finally had an escape with the truck her grandpa had given her. At least she didn't have to rely on her parents or her friends to go anywhere now.

She tugged on the truck door and slid up onto the bench seat. Annie reached towards the dash panel, aiming to straighten the old photograph of herself as a six-year-old sitting in the back of this same truck. A big red barn filled the background. A slight smile flickered on her face. Annie had fond memories of riding on Grandpa's lap and helping him drive around the fields to tend to the animals. "Grandma has all these animals to keep me busy and out of the house," he always joked.

When Mom and Dad were not watching, Grandpa would let her steer. He even let her shift from park to drive sometimes, even though it would take both of her hands to have enough strength to do it.

After he purchased a new tractor, Grandpa's 1971 red Chevrolet truck sat in his barn for almost a decade. This past summer, when Annie mentioned she wanted a car, her parents refused to buy her one. Grandpa suggested they fix up the old truck. She had worked at the farm with him every morning for the past two months to earn enough money to buy the extra parts that the truck needed to run.

It was not a thing of beauty, but it was hers. All hers. And she planned for it to take her away from here.

Tonight would help take Annie's mind off of her problems. She honked the horn as she pulled into Liza's long, dirt driveway. How she loved this house. The flowers and rocks lining the sidewalk seemed to always be in bright bloom, no matter the season.

Liza's mom had shared with her that this was where she did a lot of her praying. She loved getting her hands in the dirt, tending to each plant. "You know, Annie," she explained, "God always has His hands on you and every part of your life. He tends to you just like I tend to my flowers, watching over every detail and working it for His glory." As she switched to the next plant, she would switch the person for whom she was praying.

She must pray for lots of people, Annie thought to herself, looking at the long row of mixed colors. She wondered which plant was where she was prayed for each time, hoping it was the purple ones.

"Mom was worried that we would skip lunch, so she packed us some sandwiches. She made peanut butter and jelly, your favorite." Liza gushed as she clambered up into the truck. Her blonde bobbed hair always looked just as perky as Liza acted. She was probably the shortest girl in the upcoming junior class but had the biggest heart of the whole high school.

The sun reflected off Liza's braces as she smiled, and her blue eyes almost seemed to burst off her petite face. Annie did not understand how her face could remain so porcelain for as much time as they had spent at the pool the past couple of months.

Liza dug through the sack once she got settled. "She also threw in some chips and some homemade chocolate chip cookies. I told her we would stop at Rick's Drive-In to grab a cherry vanilla Dr. Pepper on the way."

Annie put her truck in reverse and let out an enormous sigh. "Your mom is the best! Sometimes I think feeding people is her love language." Annie was not sure what her own mom's love language would be. Maybe sharing every detail about her daily soap operas was her way of reaching out, but Annie would find every excuse she could to escape those conversations.

The directions that Annie had written from her friend had a missed turn, and they ended up having to backtrack down the highway. This allowed Annie more time to get her mind right for the party.

"I know your parents don't really tell you, but I know they love you." Liza had listened to Annie describe the fight of the day and searched for the right words to lift Annie's mood. "I just think that they do the best that they know how to do right now."

These were the same words that Liza's parents had used when trying to calm Liza's concerns about Annie one day after school last year. She and her parents prayed for Annie and her family every night before supper.

"What would I ever do without you in my life?" Annie saw the sudden ornery glint in Liza's eyes.

Both girls belted out the lyrics of "I'll Stand by You," by The Pretenders as loud as they could, claiming to always stand by each other and letting no one hurt the other. For the last couple of years, this song became their go-to comfort for each other whenever one of them felt down. It always made Annie laugh, no matter what her mood was. She had never had a truer friend than Liza.

Annie decided against arguing that her parents should have everything figured out by now. She didn't want to think about them anymore, though. All she wanted to think about was Hawk.

Dreamy Devin Hawksley. She could stare into his honey-brown eyes forever. She felt like they could see deep down to the real Annie. All her frustration about her family and her future melted away whenever they locked eyes.

They could not spend much alone time together over the summer. He was the lifeguard at the town pool, which is why Annie went as often as she could. She loved it when he wore his bright, geometric-patterned swim trunks. He was so much easier to spot, no matter where her viewpoint was. Her parents had bought a season pass for her and her brothers, no doubt hoping to keep them busy outside the house.

One weekend they were able to meet each other at the movies to see Twister when it first came out. She had told her parents that she was meeting Liza there. Hawk bought some of her favorite gummy bear candy and bought himself some jellybeans. They each nervously rocked back and forth in the theater chairs, trying to outdo the other in telling silly jokes until the room darkened for the start of the movie. He put his muscled arm around her when she got scared in the first scene as the dad was being sucked up by the tornado. She had never felt so safe as when Hawk's fingers wrapped tightly around her shoulders.

Their favorite part of the movie was watching the cow fly through the sky. They laughed a little louder than they should have, prompting people to turn around to shush them. She was imagining her grandpa's cows flying all around the farm. What a sight that would be! Tornadoes had terrified her ever since that night.

Hawk was supposed to be here for the end of the summer party. In fact, she couldn't think of anyone in their class who wouldn't be there. Despite the small class size of only fifty-three, it was still going to be quite a gathering. There weren't any other houses around for at least half a mile, so they should be safe from the authorities being called.

Annie turned just past the wildflower patch on the side of the road. A swarm of butterflies rose from the sea of colors as her truck drove past. Both girls paused, holding their breath, and watched as the butterflies settled back in.

By the time the girls arrived at Richard's family cabin on the Paluxy River, the party was already well underway. Brushing her sandwich crumbs off her new orange halter top, Annie climbed out of the truck. She checked her makeup one last time in the side mirror and readjusted the butterfly locket necklace she was wearing. It was a birthday present from Hawk. Liza ran around the front and hooked her arm through Annie's.

"Here we go! We are officially juniors now!" Liza exclaimed. "Let's go!"

Liza took off running with Annie in tow. She spotted Hawk waving to them from the deck on the side of the cabin, and the butterflies in her stomach came alive.

Grandpa's daily mantra repeats in the back of her head. *You're always one decision away from a totally different life.*

Why did she feel like her life was about to totally change forever?

1 Jasmine

End of June
Present Day

My mother has drilled into my head for the past twenty-seven years that I was born for an extraordinary purpose. Recently, she has proven not to be trustworthy, so it is possible she has been lying about that as well.

Closing my eyes, I take a deep breath as the warm breeze offers a strong cedar scent from the trees lining the curved road. The cicadas produce their high-pitched croaking sounds, seeking their own purpose in the cloak of the branches.

I glance at my hands and try to wipe the crimson color off, but the sticky blood smears around, creating a kaleidoscope of colors mixed with the dirt, gravel, and small shards of glass. As I readjust the heavy head in my lap, his eyes slowly open and focus on my face.

The sirens in the background sound closer, and I pray he can hold on for a few more minutes.

How long ago did I call 911? Ten, maybe fifteen minutes?

I glance at my leather belt that is bound around his upper thigh. Blood continues to ooze out of his torn pants. The uncertainty of his unseen wounds echoes my own buried pain.

This stranger's eyes work hard to stay focused. I've never seen eyes the same color as mine before. Instead of eyes full of fear, they look almost peaceful and somehow grateful for a place to rest his bleeding head. I find myself envious of the calmness on his face.

My life has been in such an upheaval lately. My parents. My brother. My husband, well, ex-husband of sorts. I no longer know where I belong. The man's bloody lips part as a slight moan escapes.

"Don't talk. Can you hear them? They are almost here." My mind pulls back to the reality of my situation. "Just hang on a few more minutes, and they will take care of you."

I swipe some more debris off the top of his head. His salt and pepper hair is cut short on the sides and a little long on top. By the looks of his clothes, he must be something like a mechanic.

His black pickup lies in the ditch like a toy that has been discarded to discover its final resting place. Apparently, the curvy drive through the endless cedar trees can be treacherous. My car dings, reminding me I left my door open when I stopped to help.

Suddenly, the deer that I thought was dead jumps up and quickly glances around. He darts into the trees along his merry way, vanishing as quickly as this stranger's life seems to be.

He starts again. "Please tell my wife and son that I …that I love them with my whole heart and not to be sad. Please …please let them know I will always….will always be near." He pulls in another long breath as it causes more gurgling in his throat with his effort to continue. "Tell my wife s..s…she will always be my J…J…Jelly Bean." He sputters out his dying love for his family while I'm praying with all I have that he will hop up like the deer and resume his life.

Admiration grows in me for this man. All he seems to be worried about is his loved ones. Realizing the heavy responsibility that he has burdened me with, my admiration and anxiety start a tug-of-war back and forth. I desperately cling to the admiration as my heart threatens to beat out of my chest.

It can't be about me right now.

17

I hear Mom's voice in my head, reminding me that this situation I find myself in can't be about me. Not right now.

"You are going to tell them yourself. Just try to relax." I stroke his forehead, feeling helpless, not knowing what else to do besides trying to offer comfort.

"Also, tell my….tell my wife to let our daughter know I thought of her every," he struggles as his eyes roll to the back of his head. "…every single day, and I'm so s…s…sorry that I missed…." A painful look comes over his face as he heaves blobs of blood. I pivot his head to help him clear his throat and utter a plea to God for some help.

The man's eyes roll back once again as he drifts in and out of consciousness. Faint signs of determination show across his face, hinting at an unfinished message. I hold his head a little tighter as the ambulance's lights come and go along with the curve of the road.

Suddenly, the sound jolts him back. His eyes snap open in disbelief as a gasp escapes his lips. His eyes connect with mine and begin to tear up. "I've always loved you since the day you were born."

Realizing he must be confusing me with someone else in his last moments, I play along. "I've always loved you, too." As I stroke his cheek, his eyes grow tender as they close for the very last time.

I wait patiently for the sheriff to finish at the scene and then follow up with questions for me. I double-check the words that I have written. The dying man's last words to his beloved family. The quickest paper I could find to write on was a receipt for my lunch I purchased earlier while driving through Granbury. Hopefully, the sheriff will care enough to rewrite it for them.

I suddenly feel exhausted. It must be the adrenaline dump that my brother complains about after each of his boxing matches. It really does put a drain on your whole body. I understand now and should really text him an apology for all the times I teased him about it. But only for that. Not for the other words that were exchanged the last time we spoke.

I'm sticking to what I believe, even if he doesn't understand.

I head towards my car after relinquishing the responsibility of passing a dying man's last words to his beloved family. I mutter a quick prayer for the tough night that awaits his unknowing family.

As I settle back into my car, I take a deep cleansing breath like my counselor taught me. Checking in the visor mirror, specks of blood are on my face and in my blonde hair. I know it's not my blood. I throw open my car door as all the anxiety that I had swallowed for the last hour comes forcibly back up.

Painful memories that I have worked hard to shove down resurface.

How different would my life be today if an alternate choice had been made so long ago? In a parallel universe, what would my life look like?

I instantly gain control of the intrusive thoughts. Past choices, whether mine or made for me, have caused me to end up right where I am.

And in this reality, this was not the first time a man had died in my arms, and this was definitely not how I pictured my first night in my new hometown of Glass, Texas.

I pray this move will be worth it and bring the answers that I need to feel whole again.

2 Summer

End of June
Present Day

I'm not the person I once was. At what point in my life did I allow myself to become so invisible?

The soapy water swirls down the drain, just like the childhood dreams I once had for my life. Since we started dating a few years ago, I can't decide which of us, Chad or me, has transformed more.

Maybe I'm not his number one priority after all. Is this another example of what Dad was hinting at last week?

My eyes scan the dark world outside and fall on the rock sitting on my windowsill.

Life is not at all what I imagined it would be at this point in my life. Living in a tiny house in the side yard of my childhood home was not the original plan. But I have only my own choices to blame for why I feel so invisible. If I don't change my surroundings soon, I might never feel seen again.

I grab a fresh dishtowel from the drawer. I need to stop comparing Chad to other guys. Relationships aren't the storybook romances movies portray. My parents' relationship has been a testimony to that fact.

Drying the last plate, I set it back in the cabinet. I'm not sure why I even use real plates to begin with. Lately, Chad has canceled on me more than he has shown up for our dinner dates.

His excuse tonight was that his mom needed him to come repair a fence after rounding up the loose cows. Chad never suggests his younger brother could help occasionally or even thinks of inviting me along.

I don't know how to make him understand I feel like an inconvenience when I really need to feel like I'm his priority.

My eyes go back to the rock on my windowsill.

Or I just need to accept it as it is. My options have dwindled.

"That's enough, Summer Dawn!" I scold myself out loud to the kitchen window's reflection. "Life is what it is right now. This is the life you chose for yourself. Deal with it or do something about it."

My lungs fill with a large intake of air as I work hard to recharge my mindset. I give my reflection a quick nod of agreement and walk to the bedroom.

After putting my comfy clothes on, I go back into the kitchen and open the freezer door to grab my nightly chocolate chip cookie dough ice cream. It's getting tiring eating it by myself. The house is too quiet, and loneliness is settling in as the new normal. I look up and see my reflection looking back at me.

"Okay, okay. I know. Don't complain. Do something about it." I feel my reflection is happy with this attempt at adulting.

I could call Laney to see if she wants to come watch the latest episode of Big Brother with me. She has been so busy lately that we have spent little time together.

A few years ago, we bonded over Big Brother during the summer we worked together at the Bug Zone

Kid Park. We became fast friends when we realized we shared the same sense of humor.

I quickly gather my light brown hair into a bun and grab my phone to call her. The phone rings and immediately goes to voicemail. Of course, I should have expected that. I've been sent to voicemail a lot lately.

Deciding to snuggle with my ice cream alone, I collapse on the couch. As I wait for the latest episode to start, I scan my framed pictures on the shelf, reminding myself I need to dust soon.

My eyes stop on the large black frame in the middle. The happy family that used to be us stares back. I take in each of the smiles on our faces, the faces of the former versions of ourselves before our lives fell apart. The Paluxy River flows behind us. The golden tones of fall highlight the background as the sun disappears behind the treeline. Mom's arms are wrapped around my brother, Clay, and me while our youngest brother, Dusty, is on Dad's back. That is the happiest I remember Mom ever being. She recalls it as the last year that her house and heart felt full.

It's been more than nine years since we posed for that picture. I was a senior with such a different outlook.

Life is much different now than it was a decade ago. I'm not even sure what I want out of life anymore. I just thought I knew what I wanted back then.

I make a mental note to schedule another photo session. I'm twenty-seven now, and Clay is twenty. We've changed a lot since then. Maybe that could be an early anniversary present for our parents. I'll have to ask Clay what he thinks about the idea since our youngest brother won't be in it.

Our parents always tease us that they deserve two anniversary presents since they have actually been married twice to each other. The first time was during

Christmas break of their junior year in high school, when Mom found out she was pregnant with me after one single night together at a party for the end of the summer. My dad would always say to my mom, "Annie, my favorite Jelly Bean, I wouldn't have had it any other way!"

I've always wondered what my life would have been like if she would've gone along with her mom's urging to give me up for adoption. Mom tells me that Grammy had never been very supportive of anything that she did growing up.

The second marriage came seven years later, after being divorced for four years. Being new parents at such a young age proved harder than they originally thought. According to my dad, being apart was the roughest time he's ever experienced. Mom blushes like she enjoys the fact that he was tortured without her for those "in-between years," as they call them. But she also claims it was the best thing that could've happened to them. It caused them to treasure each other even more.

Clay was born nine months later. That's when we moved into my great-grandpa's farmhouse, and they still live in it today.

My phone buzzes. It's Laney. My spoon falls to the floor as I set my ice cream down to answer. "Hey! What's more important than me?" Chad always says I have issues with being a little passive aggressive. Maybe he's right.

She doesn't take offense at my attempt at a stab. "Hey, so sorry!" Her car door shuts in the background. "I forgot to grab my phone when I got out of the car. What's up?" She was breathing heavily, as if she had just finished running a marathon.

"I wanted to know if you want to watch Big Brother with me. Chad stood me up again." I quickly realize what I am implying and try to cover it up. "Please don't think I'm suggesting you are second choice or anything! I would much rather watch it with you. He complains about how he thinks it's a fixed competition and makes fun of them when they cry in the diary room. Please? I have ice cream too!!"

At least I hope there is another container in there.

"Ummmm, well…" Laney seems to stall. *Is she with someone else?* She must be out with her co-workers or something. She's been hanging out with them a lot lately. "That sounds like so much fun, but I've already got something else going on. Thanks for the invite. I'll call you tomorrow, okay?"

I barely got a goodbye before the phone disconnected.

A brisk knock on the door abruptly wakes me up from the couch. Laney may have reconsidered. I tiptoe to the door and check out the peephole that Dad installed for me. I swing the door open.

"Chad! What are you doing here?" I practically jump into his arms like he has returned from a long trip. We haven't seen each other in person for almost two days because of his recent work schedule. "Did you finish the fence already?"

Chad gives me a quick squeeze and sets me back down inside the door. Hopefully, one day, he will carry me over this same threshold as his wife.

"It's a temporary fix for now. I told Mom I'd have to buy supplies this weekend to fix it properly. I'm going to make my brother help me. He needs to step up around the ranch." He slides by me and plops down on the couch. "How was Big Brother? How many people cried tonight?"

I playfully hit the Texas Rangers ball cap off his head as I walk behind the couch. "Want something to drink?" A mixture of cow manure and cologne hit my nose. "Chad! You better not have tracked in cow stuff on my carpet!"

He clumsily tiptoes back towards the front door to chuck his boots outside. As he opens the door, he calls out for me. "Summer, you need to come here."

As I approach the door, Dad's good friend, the county sheriff, is walking up the sidewalk. Growing up, I don't remember ever attending our annual summer cookout without him standing at the grill in our backyard. He'd always sneak a hamburger patty to our dog, who was patiently waiting, knowing the yummy treat was coming.

Taking his cowboy hat off his head and placing it over his heart, his usual contagious smile is missing.

"Hi, Darlin'. I'm afraid I've come with some bad news."

It's been eight days since Dad died, and I am astonished that the tears can still come like they do. It's been a couple of days since the funeral, and I still haven't showered. I grab the cold ice pack off my bedside table and place it over my eyes to help with the swelling.

Constantly reflecting over the details of that time will hopefully cause my new reality to set in. Chad was able to take off work and helped us with errands and decisions needed to plan for the funeral. It was nice to see him step up when I really needed him, proving he saw my needs and cared for me. I felt like his priority again. Even if it was only for a few days. I'll take what I can get.

I hated the funeral and loved it all at once. Hated the fact that we had to have it but could feel how much the town cherished Dad. I wore the little black dress hanging in my closet for occasions like this. I just thought it would be for someone else's father, not mine.

His funeral had a large turnout from the townspeople paying their respects. Mourners walked from blocks away with the church parking lot filling so quickly.

Sitting in the front row, we sang his favorite songs, watched the slideshow summarizing the best parts of his life, and told all the funny stories we could remember about him. Dad would have loved it.

Our car followed the hearse to the Glass Cemetery for the burial. Other vehicles on the road pulled over, seeing our somber car parade approaching. One man stepped off his tractor and removed his hat to hold over his heart. Moved by their show of respect, I wanted to stop and shout to each of them what a wonderful human the world just lost. But I just watched in silence.

At the graveside, Clay and I sat on either side of Mom. Her best friend Liza was directly behind her, doling out tissues when necessary. For as long as I can remember, Liza has always been a great friend to Mom.

As I watched the two of them, the lost look on Mom's face brings me back to when I was four years old. For a few months after my parents divorced, Mom and I lived with Liza before we moved to a trailer park.

When I first started taking care of Mom after their separation, she would lie on the couch all day. I would bring her tissues or a can of soda. She would mumble that her life wasn't supposed to be this way. I did what I could every day to make her laugh. I understand now that she was battling depression and will probably have that same fight ahead of her again now.

The graveside services were brief because of the summer heat. Tears were shed. Hugs were shared. And that was it. His life story was over. I've never felt so empty and lost inside in my entire life.

After all the guests left, Ryan, our next-door neighbor, and his grandma stayed to clean the dishes and put away the leftover food. He is like an older brother and has always been protective of me. Skinned knees, he would run for a band-aid. In a bad mood, he would tell me a corny joke. Didn't like my school lunch, he would share half his sandwich. I have so many special memories of running through the fields together, playing in the creek, and collecting rocks between our houses. Those were the simple days. Before real life hit.

As much as I cherish Ryan and our memories together, things will never be the same between us. We were younger then. Things were different. Easier. I'll take the blame for that. I still walk the creek before bed sometimes, looking for special rocks when life gets too overwhelming. It's just never as fun when I have to do it alone.

Ugh…Growing older is not all I thought it was going to be.

Placing the ice pack back on my side table, I look at the clock and see that it is not quite 7:00 yet. The sun has been awake for about an hour.

Six more minutes.

Ryan said he would bring me our weekly Friday doughnuts at 7:00 this morning. It is my favorite time to start the day. Seven is my go-to number for everything.

His truck pulled up a couple of minutes ago. He knows how set I am about my time. I wish Chad would take note. He just laughs at me, saying I'm superstitious.

I stare at the ceiling and slowly close my eyes, already ready for a nap. I've dreamed of Dad every night since the accident. Sometimes I'm aware of the accident in my dream and sometimes I'm not. But no matter what the scenario is, I can never reach him. I can never see his face. He's always on the other side of my dream, around the corner, or down the hallway. It's like I know he's there, but I can't get to him no matter what I do.

Last night was the nightmare kind. We had been fishing, and I was swimming across the pond to get to him. The pond never ended. I just swam and swam. The harder I stroked, the further away he was. I woke up covered in sweat. Every time I startle awake, the nightmare of never seeing Dad becomes reality once again.

I try hard to dredge up better memories of Dad, picturing him happy and smiling, attempting to chase this bad feeling away. Memories of him chunking Mom's jellybeans at me from her bowl by the couch when I would walk by always make me smile. Mom would pretend to be mad, saying we were wasting them. Dad and I would scramble for them on the floor to see who could eat the most. He was always joking around and kept us laughing all the time.

Two more minutes.

I let out a little laugh, knowing that Ry is probably going stir crazy. I love torturing him. He tortured me enough as we were growing up. A little payback doesn't hurt. There had better be some doughnuts left for me at 7:00.

One more minute.

Today is the day that I have an interview at the school to help in the cafeteria. Teaching kids has always been a dream of mine, and I hope to go back to college soon. When tragedy struck our family in my first year, I had to drop out. Once our life settled into a new normal, I never made it a priority to go back.

Anything that brought a smile to my face also seemed to bring guilty feelings. I've become talented at shoving down all my own desires and plans to the bottom of my priority list. *Is it ever going to be time for me again, though? Is that selfish of me to even think that?*

Ryan thinks that if I can get this job at the cafeteria and be around the kids that it will motivate me to start school again. It was all his idea. He's always looked out for what's best for me, and I'm trusting his suggestion. It would be lots of fun to teach down the hall from him.

Chad probably won't like it too much, but I will deal with that later. He is going to have to understand that I need a change to move on in life. A change that could alter my life positively. A change that I have control over. However, I can't handle any other changes right now. A new job is plenty. I need things to stay as normal as possible otherwise.

"Good morning, Sunshine!" Ryan comes bursting through my bedroom door.

7:00 exactly.

"I really need to get my key back from you." I pull the covers up to my chin, realizing that I probably smell after days without a shower.

"Nice hair, Summer Bummer." He thrusts his hand around on top of my head, adding chaos to the rat's nest that already resides there. "I hope the lunch lady's hair net fits over all that!"

"You are assuming I will get the job. It's not guaranteed." I grab the bag of doughnuts that he brought in. We have had doughnuts together every

Friday morning since the day he got his driver's license at sixteen, twelve years ago.

"Oh, it's guaranteed! No one is really knocking down the doors to feed a bunch of rude teenagers. What time is your interview?"

"I have to be there by 10:00. I hope you're right. Why am I so nervous?"

Ry throws a pillow at my face, just missing my doughnut. "Maybe because you know you really want this job."

"Maybe so." I shove the sprinkle-covered pastry into my mouth and chunk the pillow back at him.

He catches it mid-air and our eyes lock. My stomach takes a swirl, and I quickly look away.

I can't be reminded of the pain I have caused him over the years.

Not today.

3 Third Option

End of June
Present Day

4 Jasmine

First Week of July
Present Day

The number of cars lined up on Main Street is insane. When I visited the lumberyard a couple of days ago, the owner asked me if I was going to the Fourth of July parade. After hearing some more details, I thought it sounded exactly like something I needed to attend to immerse myself here in Glass. I have not had the opportunity to really meet anyone aside from my realtor and the man who died in my arms last week.

The patriotic energy in a small town is a sight to behold. The scene is straight out of a Norman Rockwell calendar except for the updated clothing and vehicles. Kids are running around with plastic sacks, looking for the perfect spot to catch the candy thrown from the floats. Grandparents are sitting in lawn chairs under umbrellas, trying their best to hide from the Texas sun. Everyone is wearing red, white, and blue on top, bottom or both. Some are sitting in truck beds while others are packed shoulder to shoulder to get the best view of what is coming.

The Pet Parade starts first. Kids of all ages are strutting their pet of choice down Main Street for all to see. Most of them are donned in some form or fashion of the holiday colors. Some are even spray-painted with red stars.

The very first in line of the parade must have already claimed first prize. The black-spotted goat proudly wears the blue ribbon like a tie as he struts his stuff in front of the whole town. His owner can't be over five years old. The poor kid looks like he is already over this early morning heat as his pet drags him through the street.

Laughter from the sidelines fills the air as each entry passes by: dogs, pigs, more goats, ponies. One kid is even pulling a little red wagon with two brown chickens in the back. Chicken wire has been cleverly arched over the top to prevent any escapees.

As the pet entries seem to dwindle, the rest of the parade comes marching towards us. The melody of Neil Diamond's Sweet Caroline gets louder as the high school band marches closer to where I am standing. The drum major stands in the back of a pickup truck facing the band while she moves her arms about, keeping them in beat with each other. Each face that passes by is glistening with sweat under the weight of having to carry, march, and play in this heat. I scan the faces, trying to familiarize myself knowing that I will soon have some of them in my math classes this next school year. I jump as the crowd suddenly yells, "Bum, Bum, Bum," as the song reaches the chorus. The trumpets sway in unison as they pass by, entertaining what must be the whole town of Glass.

The next group is the cheer squad and drill team. Red and white balloons line the perimeter of the trailer, with a large American flag waving off the back. Riding the float together but easily separated by different uniforms, the girls giggle, wave, throw candy, and pose for parental pictures on the sidelines, and, of course, the multiple selfies that I'm sure will be posted to each one's preferred media platform as soon as they are able. Seeing the girls brings back many fond memories of my drill team days in high school and at college.

Following the spirit squad come the football players, wearing their gray and black jerseys. Two younger guys on the team carry a banner stating that "Panthers are #1" while the other players wave to the cheering crowd and throw candy. If they exude the same amount of energy on the football field, I'm guessing they must be pretty good. Movies centering on small town football teams always portray how much their community supports them. I'm excited about experiencing it firsthand this year.

A little boy with a cowboy hat and the smallest cowboy boots that I've ever seen stands in front of me. He runs to snatch the candy off the street and brings it back. An older woman sitting in a lawn chair holds a gift bag for him that he tosses his collection into. He asks his mom where all the horses are. "Remember, they will be at the very end. No one wants to come after the horses." She holds her fingers to her nose as if a stench just rolled through. "Then we will go down to Duffie Park and ride some rides." The tiny cowboy seems satisfied enough with her answer, yet still strains his neck while looking down the street.

The parade continues as entries seem to be in similar groups with various floats sprinkled in between. There are motorcycles, scooters, bicycles, classic cars, tractors, golf carts, and even the town's fire engine. Each with its own form of red, white, and blue décor of balloons, streamers, posters, and flags. The line seems to go on and on. I question why I didn't bring a chair to sit on. I'm just very thankful for the float that was throwing out cold bottles of water.

Finally, the horses are in sight. Each one decorated to represent the holiday. Some even have shiny ribbons woven throughout their manes and tails. The little cowboy starts whooping and hollering. He takes his cowboy hat off and twirls it around over his head, hitting me in the legs repeatedly. "Here he comes! Here he comes!" The mother tries to lift him up, but he wriggles free to get closer to the street. "Uncle Shep! Uncle Shep!"

I glance up to find this Uncle Shep character when our eyes meet. My stomach immediately reacts with its own parade of butterflies. I could easily get lost in those cornflower-blue eyes. Our eyes lock only momentarily because of the little cowboy yelling louder and louder, afraid that Uncle Shep won't notice him. The horse stops, and the little cowboy's mom lifts him up to sit on the horse. Uncle Shep never looks my way again as he trots off down the street with the little cowboy still whooping, hollering, and swinging his hat around, having the best time of his little life.

The scissors slide smoothly, cutting the tape on the last box for the day. The flaps fly open since it was packed too tightly. Last night, I took a break from unpacking and watched the fireworks from my backyard. Screams of approval could be heard through the area while the townspeople watched from Duffie Park as the firefighters shot off one firework display after another once the outdoor concert of a local band was finished.

Bubble wrap falls to the floor as I carefully pull each cream-colored plate out of the box. One short of a complete set.

My fingers run along the lip of the plate, recalling the time I unpacked these at our first house. I loved that house. The down payment on it was a wedding gift from Ted's parents. My mother-in-law picked it out for us, but I had no complaints at all.

The kitchen and back deck tied for my favorite spot in the colonial-style residence. The large window above the kitchen sink overlooked the back deck and the expansive backyard filled with large trees that I'm sure witnessed many gatherings from decades of owners before us. Not only did she pick it out, but she paid for and oversaw the renovations. She had an excellent eye for décor and saw potential in overlooked treasures.

Too bad she didn't have as keen an eye for her son's potential or lack thereof.

The ding of my phone jerks me back into the present day. I don't recognize the number.

> just checking to see if now would be a good time to stop by the lumber yard said you needed some help you bought the old walsh house right

I'm not sure how time escaped me so quickly this morning.

> Yes, now would be perfect! Thank you!

I'm curious if he would even take note of the capitalization or punctuation that I used. It seems like he believes he doesn't need any. Being a teacher, I just can't make myself forget the proper way to write a sentence. Tate, the owner of the lumberyard, highly recommends this guy to do a little painting and build a couple of shelves. I guess it doesn't matter if he knows how to use punctuation for his job as long as he knows how to use a hammer and a paintbrush.

Stepping into the hall bath, I quickly glance in the mirror to see if my hair and makeup still look as fresh as they did hours ago when I got ready for the day. Grabbing the bubble wrap off the floor, I head to the garage to throw it away, making a mental note to decide what to do with all the empty boxes piling up.

A vehicle pulls into the driveway, so I scurry to the door to peek out. That didn't take very long. Of course, this is a pretty small town.

I slowly push the curtain to the side to get a peek at what old man the lumberyard has sent my way. His white pickup truck is caked with mud. The windshield wipers look like they had worked hard to keep them clean, but obviously had lost the battle.

As his long legs unfold from the truck, I catch a glimpse of his face. He isn't old at all.

It's Uncle Shep from the parade.

My lungs have forgotten how to work. I try hard to regulate my breath and dart to the mirror one more time to make sure all is well with my face. I'm not ready to be around another man yet. Alone in my house. Especially not one as cute as Uncle Shep.

I wait a little after the doorbell rings so that I don't seem too eager. Taking a deep breath, I open the door with my right hand while my left hand holds onto the silver circles on my necklace. I slowly rub them between my fingers while trying to control my breathing.

"Jasmine? Hey! Tate said you might could use some help around here with a few things. Man, I haven't been in this house for at least ten years." He brushes past me, apparently taking my holding the door open as an invitation to come on in. Maybe he doesn't recognize me from the parade after all.

"Woo Wee! If these walls could talk! One of my best friends, David Walsh, grew up here, and I spent countless days here when I was younger. I know every nook and cranny." His eyes dart back and forth as his head spins around, taking it all in and losing himself in his memories. He startles as his eyes catch me once again, jolting him back to the present day. "I'm so sorry! How rude of me! My name is Shep. At least that's what all my friends call me." His broad smile makes me nervous again.

He holds out his hand for a proper greeting. Apparently, he has never been taught that a man should wait for the woman to extend her hand first. I gently grab his hand as he energetically pumps my hand up and down, causing his rough calluses to scratch the inside of my palms.

"Thank you for coming over so promptly." I break the handshake and nonchalantly wipe his transferred sweat onto the back of my shorts. "I've got a list in the kitchen. We can sit in there if you don't mind." Before I finish my sentence, Shep is already headed down the hallway.

As we finish going over the list and measuring a few walls, Shep finishes up one more story of his younger days in this house. He glances at the backyard. "Mind if we step out back for a minute?"

I head to the sliding glass door and unlock the door. I bend over to pick up the security bar nestled at the bottom. It makes me feel safer. I'm not sure what to think about being in this big house by myself yet, although knowing I have a little security in my bedside table helps in the middle of the night.

He allows me to step through the door first and then leads me on a tour of my backyard like he is the one who lives here.

"Looks like your pool could use a little TLC." Shep grabs the pool net hanging nearby and fishes out the floating leaves.

"At my old house, we had someone come from the pool store and take care of the pool for us. Do they have that kind of service around here?" I would like to enjoy some floating days with a good book before I have to start the new school year. In fact, as hot as it is in Texas, I might enjoy this pool through Halloween.

"Glass doesn't have a pool place. Most people order their pool supplies online or drive up to Granbury to get them." He opened the skimmer and looked around for a place to dump out the contents. "However, this is your lucky day." There goes that broad smile again.

"Oh yeah? How is that?" I try to keep my face as nonreactive as possible.

"I used to take care of this pool for the Walshes when I was in high school. They would mainly pay me in all the food I ate around here but would always give me a nice bonus at the end of each summer. They found someone else when I went to college, but I bet I can remember how everything works." He began unhooking the gate that hid the large sand filter. "Or I could find out who they were using and get the information to you."

"Or perhaps you might show me how everything works and teach me what to do." I remember the pool guy was around a few times a week, and I'm not sure if I want or need to have Shep around me that much. I probably need to avoid him as much as possible when he is finished with the list that I've already hired him to do. He went to college? Then why is he just working odd jobs? I'm curious to find out, but don't want to lead him into any extra conversations. I still have a few more years left on my "break from men" stage.

"Sure, I could do that. I'll gather up the paint and supplies that I need this evening and be here first thing in the morning to get started on the inside, if that's okay with you." He stands still for one of the first times in the last hour and waits for my response.

My left hand grabs my necklace again. I turn away from him as I respond to avoid eye contact. "Yes. That will be just fine."

I lead him through the house and see him out the front door.

"I heard through the grapevine that you inherited quite a bit of money and moved here from Fort Worth to buy this big 'ole house and start a new life."

The shocked expression on my face obviously makes him feel immediate regret for letting that snippet of information slip out.

"Excuse me? How is that any business of yours?"

"I'm sorry, ma'am. I meant no harm in it. Have you ever lived in a small town before?"

I continue to stare at him, feeling lost in this conversation. "What does that have to do with anything?"

"It's just something that you have to understand about a small town. Everybody around town knows everything about everybody else. No matter what time of the day something may happen, it's pretty much old news by the time your head hits the pillow."

This is something that I will need to take into consideration. I am used to Fort Worth, where I can go unrecognized just about anywhere. I really don't want everyone around here to know about how my life fell apart.

"Another unwritten rule to know is to be careful about whom you talk about. In a small town like this, they are probably related to or could have been married to the person you are talking to." His head tilts to the right as his mouth contorts to a grimaced look.

"Thanks, I guess. That is good to know." I remember his little nephew at the parade. I can see how tight-knit this community must be. I'm just thankful he doesn't seem to recognize me.

"Sorry again, and I'll be back in the morning. I'll text you on my way." Shep folds himself back into his muddy truck. He rolls his window down for a final wave as he pulls through the circle drive. "Looks like you were enjoying yourself at the parade yesterday. We will have another one for Christmas!"

He holds his left hand up in the air for a long goodbye as he drives down the driveway. I'm just glad he can't see my face turning red. I can not handle any distractions right now in my life.

Especially not one as cute as him.

5 Summer

Second Week of July
Present Day

I check my phone once again. Today should be the day I hear something. The school board approved new hires at last night's meeting. Hopefully, they will call me and let me know one way or another about my potential hash-slinging job in the high school cafeteria.

I grab a piece of candy from the bowl on my kitchen table. The candy from the parade a few days ago helped me refill my stockpile. I even gathered seven pieces of butterscotch. One of Dad's favorite candies. I'm sure that was a sign that he was thinking of me. I had only collected six, and Laney gave me one of hers so I could have seven.

The parade was long as usual. We made fun of Ryan, as we do every year, as he passed us by in the parade. Chad finished work, then met Laney and me at the park for fireworks that night.

Nothing matches the feeling of watching fireworks overhead while lying down. Arrays of so many colors are bursting, spinning, and then the smoke drifts away as new flashes dart into the sky to continue to dazzle the town. Oohs and aahs pop up all around as everyone points out their favorite explosions. Although I can be among hundreds of other people witnessing the same glittering shower I am, I feel mesmerized and alone in a pyrotechnic world of wonder. It's by far my favorite holiday.

For six years now, Chad and I have held hands under the fireworks. I believe it is so romantic. Of course, it was a little awkward with Laney there. She usually has a date with her, but not this year.

My phone dings, bringing me back to reality. It's Laney.

> Heard anything yet? Maybe they will have another opening soon and I can come work there. Wouldn't that be a blast? We could throw food at Ryan when he's not looking 👀

My fingers work right away at a response.

> I'm picturing him with a slice of pizza on the side of his face. 🍕 Nothing yet

Sliding my phone in my pocket to keep it close, I glance out the back kitchen window to see if my younger brother Clay is still at the farmhouse. My hand instinctively grabs the heart-shaped rock on the windowsill. I rub it seven times between my fingers. The smoothness and repetition have calmed me for so many years. I should check on Mom to determine what her condition is for the day.

A few years ago, when I dropped out of college to move back home, I was hovering too much over Mom, worried about her. Her depression reminded me of when I was little, before she and Dad got back together, and I had to take care of her. She admitted she loved having me close but hated that I gave up my independence to move back to help. Our solution was finding this tiny house and placing it on a concrete slab to hold it secure in the side yard. There are a couple of acres between my house and the farmhouse. That way, Mom said I could maintain my privacy and independence but still be close enough if she was having a hard day. It seems to have worked for both of us.

I grab my iced coffee and head next door. As I walk in, my brother Clay is packing his things to get ready to head back to college in a couple of days. He found a job that allows him to move back early and get settled in before school starts.

"Hey! You excited about your new job?" I choose not to comment on his lack of packing skills.

"I am. Uncle Tate hooked me up with a lumberyard close to the campus. I will probably have to work several weekends, though, so I'm not sure how often I can come back." He glances towards the kitchen where we can hear Mom loading the dishwasher. "Are you okay with my leaving? Will you be okay?"

I've already mulled over this question several times in my head. Once again, I feel a responsibility for taking care of Mom and putting my own needs to the side.

"We will be just fine. Don't worry about us. It's time you focus on yourself. And these towels." I playfully dump his folded towels basket all over the couch and run from him as he throws one my way.

Mom is in the kitchen staring out the window towards the barn. I doubt she has entered it in the past seven years. I don't blame her.

"Hey, Mom. How are you doing today? Did you get any rest last night?"

When she turns to me, I notice her red, swollen eyes. They immediately start tearing up again. "The house will be so quiet when your brother goes back to school. He offered to take a semester off, but I told him I would disown him if so. I still hate that you never went back. You sacrificed your future life in more ways than one to take care of me. And I will forever be grateful." She reaches out to hug me.

I open my arms as she falls into them. "Are you kidding me? Now I get to have you all to myself." I rub my hands down the back of her head, stroking her tangled hair. "Once Clay leaves, it will be all about me once again. I haven't had that kind of attention since he was born."

I can't distinguish between laughs and sobs in the movements against me until she withdraws. A slight smile spreads across her face.

"Are you sure you can handle this mess all on your own?" She throws her right hand in the air and twirls like a ballerina.

"We will handle each other together, Mom. You and me." A slight smile tries to expose itself, but the sorrow quickly takes over.

"I just miss your dad so much. It wasn't supposed to be like this." Mom and Dad always talked about which of them would be the favorite of their future grandkids, hosting future slumber parties, and growing old together on the back porch.

"I know, Mom. It's not fair."

My phone buzzes in my back pocket. I pull it out and recognize the school telephone number. I hold a finger up to Mom, letting her know to be quiet for a minute.

"Hello. Yes, it is. Oh, that's great. Okay, sounds good. I'll come to the office in the morning. Yes, thank you so much. I'm looking forward to it as well. Goodbye."

"You got the job?" This is the first look of excitement I've seen on Mom's face since before Dad's accident.

"Yes! I got the job! He needs me to come in the morning to fill out the paperwork. I'm so excited! I need to call Chad and tell him!" I give Mom a look to see if she's going to be okay.

"Go! Go call him! Maybe I'll actually cook tonight to celebrate." Reality sets on her face. "Well, maybe I'll pull a new casserole dish out of the freezer for tonight. There are still so many leftovers from the funeral attendees who came from the church."

"That would be great! I don't care what we eat as long as we all get to eat together tonight."

"Just the three of us. That's all that's left now. Just the three of us." Her face drops again. There have been so many waves of emotion in the past couple of weeks.

"Yes, Mom. It's just us three, with two beautiful souls watching over us from above." She swatted at me with the dishtowel to chase me out of the kitchen.

I exchange a look with Clay as I hurry past him into the living room. We know exactly what the other is thinking. Can she hold it together this time?

It's down to just the three of us now.

6 Third Option

Third Week of July
Present Day

7 Jasmine

A Layer From the Middle of June
Five Years Before the Move
Twenty-two Years Old

The noise from the small fan on my dresser effectively drowned out the chatter behind me. I turned it down a little lower, risking ruining my makeup before the ceremony, but my bridesmaids discussing things in the corner caught my attention.

"What are you guys talking about now? Talk louder. I can't hear you!" My makeup artist paused, so I turned and faced all the friends who represented the entirety of my life.

Colleen served as my maid of honor. My best friend since the church nursery. Mom said that I was always a calmer version of myself around Colleen. The nursery workers used to let us take naps together in the same crib on Sunday mornings. Sometimes that is the only way I would stop crying. She's been my rock ever since.

Layla and I met when we sat together in sixth grade math class, nearly surrounded by all boys. Her quick wit kept them at bay for most of the year, and we bonded over teasing them back and forth. We grew even closer when we both made the high school pom team. We spent countless nights in my upstairs bedroom, dancing in front of the wall of mirrors that Dad installed for me. She could make me laugh and would always have my back. Math had been my favorite subject since that year in sixth grade, and I couldn't wait to teach it after I graduated next year. Our bond continued every six weeks as she covered up my brown roots and made them blonde again.

And then came Reese. Reese was Ted's younger sister. When Ted first brought me home to meet his family, she immediately led me to their game room to find out how her brother managed to get someone as beautiful as me to date a loser like him. She instantly became the little sister that I never had and always wanted.

Although Ted's mom insisted on a huge wedding and paying for it all, we stood firm on keeping our bridesmaids and groomsmen to a minimum. That became our sole contribution. But that was just fine with us. The overwhelming beauty of the Stone Falls Wedding Venue in Fort Worth was every bride's dream. We were only able to book it thanks to Mrs. Bertarelli's, or I guess Mom's, connections.

"I told your friends that my brother is the second luckiest person in the world because he gets to marry you." Reese walked over and gently pointed out a string hanging off a crystal cluster on the front of my wedding dress. Since I met her at fifteen, she has blossomed into a confident and beautiful young woman over the last couple of years.

"Who is the top luckiest person? Me for marrying him?" I closed my eyes to allow my makeup artist to complete the final face touch-ups before I walked down the aisle.

"No, Jazz. I am. I've always dreamed of having a big sister, and now you are about to make it official by marrying my loser brother!" I felt her hand touch my bare shoulder and hoped the welling, grateful tears wouldn't ruin my makeup again.

"Okay, that's enough, everyone. If you all don't stop making me cry on this magical day, I'm kicking you all over that enormous wall out there." I pointed to the historic stone wall beyond the window that surrounded the grounds below where I was about to become Mrs. Ted Bertarelli. "And you all have witnessed my high kicks on the field and are aware that I could do it!" I slid out of the chair and turned to face the best group of friends that a girl could have ever asked God for. Mom used to tell me she prayed for my future friends and spouse before I was even born. All the prayers had worked.

One of my favorite things about weddings was not to watch the bride walk down the aisle, but to watch the groom watch his bride walk down the aisle. In my opinion, a groom shedding tears often indicated a promising marriage.

Ted and I had been to a few weddings together as our college friends had married off one by one. Not a single groom shed a tear at any of the weddings we attended together in the past couple of years.

In fact, our first date was at the wedding of one of Ted's friends. He served as a groomsman at the wedding. I had been tutoring Ted for about three months for his statistics class. His math skills were quite lacking. Ted had laid on some major flirting during our tutoring sessions, and I held him off for a couple of months. However, when he began bringing me my favorite strawberry smoothies for each session, I knew I was in trouble. He later told me he knew his "smooth" smoothie move would eventually wear me down. Love a man with good corny dad jokes.

Now, here we found ourselves at our own lavish wedding. My name would change from Jasmine Dawn Forte to Jasmine Dawn Bertarelli. My new forever perfect name.

As Dad led me down the aisle, my eyes searched over the heads of all the wedding guests. Many of them were strangers to me but associates of Ted's family. My smile seemed artificial and forced until I saw Ted.

Here was the man who would give me the perfect life I had always dreamed of. The man who always held the door open for me. The man who brought me fresh flowers for our dining room table every other Friday. The man who greeted me with a kiss on the cheek every time I entered the room. His hand quickly moved to his face, brushing away a tear once we locked eyes. Butterflies erupted in my stomach, and my shoulders and face relaxed.

That single tear reassured me that my perfect life so far had found my perfect match for our perfect future together. This is what I have planned for all my life.

Nothing will stop me from achieving it now.

8 Summer

A Layer From the Middle of June
Fifteen Years Before the Wreck
Twelve Years Old

I vowed to myself that I would never own a pop-up camper. Mom and Dad had been arguing, trying to get it level after already spending so much time discussing which direction it should be positioned. Mom wanted it facing the Paluxy River, and Dad wanted it facing the picnic table. Dad let Mom win, of course.

If I ever have a camper when I get older, I will make sure my husband understood we are getting a fully equipped travel trailer with a kitchen, separate bedroom, and a full functioning bathroom. Just like the one that Ryan's family had.

"Hey, Summer, check this one out!" Ryan motioned me over to see his new discovery down at the riverbank. He turned thirteen a few months ago and had outgrown me by at least six inches. He constantly reminded me that he was the older one and therefore was wiser since he had more life experience than I did. I would always roll my eyes, slug him in his growing bicep, and run off, reminding him I was still faster than he was.

Mom gave me a sign of approval when I glanced her way, so I jogged down to join Ryan at the bank. My two little brothers, ages three and five, tried to follow me, and I was thankful she didn't allow them to. I loved it when I could do things just for myself.

Ryan held out a white flat rock that was a perfect circle. It was about the size of a quarter. "This is a winner!" After he shoved it in his back pocket, we both stooped over and wandered around, searching for the next rock worthy of picking up.

For years, we have collected rocks at the creek that ran between our two houses. We had begged our parents to agree to vacation together here at Dinosaur Valley State Park for the past couple of summers. Mom made it clear that she would be delighted once Dad bought her a camper, as she refused to stay in a tent again. The last time we camped here when I was two, a rare downpour caught us off guard. Mom said we were soaked after the tent sprung a leak and water seeped in underneath to soak our sleeping bags.

Although it was just a short four-day weekend trip, we were so excited to be here. I'm not sure how much this counted as a vacation since it was only fifteen minutes from our house. We've been here on school field trips, but it seemed like we never really had time to explore like we wanted. Dad warned Mom in the kitchen a couple of weeks ago to take advantage of me wanting to spend time with them because soon I would be a teenager who wouldn't be interested. I couldn't ever imagine not wanting to be with my mom and dad. Life just wouldn't be the same.

Dinosaur Valley State Park was a huge tourist attraction around here. Dinosaurs once inhabited this area, leaving lasting imprints on the Paluxy riverbeds. It's like God poured out some concrete, and the dinosaurs walked through it before it dried.

Ryan and I wagered to see who would be the first to find a dinosaur track not yet recorded on the map. Whoever won got to boss the other around for the rest of the summer. I already had a written list of all the things that I would make him do for me.

"Look at this one!" I reached down into the water and grabbed my newest treasure for my collection. "I've never seen a pink rock before." Rubbing the mud off on my t-shirt, I held up my new pride and joy for him to admire. He barely glanced at it and turned his attention back to the water surrounding his ankles. I've noticed that he has been more competitive this past year. This lit a fire in me to show him I was the best cool rock finder. I crawled on my hands and knees to get an even closer look.

Before we knew it, our pockets were each loaded down with our newly treasured rocks. We planned to show them off at supper to our families so they could vote for the best one. I knew Uncle Tate and his girlfriend would vote for mine.

Mom had prepared enough hobo dinner foil packets for everyone. They each had hamburger meat, potatoes, and carrots in them. She made them up that morning before we left the house, thinking that would be an easy meal and easy cleanup for our first night. Ryan's family brought the ingredients to make some s'mores afterwards. I hoped we had s'mores every day. They were my favorite.

"I'll beat you there!" I yelled after I had already started off. Ryan's footsteps were catching up to me. My hands held the tops of my pockets closed so I wouldn't lose any rocks along the way.

Suddenly, I heard Ryan taking off to my right in the water to pass me up. I stepped over into the water in order to block him when my foot landed on a large, slippery rock. My foot flew up in front of me, even with my nose at one point, and I ended up landing on top of Ryan, who cushioned my fall in the water.

I laughed so hard that I peed my pants a little. Thank goodness we were already soaked. Ryan stood up first, so he reached down to help me up.

The moment that I wrapped my fingers around his hand was the first time that I had ever had that tingly feeling in my stomach, other than when Dad drove really fast over a hill. I had never felt that before around Ryan, so I was a little confused. Judging from his expression, I sensed he felt the same.

I yanked my hand away and took off running toward our campsites. "I'm still faster than you!" He was still standing there, staring at his empty hand, when I glanced back his way to ensure I was winning. I vowed to myself never to hold his hand again.

After finishing three s'mores each, our parents cut us off, telling us to save some for tomorrow night. Ryan's perfect white circle rock won best find after our parents patiently oohed and aahed over our rock spread. Uncle Tate told me he liked mine the best before they left. I decided I would start my rock hunting early in the morning by myself.

"Let's ride our bikes around the circle while your mom is putting your brothers to bed." Ryan headed towards the mountain bike he received for his birthday a few months earlier.

"I don't know. I kinda just want to stay here with Dad around the campfire." I kicked a marshmallow covered with ants on the ground and looked at Dad for support and a reason to turn Ryan down.

"Go ahead, Flutterfly. We have plenty of time to sit around the campfire when you two get back." Dad used the nickname he has had for me since I was about three years old. He said it was so cute how I would mispronounce butterfly, and he never wanted to forget it. He pulled me to him and kissed my forehead. Both of my parents have done this for as long as I can remember to say goodbye or goodnight. It always made me feel so special. "I'll grab my guitar, and we can sing some campfire songs when you two get back."

Dad put another log on the fire while Ryan's dad stoked it with a long stick. Crackles sounded as tiny flames escaped into the air and then disappeared. I reluctantly headed for my bicycle.

"Hang on." Ryan turned around and headed back to his camper. He returned after a couple of minutes. "Come on, Summer. Let's go before it gets too dark."

As he ran by me, I got a sudden whiff of what Dad smells like when we go to church or some fancy restaurant. I hesitantly kicked at my kickstand and threw my leg over the seat. Ryan had already taken off and was doing doughnuts, creating circles in the gravel waiting for me to catch up. I pedaled faster to pass him without him expecting it. We ended up racing around the campground circle twice, waving to our dads each time we passed, taking turns who was leading out front.

Near the end of our third time around, Ryan slowed down enough to allow me to ride next to him. The crunch of gravel beneath our tires matched the intensity of the awkward silence building between us. I still couldn't shake my feelings from earlier.

"Let's walk down to the water and see if we can see any fish jump. Maybe tomorrow our dads will take us fishing." Ryan hopped off his bike and pointed to a spot next to the wooden post marked as campsite seven and suggested where to leave mine. I did one last doughnut in the gravel, causing the dust to swirl in the air. Unable to come up with any excuses, I parked my bicycle next to his, taking time to wipe the dust off of the handlebars.

We headed down the sloping bank, lured by the sound of the river as it drifted its way over the large rocks scattered throughout the water. A small animal scurried up the bank on the other side, seeking a hiding spot in the brush underneath the trees. As Ryan walked past, his scent surprised me again.

"Did you put on some of your dad's cologne?" I pinched my nose to convince myself that it was unpleasant. Ryan's face blushed slightly before he turned back towards the river.

Ryan picked up a few different rocks, inspecting each one. Finding a perfectly flat one, he brought his arm back and quickly flicked his wrist, causing the rock to skip three times across the top of the water before it sank to its new resting place. I silently joined him while we took turns skipping various rocks to see who could get the highest count of skips. He stepped a little closer to me, and his elbow brushed up against mine. I sensed a familiar sensation returning to my stomach.

"We probably need to get back." I dropped the rest of my rocks and turned to head back to where we left our bikes. Water splashed as Ryan chunked his all at once into the river and followed me back up the bank.

Once we reached our bicycles, Ryan grabbed my arm, turning me around to face him. "I need to ask you a question, and you can be honest with me. I won't be mad if you say no."

I had never really seen Ryan appear so serious before. He traced his fingers back and forth over the number seven on the rough wooden post, avoiding eye contact with me.

"I'm always honest with you. What's wrong?" Worry replaced the sensation in my stomach.

"You realize I'm starting seventh grade this year? I get to go to the school dances now, and I'm really nervous about it. Will you practice slow dancing with me, so I can understand what I'm doing, and tell me if I look stupid or not?" He scrunched up his face, expecting a sarcastic remark.

"Is that all? I thought you were dying or something." I slugged his arm, and he flinched even though I knew it didn't really hurt. "Are you going to sing for us or what? There isn't any music to dance to."

He reached into his jeans pocket and held up his iPod Touch. He plugged in the earplugs and then put one in his ear and attempted to put the other in mine. When he started the music, Kiss A Girl by Keith Urban came on. I just stood there because I didn't know how to dance either. He placed my hands on his shoulders, one by one, then awkwardly placed his hands on my hips. We stood still. Neither of us knew what to do next.

"Shouldn't we be moving or something?" I giggled at the awkwardness.

He convulsed his body as if an earthquake was moving through him. "Like this?"

I slugged his arm again. "No, it's called slow dancing for a reason. It's not called spasm dancing."

He shook his arms out as though trying to rid his body of his nervousness and slowly put his hands on the sides of my hips again. "It seems like we just sway back and forth."

We both started a slow swaying motion together until we fell into a natural rhythm.

"Yeah, that feels right. I can do this, I suppose." Ryan's face started looking more confident as his feet took tiny steps to the side and back to the middle.

"I believe you are a natural." I built him up, holding back a smile.

"Honestly? I just don't want to embarrass myself. But I think I got the hang of this." He added a little sway to his shoulders.

"It's really just too bad, though." I shook my head and conjured up a sad look on my face.

"What? I thought I was doing pretty well."

"It's just too bad that no girl would ever agree to dance with a loser like you!" Pushing his bicycle over, I turned to grab my bike and hopped on it. I took off on the gravel pathway to head back towards our campsites before he reached me.

"Summer Dawn! I'm going to get you!!" His voice trailed off as he struggled to get his bike upright.

I pedaled with all my might, unsure if I was trying to outrun Ryan or outrun the butterflies that were awakening in my stomach again.

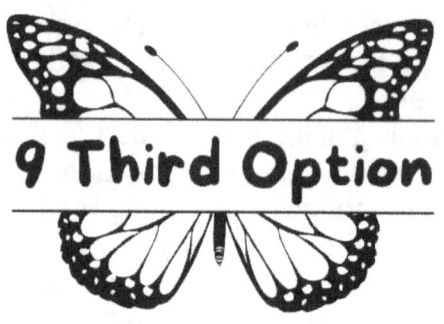

9 Third Option

**Middle of June
Ten Years Ago**

10 Jasmine

Middle of August
Present Day

I step into the hallway and shut my classroom door. Placing my feet onto the black paw prints painted on the floor at the door entrance, I close my eyes and try to reset my mind.

My hand reaches for the doorknob. As the door opens, I try my hardest to pretend that I am seeing my classroom for the first time. I want to see what my future students will notice as they walk into my math class for the first day of school next week. I want it to be perfect.

The fresh scent hits me first. I always start out each school year with a crisp, clean scent. I want my classroom to be inviting as each student walks in. The changing seasons and holidays will bring distinct scents. My classroom at my previous school always smelled wonderful, even after lunch, which is quite an accomplishment. Especially here in Texas.

My eye is immediately drawn to the bulletin board on the side wall that states, "Calculate Kindness Into Every Day." The bold khaki letters are accented with a string of lights and a large black cardboard calculator with the school year painted across the screen. Even though my focus is to improve their math skills, my second goal is to ensure they sense love and acceptance in my classroom. That phrase should help set the tone in the right way to start off the school year.

Upon entering, I observe the neutral tones integrated into every part of the area. Sheer cream curtains hang at the room's rear windows. They help with a cozier atmosphere while still letting some light in.

Two ivy plants sit on the shelves in the front of the room by the whiteboard. The lady at the local nursery said they are easy to care for and help reduce stress and anxiety. My bulletin boards have soft colors with twinkling lights wrapped around the edges. I added my finishing touches today with the low-light lamps in each corner of the room.

I can throw in a couple of yoga mats and have a functioning yoga studio atmosphere. Math is so stressful for some kids. I'm hoping this approach will make a difference this year.

Satisfied with how my vision came to life, I sit down at my desk and notice I have a missed call from Mom. She and Dad keep trying to visit, and I continue to come up with excuses. I can't deal with any more arguments right now.

Setting my phone aside, I glance over my class rosters. There was a flute player at the parade whose shirt sat snug around her middle, looking like she might be pregnant. I hope she is in one of my classes, and God will allow me to be there for her for some extra support. I begin praying over each class roster that I will be sensitive in meeting each student where they are academically. My prayers continue requesting that God will give me the wisdom in how to handle situations that may come up during the year and that my reactions will point the students to Him.

"Are you taking a nap?"

Startled by a deep voice, my head pops up to see Shep standing in the doorway.

"No, actually, I was just praying over all my students' names for this next school year." *What is he doing here?* Maybe he built some shelves for a teacher here. He proved himself to be pretty handy with the projects around my house in the past few weeks. I tried my hardest to avoid much conversation with him each time he came over to work.

Shep's hand flies to cover his mouth as his eyebrows arch up as high as they can go. "I'm so sorry! Didn't mean to disturb you. I wanted to welcome you to our hallway."

"Our hallway? Did you go to school here?" I stand up and begin gathering my things to take home. I can take this back up with God on my back deck this evening.

"I sure did. They loved my always infectious charm so much that they hired me back after I graduated with my education degree, with an emphasis on industrial technology. I teach a couple of doors down from you. I've taught here for six years now." He points down the hallway.

"You are the teacher for Tool School?" Each time I pass by the banner, I have wondered who came up with that name. Now I know. Uncle Shep.

"Yep! Do you like the name? I came up with that all by myself a couple of years ago." He puffs his chest out a little more than normal as the corners of his eyes crinkle with his wide smile. "I teach wood shop, technology education, and an introduction to construction. You must take wood shop first, though, to learn how to use the basic tools before you can take construction. In my other hours, I coach weightlifting and then whatever sport is in season. Currently, I am an assistant coach for the football team."

I close my mouth, realizing that it must have been hanging open in shock. I'm still trying to process the fact that he is a teacher here. And will be a couple of doors down the entire school year.

And I had done such a great job of avoiding him up to this point.

"So, you only remodel on the side? I thought that was your full-time job."

"Oh, no. Mainly just in the summer. Most coaches have an extra job in the summer for some additional income and to help stay busy. But some jobs that Tate sends me from the lumberyard, I work into a class project. That is, if the people aren't in a hurry to have something done. All they need to do is pay for materials, and the labor is free, so we usually have a good list to choose from for our class projects. The list seems to get longer every year."

My mind is swirling.

Shocked that he is a teacher.

Impressed by his Tool School creation and the way he has incorporated the community for real-life learning.

Taken aback by how his sky-blue eyes seem to get brighter as he talks about his classes.

Yikes. I'm going to have to take the long way from the parking lot now to avoid walking by his classroom every day.

"I have to run. Sorry again for disturbing your convo with the Big Man Upstairs. I left my keys in my classroom, and I'm late for football practice. You are coming to the scrimmage next week, aren't you?" He steps backwards down the hallway. "The whole town will be there!"

"Yes, I should be there."

"Great! I'll have the guys score a touchdown for you!" He darts off towards his classroom, causing a whiff of his musky cologne to sweep inside my doorway. I can already tell that this will be a difficult hurdle in my way of finding the answers I came for.

I'm pretty sure that even if I didn't know where the football field was, I could find it just by following the noise in town. The scrimmage is against the Glen Rose Tigers, the town to the east of us. Both towns are very similar in size, and because of the close proximity, they are staunch rivals in all sports. But football seems to be the one that the whole town gets excited about. Coach Sheppard explained to me one morning before school that even though this scrimmage doesn't count for any school statistics, it counts for morale for the entire season. Both teams will play each other officially later in the schedule, but the winner of this first battle gets bragging rights until then. It has been a scrimmage tradition for decades.

Last night, I drove to Glen Rose with Macee, who teaches English next door to me. She invited me to go with her to Ladies' Night at the Glen Rose Downtown Square. They were having a "So Long Sweet Summer" celebration at several of the boutiques. We shared some brisket nachos at the Sexton Mill overlooking the Paluxy River and then visited several stores on the Square. I needed to buy a few Panther shirts and also found several items I decided I couldn't do without. Glen Rose's high school jazz band was on the square playing music for entertainment. It was quite an event. Macee said they have something a few times a year, so we plan to go back again. I'm going to enjoy teaching with her. She has made me feel like I belong here.

Classes started yesterday, and I already love them all. Teaching in a small town differs completely from teaching in Fort Worth. All the kids already knew my name, where I moved from, and even whose house I had bought. Shep was right. News gets around fast in a small town.

I've been addressed by name nearly every time I walk into a different store here in town or, "How do you like the old Walsh house?" or even, "It's a lot different way of living here than Fort Worth, huh?" I've stopped being surprised that everyone knows my business and simply started going along with it.

As long as they don't learn about my past business.

I show my teacher pass at the gate and head to the twenty-yard line on the north side. Macee invited me to sit with her and her boyfriend.

I've attended countless football games throughout my school years, from cheering on my brother at his games in Fort Worth through dancing on the field at Texas A&M, but I have never attended a small-town football game. They most certainly could rival the intensity of a college event.

I quickly dodge a group of little girls running around wearing the tiniest cheerleader uniforms I've ever seen. The

65

stands are a sea of black and gray shirts with shaking poms, and the sound of cowbells are scattered throughout the crowd. The rowdy student section is next to the band. Many of them have empty water jugs filled with beans to create as much noise support as possible. The band members are setting up their positions and preparing their instruments. They each wear khaki pants with a black polo shirt tucked in.

A football lands at my feet. A young boy wearing a football jersey with the number 25 runs to snatch the ball. He jogs quickly back to one of the mini football games happening just beyond the end zone. Thunderstruck by AC/DC plays over the loudspeaker, and the aroma of grilled burgers wafts my way with the welcoming breeze. I pass a table selling raffle tickets for a football signed by the entire team. It's like a huge tailgate party with the whole town. It truly is a sight to behold.

Macee waves me over and pats the blanket spread out on the bleacher seat. "You made it! I'm so glad you could come."

"Wow, I'm guessing Glass likes a little football action, huh?"

Macee's boyfriend stands up and offers his hand to help me meander through the people to my seat. "Hi, I'm David. Welcome to Glass. I hope you like your new house. It's my childhood home. Lots of fun memories I've made there."

"Hi, thank you so much. I'm loving it so far. The house is splendid. You guys will have to come by sometime." I take a seat next to Macee and let out a little sigh.

"I'm sure this can be a little overwhelming for new people." Macee looks at me with her eyebrows raised, questioning if I'm okay. I had shared with her last week as we were getting our classrooms ready that I fight off anxiety at times. It gets worse during stressful times, and the first week of school is always stressful.

"Oh, I'm good. No, this is just…. I'm impressed with the fanfare in such a small town." I glance down at the field where students of all ages gather in two groups on the field to form a spirit line. At the front is an inflatable tunnel with a side profile of an enormous black panther on the side wearing a gray football jersey. The panther's large white fangs and claws look ready to battle anyone that dares to challenge its mightiness.

On the other side of the field, the visitor stands are bursting at the seams. A sea of red lines the fence, with the sideline coaches ready to yell their opinions towards the field. The Glen Rose Tigers football team gathers to run through a massive tunnel created by a large inflated red and black tiger with white fangs posed and ready for the attack.

"Looks like it is going to be a battle of the jungle cats around here." A huff of a laugh escapes as I turn to see if they appreciate my lame attempt at a joke.

Macee gasps and gets out her phone. "Ooh, I like it! I'm going to jot that down as an idea for the matchup game later this season." Macee apparently helps contribute to the countless spirit posters all over town.

David reaches over Macee and taps me on my leg to get my attention. He points down to the field. "Shep wants your attention."

I turn my head and see Shep jumping up and down, waving his arms, looking in my direction. His smile broadens as we make eye contact, and I give him a little wave. He turns and runs off the field towards the football boys gathered in the corner behind the tunnel.

"You must be the missing ingredient." David looks at me with his eyes narrowing, as if he is deep in thought.

"What do you mean, 'missing ingredient'?" I despise the fact that my stomach does a little flip fearing his answer.

"Shep has had a little extra pep in his step in the past month. You must be the reason." A smile breaks out on David's face as though he has figured out a mystery. "And by the look on your face, you must feel the same way."

A rush of heat suddenly floods my body, and I can feel my face turn red. Macee slaps David on the knee. "Oh, David, stop that. You are embarrassing her. Besides, you are a little late to the party. We teachers have already placed a bet on who can predict when they will go on their first date." Macee turns to face me. "We've all noticed how Coach Shep has changed his hallway routine to walk purposely by your classroom door whenever he can."

My eyes widen in disbelief and horror. They've all placed bets on me?

"Don't worry," Macee continues. "I peg you as pretty strong, so I'm guessing it will take him a few months to wear you down. I bet it would be at least Thanksgiving Break before you give in." A large grin spreads over her face as she nods in agreement with herself and makes me laugh.

"Thanksgiving? More like never." I glance back down at the corner of the field to see Coach Shep. He is standing in the middle of his football players, who are circled around him, all on bended knees. Shep's hat is off in his hand with his head bowed, obviously praying over his players.

I let out a little sigh. *This might be harder than I thought.*

The Glass Panthers succumbed to the Glen Rose Tigers with a score of 21-7. David mentioned during the game that the Tigers were ranked number two in the district. The Panthers had only won against them twice in football in the past decade but seem to be optimistic about their chances every new season. He said we will play them at their stadium for a district game in the next few weeks.

I follow Macee and David down to the field because it seems like the whole town is headed that way. I spot Pennie, a girl from my homeroom class, running to greet a football player. He must be the father of her future baby. He leans down and kisses her tiny bulge before he swoops her up to twirl her around. Pennie leans back, allowing her long auburn hair to flow around in a circle. They seem happy, but how will they manage the baby once it gets here?

Once we find a stopping point near the end zone, I spot Shep walking our way. How does someone look even cuter when they are all covered in sweat? He has a dark smudge on the side of his face. I instinctively reach up to wipe it off for him before I realize what my hand is doing.

Shep grins and apologizes for being so sweaty and dirty. "The boys played hard tonight. I don't really have any complaints. The Tigers just came in ready to roll."

"I do love to watch a good football game, but I have to say that I witnessed something that I've never seen tonight." Shep looks at me with a questioning twinkle in his blue eyes, waiting for an explanation. "I've never quite seen a coach as enthusiastic as you seem to be after almost every single play."

A shade of red spreads over Shep's face as Macee and David laugh at his expense. "When the game gets a little long to watch, we focus on Shep to be entertained." David joins in the fun.

Shep spreads his stance in a defensive mode and crosses his arms over his chest. "I'll tell you what. When I get into my coaching mode, something takes over my whole soul. People have sent me videos before of me jumping up and down, chest bumping the boys after a brilliant play, throwing my hat down on the field, or even the referees chasing me back behind the line when I get too excited. Most of the time, I don't even remember how I acted!"

"Just another reason we love you, man." David slugs Shep on the arm, which just makes me notice how big his biceps are once again. "Hey, we are going to head that way to save a booth. Want your usual to drink?"

"Yes, thanks! I'm going to go shower real quick and make sure the boys have cleaned up the locker room. I'll head that way as soon as I can. Are you joining us?" Shep points at me as he begins to walk backwards.

My eyebrows shoot up with a questioning look at Macee.

"We always meet at Bella's Pizzeria on Main Street after every home game. Come join us! It's always lots of fun."

Macee could sense my hesitation. "Come on, we've had a long week with school starting and all. Come have some fun with us."

"Okay, I'll come for a bit but probably won't stay too long."

Shep lets out a little whoop and runs off. "Don't leave until I get there!" He stops to high-five the little cowboy from the parade and snatches the cowboy hat from his head. Wearing it, he gallops around as if on a horse. The tiny cowboy slugs him in the knees, winning his prized hat back. Shep hugs the older lady standing with the boy. She reaches up and pats Shep's cheeks before sending him on his way.

I turn around and see both David and Macee looking at me. "What? Can't a girl just want some pizza?" I hook arms with Macee and lead her towards the parking lot.

"Not one word, David, not one word." I give him my best teacher look, daring him to say something.

He slides his fingers across his lips and throws the pretend key over his shoulder.

What have I just agreed to?

By the time Shep gets to Bella's, the restaurant is full. We've snagged a booth in the back on the opposite side of most of the teenagers. There is a wide mix of students: football jerseys, band uniforms, cheer uniforms, and many more with a variety of Panther Pride gear. I admire how they all mix and don't segregate according to school interests. I point Pennie out to Macee and ask if she knows her story.

"That's a sad story, actually. Her mom passed away a couple of years ago from cancer. She lives with her dad, but he's not really involved as much as he used to be. There isn't much supervision. We all think he is dealing with his own grief. Her boyfriend, Tony, is a pretty good kid. He's a senior too. I heard that after graduation, he will go to work for his dad at the family's automotive shop. I'm pretty sure the baby is due in November."

"I wonder if she needs anything. I've noticed her working some mornings in the cafeteria, cleaning tables."

"Yeah, the school has a work program that hires disadvantaged students who need to earn some money." Macee takes another bite of her pepperoni pizza. A chunk of pineapple falls off into her lap.

"I'll get some more napkins." Shep hops up and saunters to the counter, giving out knuckles here and there along the way.

David catches me watching Shep. He wiggles his fingers at the corner of his mouth and then slides his fingers along his wide smile as if he has just found the key to unlock his lips. I quickly give him my teacher's look again, and he slides his fingers quickly back across his lips, tucks the key into his shirt pocket, and gives me a wink.

I grab the chain at my neck and slide my fingers down to find the charms tucked inside my t-shirt. My finger traces around each circle interlocked within each other.

Big circle, little circle, big circle, little circle.

Shep comes back with a handful of napkins and another drink for himself. This would be his third refill. I notice the teenagers on the opposite side looking at us. They seem to whisper and stare, and I suddenly realize that Shep and I must be the topic of their conversation.

I need to get out of here. I reach for my purse under the table. "I really need to get home. I've got an early day tomorrow. Thanks so much for inviting me to come with you all."

Shep slides out of the booth to let me out. "I'm glad you agreed to come. You can make this a tradition to join us anytime. I sure would like that."

I lay some cash on the table, not wanting him to think this was a date. "I'm not sure. I will just have to see. This should cover my part and some of the tip." I brush my pants for any hidden crumbs before I head out the door.

"Let me walk you to your car," Shep starts to follow me.

"No, I'm fine, really. You stay here and finish up that pizza. Looks like you have one piece left." I point to the nearly empty pan of pizza covered with just about every type of meat one can think of. Shep stands there looking like he's not sure what to do.

"See you Monday," Macee calls after me as I walk away.

"Bye, thanks again!" I give a wave and pretend to fidget around in my purse in order to avoid the teenager stares as I head towards the door. As I pass Pennie's table, she waves goodbye to me, and I give her a quick smile in return.

When I reach my car, I peek back into the windows of the restaurant. A swarm of teenagers surrounds the booth that I just left. Many of the football players give Shep knuckles. I assume they have something to do with me. With the car started, I head out of the parking lot. *What was I thinking? I shouldn't have ever agreed to eat pizza. I want to go to the next football game, but I am going to need a good excuse to avoid Bella's Pizzeria next time.*

I grab my necklace again while I wait at the one red light in town.

Big circle. Little circle. Big circle. Little circle.

I don't understand what this attraction is that I'm fighting off towards Shep. He does not come close to checking off any of the boxes that Ted did. Of course, that is now a moot point considering how that turned out. None of this matters anyway, because I am far from ready to start a new relationship.

I moved to Glass on a mission to find some answers about my past. And when I am ready to pursue something new, Coach Shep does not come close to the perfect type of man that I need in my life.

11 Summer

End of August
Present Day

I reach over to hit snooze on my alarm. Seven more minutes and then I need to get up. This has been the longest week ever. *What was I doing getting a job that I have to get up so early for?* Being at the school has been a lot of fun, though. It feels so natural to be there. This new self-preservation mode might just work.

When school started last week, Chad sent me flowers to congratulate me on my new job. That was so sweet of him to think of me. The manager of the cafeteria said I couldn't keep them in our work area though because of some state regulations, so she stuck them in her office on her desk. I kept making up excuses to ask the manager questions all day so that I could admire it.

I focus on the wildflower bouquet that now sits on my kitchen table. They remind me of how he tries to show me he loves me. I need to put some fresh water in them this morning and pull a couple of old ones out. It's been over a week. In fact, I think I will pinch off a few petals to lay on the kitchen windowsill by my special rock to dry out.

Dad found this beautiful crystal decanter that he gave me during my eighth-grade year. I've been

73

keeping dried flower petals in it ever since to preserve the special ones. White petals from various homecoming mum corsages. Dad bought me beautiful pink roses for my sixteenth birthday. A couple of purple and red petals from each year of my prom wristlets. Special flowers that I collected from walking along the creek with Ryan next to our house. The ones I kept out of the casket spray from the funeral should be dry enough now to add to it.

I sure do miss my daddy. It's funny how different things will trigger a memory out of the blue. The other day I started crying in the grocery store when I passed the bakery counter. Dad would always buy my brothers and me a special cookie at that very spot every Saturday when we would all go grocery shopping. Mom was with me, and she started crying too. It reminded me of when she was sad after she and Dad separated when I was little. We stood there and held each other in front of the bakery counter, with rows of freshly baked cookies witnessing our breakdown. The smell of chocolate and brown sugar whirled around us as we cried. Mom ended up buying one for me. I brought it home and sat on my couch with a picture of Dad and ate it. *How can such precious memories hurt so badly?*

My alarm quietly starts singing to me again. It's U2's song "Beautiful Day." One of Dad's favorites. He would belt it out in the car on the way to school every morning and make all of us sing along. If we refused, he would threaten to pull up to the school, windows down, and have the song blaring just to embarrass us in front of our friends. Now, I start off every morning listening to it.

I pick up my phone but don't stop the song from playing. I need this song stuck in my head today. Heading to the bathroom to get ready, I contemplate whether it's possible to train myself to become a morning person.

Ryan hands me a doughnut over the cafeteria counter where I'm serving up biscuits and gravy to the high school students. "Happy Friday! How was your first full week?"

I grab the doughnut before my manager sees and stuff the bag in my apron pocket. "I'm exhausted. Hopefully, I can sleep all day long tomorrow."

"I was hoping we could go mudding tomorrow like we used to. We never hang out anymore."

I shrug my shoulders apologetically as I slap some more gravy on a tray for a girl in line who wrinkles her nose in disgust.

"If you can't make it tomorrow, just let me know when would be good for you. I'll understand as long as you come to the football game tonight. You'd better not miss it. I'll be looking for you up in the stands."

"What are you thinking about tonight's game against the Grandview Zebras? Did the loss last week set them on fire for a win?" I hand over a plate of breakfast to the next student in line. Pretty sure he rolled out of bed about ten minutes ago. He turns to pay the cashier, and his bedhead in the back proves I'm probably right.

"They are fired up. I believe our chances are pretty good tonight. Are you and Chad coming to Bella's Pizzeria afterwards? Missed you guys there last week."

"I think so! I was too exhausted last Friday night after the game. All I wanted to do was get home, check on Mom, and crawl in bed. You need to stop by and see her sometime. She would love that."

Ryan is definitely one of Mom's favorites. His goofy demeanor can always get her to smile.

"I'll do that! Maybe Sunday after church. Would y'all be interested in going to church with us?" Ryan reaches over the counter to sneak a biscuit when the other cafeteria ladies aren't looking.

"No, I don't think so. We haven't been to church in so many years. The roof would probably cave in on us if we went." Seven years. It's been seven years and Mom still refuses to go. And after Dad passed away, there is no way I could get her through those doors now.

"Okay, well, let me know if you change your mind. My pew is always open for ya!" Ryan heads towards the door to go to class and prepare for the day. "By the way, that hair net is," and he blows a chef's kiss my way.

Acting like I'm going to pelt him with a biscuit, he turns away laughing. I've enjoyed hearing that laugh again every day.

I glance around the cafeteria at all the students sitting at the tables. Pennie is sitting at a table with a guy's arm around her. He must be the father of her growing bump. She wipes some biscuit crumbs off his football jersey. She has been coming into the cafeteria early on Tuesdays and Thursdays to wipe off tables to earn some extra money. I should really work harder to be nicer to her.

The kid with the bedhead has his head down on his arms. No doubt he is catching a little more sleep before he is ushered off to first period.

I always dreamed of having a career surrounded by high school students, just not in this capacity. Maybe one day I will go back and finish my education degree. I can feel it in the depths of me. This is where I belong.

My phone buzzes as I'm placing the last gravy pot on the shelf. It's Ryan.

Just need to ask you a quick question you don't owe me an explanation I just would like an answer

That's weird. I quickly type a response before my manager notices I'm on my phone.

What?

I hide the phone on the side of the counter while I wipe it down. The three dots signal his question should come through soon. *What does he want to ask? Since when does he not want an explanation?* The three dots disappear, and his message pops up.

are you happy with chad

The question catches me off guard. *Why is he asking me that? Of course, I am. Aren't I?* We've been dating for over five years now. Everything seems to be *fine. Of course, I'm happy. I haven't been ready to get married to Chad until lately. With Dad passing, I realize how brief life can be. I shouldn't put Chad off anymore. He's wanted to get married for a couple of years now. Why is he asking me this? Does he know something I don't? Is he just being protective? I know he really doesn't like Chad. And the feeling is reciprocated. They are both going to have to deal with each other.*

I type a three-letter response to his odd question and hit send.

> yes

> that is all I need to know

I stick my phone in my pocket without typing an answer back.

My eyes open wide enough for me to see the time on my phone. 9:32. Ugh. I was hoping to sleep in at least until 10:30. The morning sun shines in my window. I forgot to pull the curtains when I went to bed last night.

Chad brought me home after a night of football and pizza. I felt awkward at first because of Ryan's strange question yesterday, but he acted as normal as could be. Chad always cuddles up to me a lot more when Ryan is around. It's like he wants to make sure that Ry has no question that I am taken or something. Ryan definitely knows what buttons to push to get Chad stirred up. He kept talking about childhood memories of our growing up and all our adventures. Chad would come back with comments like, "Well, when Summer and I have kids one day…." And then Ryan would share another one. At least they pretend to like each other in front of me.

I roll out of bed and pull my hair up into a bun. Clay was supposed to come in from school this weekend but ended up having to work. Mom and I are going to run into Glen Rose for the day and do some shopping.

I step out onto my tiny porch and let the sun warm my face. *How can it be so hot this early in the morning?* Mom is swinging on her porch swing, so I head over to wrap up details for our girls' day.

"Good morning, Sunshine!" Mom smiles and waves me over. She pats the seat right next to her. I cuddle up to her and lay my head on her shoulder. I've discovered that it doesn't matter how old you are, there's nothing that makes you feel young again like cuddling up with one of your parents.

She's humming a tune that I don't recognize and sipping on her coffee in between hums.

"You seem to be in a good mood this morning." I take her coffee cup from her to steal a sip.

"I had such a great dream last night. Your dad and I were sitting together in church, and the choir was singing this beautiful song. I don't recognize the song, but I can't get the tune out of my head." She hums a little louder. "I haven't had that kind of peace since your…. well, in the past seven years." Steam escapes from her mug when she takes another sip. She goes back to humming again, and I nestle the top of my head into the crevice of her neck, listening to her hum away. Flashes of when it was just her and me taking care of each other quickly run through my mind. I've always felt responsible for ensuring she was happy.

Ryan's question haunts me again. *Am I truly happy with Chad?* I dreamed last night that Ryan and I were eating at a restaurant and Chad was our server. Ryan left a twenty-dollar bill as a tip, and Chad wadded it up and threw it on the ground at his feet. I was bewildered as to why he would do that? What could that have meant?

A monarch butterfly flutters up to perch on the red and yellow lantana in the hanging basket on the porch. We both freeze and sit still not to scare it away. It flutters around from bloom to bloom and then erratically circles underneath the porch next to us. As if it has somewhere it has to be, it suddenly takes off, soaring up into the sky.

"I heard that someone has started a butterfly farm a couple of miles down the road. I wonder if that one is from there?" I nestle a little closer, not wanting this moment to end.

Mom takes another sip of her coffee. "Not sure. All I know is that hanging basket is the last thing your father gave me before he… you know…. left. He said he bought it because he knew how much I loved watching butterflies."

I look up at Mom as a single tear rolls down her cheek. I stretch my arm around her shoulders and pull her into me, reversing the roles once again of who comforts whom.

Mom and I round the last corner of the town square in Glen Rose. Our arms are heavy with bags, and our wallets are lighter than when we started. Retail shopping therapy works every time. We saved our favorite store for the last: Front Porch Designs on Walnut Street. We hurried through the other shops to spend the rest of our time and money at this sweet establishment.

As we walk in, Traci, the owner, greets us. She has such a genuine and sweet demeanor. She offers a spot to put down our packages if we want, so that we may walk around with open arms. Mom is drawn to the jewelry section while I walk over to the new fall décor that has been set out. Every year I say that I'm going to decorate my front porch for each season like Ryan's grandma does, and I keep putting it off. Hopefully, I can find something to help motivate me to do it this fall season. One thing I have learned over the past seven years is not to put things off. No one knows when his or her last day on this earth might be.

The cutest little baby bibs are displayed on a table. Pennie comes to mind. There is something about her I am pulled to. I need to be nicer to her the next time she is working. I chose a bib that says, "Feed Me and Tell Me I'm Cute." However, buying her a gift before we have really ever talked might be too awkward. I set it back down on the pile.

After meandering around the store for what had to have been about thirty minutes, taking it all in and making our selections, we head to the counter to check out. Mom has found a dainty silver necklace with a silver butterfly sitting on top of a flower.

"I'm getting this to remember this day. It is the first day in a long time that I have felt almost normal again."

I grab the necklace from her and place it in my pile next to the specialty jellybeans I found for her. "Please let me buy it for you. Then it can be that much more special."

Mom bends me forward and kisses me on the forehead. She doesn't put up an argument about my paying for it. "I am so very blessed to have you in my life! I wouldn't wish it any other way!"

I give her a quick squeeze, understanding the meaning behind her comment. She and Dad have always been open about how they got pregnant with me in high school and the options they faced. Mom's parents weren't supportive at all, causing her to move out into a camper on Grandpa's farm. Several years later, when my brothers were born, her parents started talking to her again. They had apologized for not being available when I was younger, but Mom had a very hard time forgiving them.

Traci noticed Mom looking at an open journal on the counter. "That's our prayer journal. Please jot down any prayer requests that you may have. When we close up every day, I take the journal home, and my husband and I pray over all the requests in it. Sometimes people even come back and share with us how God worked in their lives, answering their particular request." Traci gave a sweet smile to Mom.

"Oh, no, that's okay. Thanks anyway. I'm not really sure if I believe in that anymore." Mom grabs her bags and takes a step back so I can finish my transaction. The wrinkle between her brows becomes more visible as she sinks into deep thought.

"Sure. I understand. Just know that it is always here if you ever change your mind." Traci hands me my receipt and tells us to have a blessed day, seeming to pick up on the pain in Mom's voice.

We head out the door when Mom suddenly stops. A butterfly circles around her head. She watches it as it hovers over the hanging basket of flowers by the front door. She sets her packages down on a bench. "Watch these. I'll be right back."

I try not to stare to see what Mom is doing back in the store. I hold my phone up in front of my face to mask my watching her through the storefront window. She talks to Traci, and they walk back towards the counter, causing me to lose sight of her. I sit on the bench waiting for a few minutes until Mom finally comes out.

Walking to the car, I struggle back and forth about whether to ask her what that was about or to allow her to have her private moment. We set the packages in the back seat once we get to the car, having been silent the whole walk there.

As we head around a curve driving back towards Glass, Mom breaks the silence. "I told her briefly about what has happened and about my dream last night. I wrote a prayer request in her journal, and she promised to pray for me."

I kept silent, allowing her to process her thoughts and hoping that she will share more of them with me.

I finally couldn't stand it anymore. "Do you mind if I ask what request you wrote?"

"I just wrote one word."

"What was that?" The curvy road keeps me from looking at her expression while she sits there staring out the window.

"Church."

I slowly nod my head without a response, uncertain how I feel about her prayer request.

We sit in silence for the rest of the ten minutes that it takes to drive back home. When we pull up at the farmhouse, I let her out and help her carry in her packages. She thanks me again for the shopping day and the necklace. She's going to go take a bubble bath to wash off all the sweat from the day and eat the specialty jellybeans I bought her.

I pull my car closer to my tiny home and sit there in my own thoughts.

Would Mom really want to go back to church? After all these years? What would everyone think when we come waltzing back in the doors after seven years of absence? I can already feel the judgment that some people would probably have toward us. All the whispering and talking behind our backs, wondering why we have graced them with our presence suddenly. *Nope. I can't do it. I'm sure this is another one of Mom's whims that will pass in a day or two.*

I reach for my door handle to open it and freeze in place. Tiny little eyes stare at me as they perch on my side mirror. The butterfly and I study each other, taking in every detail, until it unexpectedly takes flight. I watch the orange spot until it disappears towards the back of my house.

I get a sinking feeling in my stomach that we might start back to church soon.

12 Third Option

**First Week of September
Present Day**

13 Jasmine

A Layer From the Middle of July
Three Years Before the Move
Twenty-four Years Old

I was frozen in place. More out of shock than pain. Judging by his expression, Ted was just as shocked as I was. Neither of us quite knew what to do next. His face suddenly filled with remorse. He fell to his knees and started hugging mine.

"I'm so sorry, Jazzy. I don't even know where that came from!"

I did.

"I've done nothing like that before when we've argued. Not even when my brothers used to make me mad. I'm so sorry. Please forgive me! I promise I will never do that again!" He suddenly jumped back up as fast as he had fallen down.

"Just hit me back. Right here in the kisser. Hit me as hard as you can. Or you can hit me in the stomach. Just haul off with all your power and punch me. Not too low because you know we want to have kids one day." He scrunched up his face, ready for the blow.

I turned and walked straight to the kitchen to grab my purse and started towards the front door. I didn't even realize we were arguing. I considered it merely a discussion.

"Jasmine! Wait! Wait! Don't go. Where are you going? Please don't leave. Let's just talk. Come on." Ted plopped down on the leather couch and patted the seat right next to him.

I stared at him with a deadpan face. My stinging cheek reminded me of why I was headed out the door.

"You probably don't want to sit by me. Here, I'll move." He sped over and sat in his recliner, never taking his eyes off me. His entire body trembled. My calm composure surprised me.

His move put him further away from the front door, so I turned and walked towards escape once again. I knew he cared way too much about what the neighbors would think and would never continue his begging outside.

"Jazz, no, no, no, no! Don't leave! Where are you going? Please stay! I'm so sorry. I will never do that again."

And that turned out to be one of his biggest lies ever.

We never really discussed the first hit. I came home the next morning, having spent the night with Layla. She had always made me feel safe ever since she protected us from the boys in our sixth-grade math class. I informed her that we had argued and needed some time apart. I tried to hide the left side of my face from her, but I'm sure she caught a glimpse. She never asked me about it. I don't think I could've brought myself to admit I had been wrong about him.

When I walked in the front door of our house the next morning, the smell of bacon swept away my anticipation and replaced it with a bit of hope. Ted had cooked my favorite breakfast, hoping I would come home. He pulled a chair out for me, and that was it. It was in the past.

I managed to hide the bruise with makeup. Thank goodness it was in the summer, so my tanned face absorbed a lot of the off-color. Despite the Texas heat, I left my long blonde hair down for a few days so I could use it to conceal the spot if I felt like anyone was looking.

Ted magically turned into the perfect husband again after that. It was like we were dating again. Doors were being opened. Flowers were sent randomly to my classroom. Weekend getaways were about once a month. Notes were left on the bathroom mirror. And the restaurants. I loved eating out all the time. He really made me feel loved and cherished.

He confessed to me once when we dated that he witnessed his father strike his mom when she allegedly defied him. He and his brothers also received consequences for not meeting their dad's high standards. His dad always expected perfection.

Ted had vowed he would never be like his dad.

A Layer From the End of April
Two Years Before the Move
Twenty-five Years Old

The second time he hit me shocked me more than the first time. I genuinely believed he would never raise a hand to me again.

He hit me much harder this time. And this incident didn't stop with one hit.

We had been arguing about money in the kitchen. Arguments were becoming more frequent. I oversaw the bills, and all his wooing of me over the past year was adding up. He bought me an expensive diamond bracelet for my birthday the week before. I knew we were going to have some added expenses soon. Ted told me I was ungrateful, reprimanded me, and started the death stare. I simply turned around to tend to the dishes again, and that set him off.

The next thing I knew, his hands were wrapped around my neck. He twirled me around, causing one of our cream-colored wedding plates to crash to the floor. He hit me with his right hand again, just like the first time. Only this time, he missed my cheek and hit me right in the eye.

Hard.

When my head turned back to face him, it was not my husband standing in front of me. I didn't recognize the rage in his dark brown eyes. They appeared as two dark holes that led to the depth of his tortured soul. His nostrils were flared, and his gritted teeth caused speckles of spit to fly at my face with his heavy breathing.

Suddenly, he grabbed my hair, slung me to the ground, and started kicking me. My legs drew up instinctively into a fetal position as I begged for him to stop. He had turned into a crazed man that I didn't recognize.

This was not the perfect man that I married.

The last thing I remembered from that night was staring at the small present on the kitchen counter I had carefully wrapped for him earlier in the day. The present that was going to change our lives forever. The gift that revealed to him he would become a father this upcoming fall.

14 Summer

A Layer From the End of July
Ten Years Before the Wreck
Seventeen Years Old

The end of summer break had come. The next day started my junior year and Ryan's senior year at Glass High School. I certainly would miss him next year. I no longer needed rides since I could drive myself now. I would miss our morning karaoke concerts, and our Friday morning stops at the doughnut shop on the way to school.

Yesterday, we agreed we needed to celebrate the last day of summer with a picnic by the creek today. We had been meeting at the creek between our houses since I had turned nine and he was ten. Until then, our mothers were always there with us. That marked the year that my youngest brother, Dusty, was born, and I believed Mom only agreed to allow us to do that to have one less kid in the house. As an only child for seven years, I found it challenging to deal with the noise produced by a two-year-old and a newborn.

Ryan had already arrived at our usual spot on his side of the creek. Dad constructed a little bridge for us to use after Mom's constant complaints about my wet shoes from going back and forth. I crossed the bridge, sliding my hand along the handrail as I had done so many years before. On my other arm, I had my picnic basket containing drinks and goodies for the day. He would be surprised I made his favorite no-bake cookies for him last night.

"Welcome to Sheppard Land," he proclaimed in the most royal voice he could muster. With one arm behind his back, his other arm made small circles in front of him as he bowed to me.

"That's quite a welcome, Your Majesty." I curtsied in return as he grabbed the basket.

"What do we have here?"

"Not so fast, Ry! There might be a surprise in there for you later." I snatched the basket back and hid it behind me, knowing full well that he could easily overpower me to take it.

Luckily, he obliged, and I sneaked a peek in the basket and took an exaggerated whiff just to tease him.

Without words, we headed east up the side of the creek bed, watching for copperheads as we walked. Ever since our run-in with one a few years ago, Ry always made sure he carried a big stick and walked in front to keep me protected.

We wound along the worn pathway and found our way to the largest pool area. Spreading out the blanket in its customary spot, we settled down, eager for a drink.

"I can't believe how hot it is so early this morning." Ryan gulped down half of his water bottle without taking a breath.

"That is why I wanted to have an early lunch. Remember our younger days when we would hang out here? It couldn't have been this hot."

"Oh, it definitely was. We stayed cool, playing in the water constantly."

"You mean like this?" I reached over and swatted a handful of water towards his arm.

"No, more like this!" He jumped up and cradled me in his arms as if I were a weightless rag doll. He started a countdown to throw me in.

I protested loudly, pounding my fists on his chest, and he slowly put me down. My feet searched for the ground as my body slid down his.

I suddenly experienced a warm sensation developing across my body. Our eyes met, and his gaze lingered a bit too long. My chest felt constricted. I didn't quite understand why my body was reacting this way.

"Guess what I made for you?" My voice betrayed me with a high-pitched tone. I cleared my throat and quickly stepped away, heading for the basket. I pulled out a baggie of his all-time favorite cookies and made sure that I held them at arm's length between us, too nervous to get close to him again.

He took the bag, narrowing his eyes. "You can't deny that you didn't just feel that between us. You've known about my feelings for you over the years. Why won't you give us a chance?"

"Ry, you understand why. When we were younger, we dated, but it didn't work out." I sat on the blanket, unable to look him in the face.

"Summer, it was the seventh grade. Give me a break. I've matured a little since then." Ryan sat down across from me and quickly polished off three cookies.

"Hey, slow down there on the cookies. You know I only packed seven. Four for you and three for me." I snatched the bag and grabbed a cookie.

"Yeah, yeah, I know the drill. Tell me again why you are obsessed with the number seven?" I sensed his expression without seeing him. He was familiar with the answer, despite his constant questioning.

"Because that is the age I was when I met you." I tried my best to add annoyance to my voice, afraid that it might betray me again with a longing sound. "I was incredibly lucky to find a best friend and big brother I'd always wanted." I glanced up at him so I could see his reaction to my next comment. "Boy, was I wrong."

Ryan's laugh had become much deeper over the past year. His eyes squinted when he smiled, like they did the first summer that we met. Little crinkles at the corners of his eyes have formed. I considered how distinguished he would become with age.

"I'd throw the last half of this cookie at you, but I don't want to waste it." He dropped the last of his portion of the cookies into his mouth, which was open like a baby bird. He didn't even attempt to chew it.

"It made things very awkward for us. You ignored me around your friends. It took a year after we broke up to feel normal again. That was one of the worst years of my life. You are a crucial part of my existence, and I really don't want to jeopardize that again. Especially in your senior year. Life will forever be different after you leave for school next fall. Talk about a Summer Bummer. Next summer will be the worst of all."

He gifted me with my special name the summer that we decided to "date." I overheard him calling me that to one of his friends, and that night I broke up with him. It's been his term of endearment for me ever since, knowing that it gets me going every time.

Ryan grabbed a couple of rocks off the pile he had created on the side of the creek bed and rubbed them back and forth between his fingers. I have longed to intertwine those fingers with mine, but my fear always wins out over my heart's desires.

"I'll tell you what. I realize at our age we are not at a place to be serious, but I already know that you embody all the characteristics that I want in a future best friend, wife, and mother for my kids. Waiting for you until you are ready is my top priority, whether that is next week or ten years from now."

He threw one rock into my lap. "Can you tell me what that rock looks like?"

As I lifted the rock, I felt the smoothness that centuries of water flow had created during its time here. My finger rubbed along the edge and dipped down into the small crevice at the top. "It looks like a heart."

Ryan straightened, his expression growing serious. He held up a second rock like the one that I was holding, crevice and all.

"We have collected special rocks here for years. I have them stuffed in my drawers and have shoeboxes full of them in my closet. I know you do too. Keep that heart-shaped rock in a special place. Remember this conversation each time you see it, knowing I never want to be without you. And I hope you feel the same way too. The ball is in your court now, Summer. You hold it or toss it back whenever you are ready, and I'll be standing here waiting to catch it."

I had never seen Ryan so serious before. His presence defined my life; I couldn't envision my future without him.

Which was the exact reason we could not risk a dating relationship.

"But I will tell you one thing." Ryan leaned closer to me, and I was afraid he was trying to seal it with a kiss. "I am sick and tired of waiting for you to eat this last cookie." He grabbed the baggie and dumped the contents into his baby bird mouth once again. Crumbs and all.

There was the Ryan I loved. Why did the thought of exploring love with him scare me so much?

15 Third Option

**First Week of December
Eight Years Ago**

16 Jasmine

Middle of September
Present Day

Another week is complete as I put away the last stack of graded papers and prepare to lock up for the weekend. I've dreaded this week coming to a close. Changing the date on the board to prepare for Monday forces me to face the dreaded date that is ingrained in the back of my mind. It reminds me of the "what ifs" in my life. *What if things had worked out how I planned? What if Ted had lived up to his true potential and not succumbed to his buried anger? What if I had never discovered the truth about the many things that have set me on this alternative path? Where did I go wrong to lose my perfect life that was planned out right in front of me?*

Reluctantly, I write the date on the board and stare at it with a longing that will never happen. This life is my new reality. I head to the sink to fill a cup with water. One month of school has passed, and I'm feeling more confident about my decision to start over in Glass. I'm only here because of what has happened in my world recently. Small-town life is starting to suit me. I've never been called ma'am so many times in my life. When I received my first paycheck, I felt guilty because of the ease of teaching here. My teacher friends back in the Fort Worth school system are receiving the same amount that I am, but they must deal with so much more paperwork from the district and attitudes from their students. I have more lessons to plan since I teach three different math classes, but the exchange has been worth it.

One more detail about teaching in a small town is I get to know my students better. Every time I water the ivy plants in the back of the room, I think of Pennie. She always comments on how her growing belly is only outdone by how much the ivy has grown since school has started. I see Pennie a lot outside the classroom. Her belly is slowly growing, although from the back you can't even tell she is pregnant. I kept her after class one day last week because I had noticed her crying. She confided in me how hard it was for her to be pregnant. She didn't mind the whispers as she walked down the hall. Her real friends stuck by her side as the fake ones fell away. She was almost grateful for that.

However, she admitted the hardest part was how the relationship with her dad had dwindled since her mom passed away. He had sunk into a dark shell. Pennie had tried her best to be there for her dad, but since she got pregnant, she feels he has sunk even deeper. They hadn't had a fight or anything, and she was almost desperate for one, just so she could see that he cared. I assured her that her dad cared, but he was just having a hard time himself. She should try not to take it so personally, even though that was much easier said than done. I was sure she could find a way to talk to him.

I asked her once whether adoption had ever been an option. I assured her that what would make her a wonderful mom was making the best decision for her baby, whatever that may be, whether she kept her or gave her up for adoption. She said that she and Tony wanted to make it work. Her eyes twinkled when she said she was looking forward to seeing herself in her baby's eyes. That comment hit hard.

My heart broke for her. I could feel jealousy creeping in over the fact that I lost my baby, and she gets to keep hers. However, looking into her face that day and hearing how excited she was to keep this baby brought up some other feelings of my own that I wasn't expecting to deal with just yet.

My emotions have been off the charts with the upcoming date on the calendar.

The last of the water drips from the watering cup into the ivy plant at the front of the room as I prepare to lock up for the weekend. Pennie is right; they seem to have doubled in size since school started. I start across the room to turn my lamps off when I notice a dark figure hovering at my doorway. Startled, I drop the empty watering cup and let out a gasp.

"I'm so sorry. I didn't mean to startle you." A mixture of hesitation and regret falls over Shep as he steps through the doorway.

"That's okay. I thought everyone had already left by now." I pick the cup up off the floor and smear the water droplets around with my shoe. "I thought you would already be on your way to the football game. Aren't you guys headed to Godley this evening?"

"Yeah, it's a short drive, so we didn't have to leave as early. I left my lucky rock in my room, so I ran back in to get it." Shep pulled a small smooth stone out of his pocket and held it in the air. "I've always loved collecting rocks. When I get a little nervous on the sidelines, I like to fiddle with the indentation on this one. It reminds me of what is to come." He pushes the rock back down into the safety of his front pocket.

"Good luck tonight. I really don't think you guys need much luck though, as well as you all have been playing." I head back to my desk to gather my things and avoid as much eye contact as possible.

"The guys have been doing great! Losing to Glen Rose in that first scrimmage lit a fire under them. They are practicing for revenge when we meet up with them again at the end of October. That seems to be their motivation for every game." Without looking, I can feel a charming smile spreading over his face. The smile that I have worked so hard to avoid the past few weeks.

"I can hear the boys talk about it occasionally in class. They really take the rivalry seriously, don't they?" Out of mannerly habit when talking to someone, I glimpse at Shep and

98

realize that he has moved closer to me. I can smell his musky cologne, and my insides tighten. I take a step back and draw in a deep breath.

"Jazz, you have been trying to avoid me lately. I'm not sure what I have done. We had such a fantastic time at Bella's Pizzeria after that first game. It just wasn't the same the last couple of Friday nights without you there. I really enjoyed what you added to our conversations." He looked down at his feet and seemed to awkwardly drag his shoe back and forth as though he couldn't decide whether to stay or run away. I've never seen him appear so unsure of himself before. *Have I made the right decision in ignoring him?*

"You won't look at me in the hallway anymore and seem to avoid me in teacher meetings. If I've made you mad, I'm sorry. Just tell me what I did so I can apologize." A pained anticipation glosses over his face as he looks back my way. He stands there looking so vulnerable and sincere, like a little boy apologizing for breaking his mom's favorite vase.

Thoughts ping-pong back and forth in my mind. *He has the potential to be a great friend, and I enjoy his sense of humor. Am I willing to lose that over my fear of getting too close and distracted from why I really moved here?*

"Oh, Shep, you have done absolutely nothing wrong. There has been a lot going on in my life the past couple of years, and honestly, I've enjoyed the quiet time I have found here in Glass. I have some things I'm working through. I really need to focus on myself and figure out where I go from here." I feel a responsibility that he feels guilty when he has done nothing wrong except be so nice.

And look so cute.

And smell so good.

Shep's face relaxes a little as he takes a step back, holding his hands midway up in the air. "I get it. I totally get it. I've been there before. You don't have to share any details about your story. I know that I've had times in my life like that too, so I get it." His confidence seems to slide back as the worried expression disappears. There is the Shep I'm trying so hard to avoid.

His pocket buzzes as he reaches for his phone. "I've got to run. The bus is waiting for me out front." He shoves the phone back in his pocket after typing a quick response. He begins to step away and just as quickly steps forward towards me.

"I totally hear what you are saying about not getting close to anyone right now. I'm begging you though, please allow me in your friend zone. That's all I'm asking for. The privilege of being your friend. I've enjoyed our conversations so far, and I really don't want to lose that. You are so easy to talk to. Promise me you will consider coming back for pizza next week after our home game." His hands clap together in the begging mode as his head bows in submission to my coming hopeful answer.

A little giggle escapes my lips. "Okay, okay. I hate to see a grown man beg. Especially when his school bus is honking for him outside." One of the football players plays a little tune on the bus's horn, getting all ramped up for the game.

"Great!" Shep's eyes seem to renew their twinkle, and he gains a little bounce in his step on the way to the door. "I'll get the boys to score a touchdown for you."

My head juts forward in disbelief, like he hasn't heard a word I just said.

"Not in that way." Shep laughs and imitates my head jutting. "Just a friend zone touchdown."

He turns and disappears as his sprinting echoes down the hallway. The battle cry blares louder from the waiting bus of teenage boys raring to bring home another victory.

I turn into my driveway as the mailman pulls up to my mailbox. The Walshes had built one out of stone with an opening filled with flowers at the base. However, they are wilting from a lack of water. That describes my insides perfectly. I need to make sure I am replenishing for myself everything I have been giving out for others. The mailman steps out of his vehicle to hand me my stack of mail.

"Ms. Forte, I presume?"

"Yes, hello. Thank you so much." I take the pile and notice Mom's handwriting on the top letter.

"I'm glad I ran into you. My name is Frank Young. You have my daughter Pennie in class this year." A flash of pride momentarily interrupts the sadness in his eyes.

"Yes, she's a great young lady. So polite and smart. I've really enjoyed getting to know her."

"Thank you. She looks just like her mother did." His shoulders sag as he is bombarded with his own personal memories. "Sorry to keep you, but I just wanted to thank you for taking extra time with her. She left me a note the other day that opened up a conversation between the two of us. She told me you were her inspiration for writing the note. I've been so wrapped up in my own sorrow that I didn't realize how she felt she had lost two parents instead of one."

I attempt to put my teacher/counselor hat back on as he fiddles with a button on his shirt. "I am so thankful that the two of you could start a discussion about everything." His chin raises a little higher as he takes a deep breath. A bit of his sorrow falls away. "Like I said before, she's a great young lady and will be a super mom, especially if she feels like you are in her corner."

Frank's squinting eyes stare back at me. His head nods slowly as his inside wheels turn. I place the gearshift into drive.

"It was so nice to meet you, Frank. Thanks for always delivering my mail!" I slowly start up my driveway as he heads back to his mail truck.

"You too, Ms. Forte. Welcome to Glass." He climbs back into his seat, giving me one last wave.

Entering the kitchen, I shut the garage door behind me. I add Mom's latest letter to the unread pile on the counter. We have our obligatory weekly phone calls. Each week, they ask when they can come for a visit, and each week I come up with a different excuse. I know that is what the letters are for because I refuse to have a face to face with her right now. It's like she doesn't want to understand why I need to do what I need to do.

My new little black kitten, Pookie, comes scurrying around the corner to meet me. She runs in so fast that her furball body ends up sliding past me on the tile floor. I reach down to grab her, and she immediately rewards me with her soft purrs and rubs the top of her fuzzy head underneath my chin.

Last week while on the phone with Mom, she talked me into getting a pet. I was telling her how well everything was going, but this big house was too quiet. I had left the music on for some background noise, but it still felt lonely. After realizing she was losing the battle to convince me to move back to Fort Worth, she suggested I get a pet. I always wanted a kitten when I was little, but Mom was too finicky to have an indoor animal. Surely, a kitten would be easy to take care of.

I set her in her favorite spot near the window to watch the birds, so I can freshen her water and give her some more food. My oldest friend Colleen is driving into town this evening when she gets off work, and I'm excited to have a girls' weekend. It is very much needed. We plan to live it up like a couple of teenage girls with money and no curfew. I had invited Layla also, but she already had plans. Maybe we can all get together closer to the holidays.

I step outside to sweep off the deck. Even though I am tired of the hot weather, I'm thankful that this weekend will be warm enough to enjoy my pool. I'm impressed with myself and how I have kept up with it. Shep set up a maintenance schedule for me to follow, and it has worked out well. The clear water looks so inviting. The solar light string that I hung up on the back side of the pool will give us just enough light to enjoy some time out here after we get back from a late supper.

Remembering that I need to change the sheets in the guest bedroom, I head inside. Pookie meets me at the sliding glass door, and I sweep her up again to get a few more cuddles. Setting her on the bed, I cover her up with the sheet. Her moving body looks like a cartoon mole tunneling its way under the top layer of the soil. She reaches the end and pokes her head out and then quickly pulls it back in, sitting in a crouching position. I trace my finger back and forth near the opening, waiting for the imminent attack. She darts out, swipes at my finger, and pulls her head back in. We continue this game a few more times when I unexpectedly yank the sheet off her head. Her tiny head darts left and right, looking for cover when I sweep her up and hold her close. Her purring picks right back up, and my heartbeat falls into rhythm with it.

It's not lost on me that I should be playing hide and seek with my own child and not a cat. I always thought it would be a little girl with honey-brown eyes like mine. She should be the one I'm playing peek-a-boo with, not a kitten. Pookie paws at the circles on my necklace.

"It's pretty, huh? That was a surprise gift from someone very special. Maybe you can meet him one day." I scratch the top of her head as she continues to be focused on one of the most prized possessions I own. "You like it? Me too. This big circle represents me, and the little circle represents my baby that I lost." I can feel warm tears slowly rolling down my cheeks. "Even though she isn't here with me, we will be intertwined forever, like these circles." Pookie tilts her head as I spill my innermost pain to her.

"My baby would've been two this weekend if she'd been born on her due date." I hug Pookie a little too tight, seeking some comfort from her. She squirms to be put down. I put the sheet back over her head and step away to the bathroom to blow my nose. I'm so thankful Colleen can come and spend this weekend with me. I really don't want to be alone.

The bacon and coffee aroma wakes me up. I slide into my house shoes and follow the smell into the kitchen.

"Morning, Sunshine!" Colleen grabs a mug and pours some steaming hot coffee to get me going.

"Wow, can you come stay every weekend with me?" I snatch a piece of bacon from the plate and savor its goodness. Colleen stirs a pot of gravy on the stove. "Biscuits and gravy? Where did you get the stuff for that from?"

"I snuck it in with my luggage last night and put it up when you were changing. I wanted to surprise you this morning." Opening the door to the oven, she checks on the biscuits and sets out a trivet.

"You are my guest. I should cook for you." I snatch another piece of bacon when she looks away to grab some plates.

"I know, but I wanted to do this for breakfast, just like your mom used to make for us when I would stay the night. Besides, you treated me to supper last night. This morning, it is my turn."

My eyes open wide as I remember the countless sleepovers at my house or hers that we have had over the years. "Remember how Dad would always insist on sliced tomatoes to go along with the biscuits?"

Colleen opened the refrigerator and pulled out a plate of freshly sliced tomatoes. "Straight from my grandpa's farm!"

"Man, I've missed you." I say a silent, grateful prayer to God, thanking Him for blessing me with such a great friend for all my life.

"I've missed you too! Now, let's eat up because we have some shopping to do!" We filled our plates and sat out on the back deck. Too late to enjoy one of God's beautiful sunrises, but He certainly made a magnificent sight beyond my backyard to behold.

We stopped by my car to dump off our armload of packages before heading to the stores on the other side of the street. Thanks to so many tourist attractions near Glass and Glen Rose, the towns do not lack cute boutiques and gift shops.

"The architecture of these buildings amazes me." Colleen stops to trace her fingers across one fossil embedded in the wall on the front of the town's salon. She was an architectural engineer at the University of Texas at Austin and at the top of her class. A job was waiting for her after graduation at one of the top architectural firms in Fort Worth. I'm impressed by how quickly she has gained more responsibility over the past few years there.

"This really is a young town. The patchwork of these buildings is phenomenal. Notice how he wove the pieces of petrified wood and stone together. And then he sprinkled fossils here and there in between with the limestone. It's just exquisite." Colleen twists her head back and forth, taking in all the intricate details of each wall as we pass by. The jagged texture of the petrified wood entices her to trace her finger along its edges.

"You know, Jazz, this is how God works." She stops and looks directly at me. "He is so good at taking all the broken pieces in our life and piecing them together to create something beautiful."

I slowly nod my head in agreement, thinking of all the broken pieces in my life lately. But I'm still waiting for the beautiful part.

We come to the storefront of the Sweet Pea Boutique. An array of pastel baby clothes hangs on a cute little clothesline in the window. The colors of blue and pink alternating with the tiniest of socks hanging in between each one.

Bells chime as the door opens and Pennie walks out with two of her friends.

"Ms. Forte! Hi!" Pennie holds up a brown gift bag tied off with a pink and blue gingham ribbon. "My friends wanted to take me shopping. We picked out the softest blanket for the baby." She pulls out a light green muslin swaddle blanket.

"That's perfect. The baby will love it." I plaster a smile on my face, hoping it looks genuine.

"Now I'm going home to practice with my old baby dolls." Pennie shoves the blanket back into the bag. "See you Monday!"

"Bye!" The three friends interlock arms and jump over each crack on the sidewalk. I turn back to the window and contemplate whether I should go inside and buy her something. The clerk might tell me the other items she looked at. Instead, my attention goes back to the tiny little socks, and I get lost in the trance of what could have been.

"Sometimes I get so mad at God that He didn't allow me to keep her. I've always thought she would've been a girl. What can He do with that broken piece?" Colleen puts her arm around my shoulders as we take in the tiny clothes that someone else's baby will wear one day. Just not mine. My fingers reach for comfort. Big circle. Little circle.

"I know. It just doesn't seem fair sometimes, does it?" Colleen has been with me through all my good times and hard times in my life. I'm silently thankful that she just allows me to be mad about it for a minute.

My focus shifts from the baby clothes to my reflection in the glass window. My aches from the previous years bare themselves through my eyes when I'm not careful. The heaviness of my heart shows all over my face when I allow myself to be real. Sometimes it gets so hard to push through and function every day. It is just not fair. This is not how my life is supposed to be. I've been good all my life and made good choices. *Why is God punishing me?*

The words Mom told my brother and me all our lives intrude on my thoughts of self-pity. "Do you see any cotton candy anywhere? Life is not a fair." My eyes roll remembering her constant attempt to compare life's fairness to the county fair. She always expected perfection from everyone around her.

After a couple of silent moments of daydreaming of what should have been, I take in a deep breath and let it out slowly. Mom's other words of wisdom also enter my thoughts, causing a layer of comfort to soothe the pain. She constantly assures me my baby, whom my empty arms ache for, is in the loving arms of Jesus waiting to meet me one day. I choose to settle for this peace and let the anger wither away.

I turn to face the next store. "Okay, let's move on. I've still got some money to spend."

Colleen picks up her packages and takes a couple of quick steps to keep up with me.

"How about some chocolate?" I already know what her answer will be.

"Thought you would never ask!" She links her arm in mine, and we head next door to The Rolling Pin.

After making an almost impossible decision of what to treat ourselves to, we head to the sidewalk and sit at one of the cute bistro tables so we can indulge in our bakery confections and hand-mixed sodas.

"Well, my, my, here comes a tall drink of water." Colleen pulls her sunglasses down slightly to get a better view somewhere behind me. I turn my head to see who she is drooling over. Of course, it's Shep.

I quickly turn back and duck my head, but apparently not fast enough.

"Jazz, hey! I thought that was you I saw earlier." He holds his hand out to Colleen. "Hi, I'm Shep. I teach down the hall from Jasmine at the high school." His eyes crinkle at the corners with his smile. I should tell him congratulations on their win last night over Godley, but I would love to keep the conversation to a minimum.

Colleen gives me an accusing look, as if I have been keeping a secret from her.

"Hello, I'm Colleen. Jasmine's friend since we learned how to crawl together in the church nursery."

Shep pulls up a chair from a neighboring table and makes himself comfortable without being invited. He apparently has never been taught proper etiquette. Maybe I should offer to teach that as an elective at the high school.

"That reminds me; I've been meaning to tell you that you ought to come visit my church if you haven't settled on one yet." He finds a cookie crumb that had fallen to the table and tosses it in his mouth.

"Yes, Jazz. That sounds like a splendid idea." Colleen raises her eyebrows at me, enjoying this uncomfortable situation way too much. She tosses a cookie crumb in her own mouth, imitating Shep's enthusiasm about it all.

"Don't get me wrong, I have a great relationship with God. I talk with Him all the time, but I don't really do the church thing anymore. I haven't been in a couple of years." I break off a piece of my pastry and chuck it towards Colleen.

Shep catches it mid-air and tosses it into his mouth. "Well, you are missing out. Our singles group is fantastic, and we meet often. I've made some great friends there. You need to check it out. Macee and David go to some of them too. The four of us had so much fun that one night after the football game. It would be a blast."

Colleen did a horrible job of trying to hide any kind of surprise on her face. "The four of you have been out before?" Her finger wagged between Shep and me, connecting us with some invisible attachment.

"Oh, just as friends." Shep leaned closer to Colleen as she took a sip of her soda. Covering the side of his mouth with his hand as if he were telling a secret, he whispers loudly, "I'm in the friend zone."

I can feel the rush of heat on my face as my eyes roll dramatically to show how annoyed I am. Colleen chokes on her soda from the laugh that bursts out of her at my expense. Droplets of red strawberry soda go everywhere.

Shep hops up. "I'll go grab some extra napkins. Because I'm a great FRIEND to have." He winks at me before he heads inside.

"Jasmine! Are you crazy? You friend-zoned him? He is so into you. Did you see the way he looks at you?" She wipes the soda droplets from her chin with her palm. "You've been single for over two years now. It's time!"

"Yeah, and Ted was really into me too, and look how that turned out." I knew my comment would totally kill the playful mood at the table, but it was the truth. "I'm just not ready yet."

Shep returns with a handful of napkins and a wet rag. He hands the rag to Colleen. "I got this for your shirt. I had them put some club soda on it for you to dab on so hopefully it won't stain."

"That was very thoughtful of you. Thanks, Shep." Colleen dabbed at the spots on her shirt while Shep wiped up the table and gathered all the trash. "You are a great friend, aren't you?" She looked my way, defying me to say anything.

"The best FRIEND you could ever wish for!" Shep wadded up the trash and shot it towards the wastebasket, sinking it right in the middle of the opening. He turned and winked at me before he waved goodbye and headed off down the sidewalk. All I could do was roll my eyes once again.

I set out the leftover fried pickles, sliced brisket, and hushpuppies that we brought home from the Loco Coyote Grill on the poolside table. I've been wanting to eat there since I received a flyer at the Fourth of July parade but didn't want to go by myself. The live music was a pleasant surprise. We sat on the outside patio while waiting to be seated. It had a very relaxed atmosphere and was just what we needed to end the day. The portions were so much larger than what we were expecting, so we brought home the leftovers to munch on while floating in the pool.

Colleen walks by, and I pluck another sawdust particle out of her hair. "You would think you had laid down on the floor for a bit by all the sawdust that I've picked off of you."

She gave her hair a good shake. "That place was so much fun. We will have to go back. I couldn't believe the number of people waiting for a table. I knew it would be worth the wait when I saw the crowd." She popped another fried pickle into her mouth. "I'll meet you at the pool."

She grabs a chair floaty and artfully slides into it after getting into the water. She sets her water bottle in the cupholder and lays her head back with a heavy sigh. "I would be out here every single night if I had a pool like this. And you have great privacy in this backyard. The mountains are your neighbors over your back fence." She waved her arm towards the back of the pool as if I wouldn't know what she was talking about.

"It is a great find. I really shouldn't have purchased such a large place, but the price was a steal, considering the size and location. I thought either it would be a great place to start a family one day or else a brilliant investment to sell when I am ready to move on. Win-win for me!" I try to slide onto the floaty as gracefully as Colleen did, but end up dumping my water bottle out.

"This would be a great place to raise a family. Speaking of family, any news on that?"

I'm not sure if she is talking about my family in Fort Worth or the other family situation.

"Is your mom still mad at you?"

"Not really. She is still hurt by any possibilities that may come out of it, but she's talking to me. She's the one who convinced me to get Pookie." I swirl my legs in a circle causing my floaty to do a slow spin. I lean my head back just enough to feel the cool water on my head.

"Pookie is adorable. She almost makes me want to go get one for myself. Isn't that the name of Garfield's teddy bear?"

"Yes. I always loved Garfield growing up. Mom would never let me have a cat. Now, I do."

"Look at you making your own adult decisions." She swats a brief splash of water my way.

"Yeah, look at me."

We sit in silence, marveling at how bright the stars are out here, away from the city lights. They make my problems feel so small.

Colleen lightly kicks her feet, causing her floaty to come closer to mine. "Hey, Jazz, I really do hope that you find the answers you are looking for here in Glass. I have a good feeling about it."

"Thanks, Collie." I lay my head back down and stare upwards into the stars. In this great big world that God created, perhaps I will find what I need in this little town to make me feel whole again. I'm learning in my life that nothing is perfect, but maybe I will discover what my extraordinary purpose is. All my research has led me here. Now it's just up to God to put the rest of the pieces together.

17 Summer

End of September
Present Day

Chad's face is frozen in terror. His body is in a full running pose, yet he stands as if time is standing still. Standing next to him, I can't keep a straight face.

"Summer, look like you are terrified!" Laney impatiently holds up my phone, waiting to take a picture of us. My giggles won't stop.

The life size T Rex lurking behind us bares its large yellow teeth while we attempt to pose a running away picture. It's the classic picture that all visitors take here at Dinosaur World. Ryan and I used to be competitive as to who could appear the most terrified.

"Okay, give me a minute." I take a couple of deep breaths to control my laughter and strike the most frightened face I can come up with.

Laney takes several pictures and hands the phone to Chad. "Take some of Summer and me." Chad grabs my phone. Laney jumps on my back while I pretend to run away carrying us both to safety. I'm so thankful she got to come today. It seems she's been so busy lately with plans with some of her co-workers that we've hardly seen each other.

After a few poses, Chad hands my phone back to me and is suddenly upset.

"What's wrong? You mad we came up with a better scenario pose than you did?" I attempt to slug his arm, and he quickly grabs my wrist.

"I told you I don't like it when you do that." He lets go of my wrist and stares at me. I can tell that anything I say next won't be the right thing.

"Loosen up, Chad. We're supposed to be having fun today. I have so many fun memories of coming here when I was a kid." In the few years since Chad moved to Glass, he had never visited Dinosaur World. It was always such a magical escape for me growing up. Ryan and I even worked here together for a couple of summers. I link my arm through his. "Come on, let's go mine for some special rocks. That was always my favorite thing to do."

Chad pulls his elbow up, causing my hold to let go, and juts his chin forward at me. "You mean your and Ryan's favorite thing to do? He texted you when I was taking your picture and asked if you found any good rocks yet." Chad walks away, going against the one-way path rule.

"Chad, you are being ridiculous. We grew up together. Of course, we are going to make lots of memories together. You want me to just cut him out of my life completely?"

This stops Chad right in his tracks. He slowly turns around, glaring at me. One can almost see his thoughts ping-ponging back and forth as to what to say.

"I would never ask you to cut him out of your life. That's not you. If you did that, I would question whether you were the person I really thought you were. You are one of the most loyal people I know. I get it. But it gets so old knowing that every single thing in your life has a Ryan stamp on it. I want to be with you. Not your memories of what you and Ryan always liked to do. Will you ever understand that?" His nostrils flare as he breathes heavily, waiting for an answer.

I turn to Laney for some advice. She simply raises her eyebrows and turns to read the plaque, educating her with everything she needs to know about the stegosaurus.

"I'm uncertain how to be me without memories that include Ryan." A big huff escapes from Chad's mouth, and he throws his hands up in the air. "But I'm all about finding new ways to make memories with you and only you." I walk up to him and intertwine my fingers in his. "Ryan is in all of my past memories, but I choose you to be in all of my future memories."

His body relaxes a little bit. This is a good sign, and I try hard to summon up some more wise words.

"How about when we finish here with all the dinosaurs, you and I go to that new restaurant in Glass, The Whispering Walnut, and each pick out our own appetizers to share? I've never been there with you know who." We both smirk at the same time. "We can sit and come up with some other new things for you and me to do together that neither of us has ever done before. Sound good?"

Chad bends slightly forward to kiss me on the forehead. "The only other man who has ever kissed me on my forehead was my daddy. And I really miss those kisses." Chad pulls me close and softly presses his lips on my forehead again. My body melts into the concave of his body, and he holds me there among the prehistoric giants.

A group of screaming young boys rushes by and has to part on either side of us while we occupy the middle of the pathway. They are all wearing dinosaur birthday party hats. I choose not to tell him about my memory of when Ryan and I shared a birthday party here when I turned nine and he turned ten. We wore the same hats.

Where did you go? I turned around and you were gone

Hey! You want to go see a movie this weekend? Chad has the weekend shift so we can pick a chick flick

Laney are you ok? You know I can see that you read my messages, don't you?

Staring at my phone has not helped at all, so I set it on the counter. Maybe Laney has a new boyfriend. She has seemed distant lately. I've been too wrapped up in my own issues to ask.

From my kitchen window, I notice Mom and her best friend Liza on the porch swing. When I notice Mom swiping at her eyes, I decide not to go over there and interrupt. Liza has been great about checking on Mom and keeping her busy doing things. They have even started an art class together.

It's been about a month since our shopping trip, and Mom hasn't mentioned church again. I'm afraid to bring it up because I don't really care about going back. God has taken too many things away from my family for me to go sit in church and hear all about His mercy and grace. Or to watch people singing about Him.

Do I believe in God? Yes. Do I believe He is all love and goodness? Nope. Sometimes I picture Him like a puppet master pulling our strings and playing with us like I used to play with my Barbie dolls. Forcing them to do whatever I wanted and whatever tickled my fancy for the moment. Then, I would throw them to the side and pick up different Barbie dolls and make them act out a different scene according to my whim.

That's what I feel like for Mom, Clay, and me. God did what He wanted to the other members of our family and has thrown us to the side to go lord over someone else. As far as it goes with God, I feel alone, abandoned, and forgotten about. Why would I want to go sit with a lot of other people faking it through life? This is a small town, and everyone knows everyone else's business. Good and bad.

My phone dings. It's Laney. Finally.

Sorry I got called into work. I had to leave during your love fest amongst the dinos. 🦖 Chick flick sounds great!

I should've known. Chad has really made me paranoid about some of my other relationships. I shouldn't have jumped to conclusions about Laney. She's been such a great friend since I moved back home when I had to drop out of college. She had just moved here to live with her grandma and didn't know anyone. We met when we both worked at The Snack Shack for that first summer at The Bug Zone. It's an enormous park for all ages that is probably our town's biggest attraction. Ryan and I would ask to go there every weekend when we were younger. Chad and I may have to head up to Granbury to find something new to do that I haven't been to with Ryan before.

Ryan. Ugh. Sometimes I believe he possesses the other half of my brain. He knows how I am going to react to things, and I can just as easily predict his reactions. He will not react well when he notices I'm avoiding him. That's really the only way I see this working with Chad. I'll just quietly cut Ryan out and try to watch how I say things. I can do that for Chad.

We are planning to get married someday. I must move on and away from my childhood things. I'm an adult now and need to make some adult memories. I can do this. It's just going to be so hard to do in this small town where around every corner I turn holds another Ryan memory. Maybe Chad and I need to move away. We could go to Dallas. There are so many opportunities there. I could start back to my college classes like Ryan suggested…. *Ugh… this is going to be impossible.*

The ice cream bowl clatters as I set it on the kitchen counter. My reflection catches my attention with her judgmental look. "What?" I ask her. "It's not like Ryan would want a serious relationship with me again, anyway." My reflection concedes in agreement.

Today calls for an early ice cream treat. It might even be a two-serving night.

I'm so glad this week is almost over. Pennie walks into the back of the school cafeteria to refill her tub of water. Her nose scrunches up from the smell of the pancakes I burned earlier. She missed yesterday morning because of a doctor's appointment, so she is helping today to make up for it. She catches me staring.

"Hey! Let me get a cart for you. You probably shouldn't be carrying that heavy tub of water." I empty a rolling cart near me and roll it to the sink for her.

"Thanks! That will help a lot. I even thought about setting it on this growing belly." She rubs her tummy in circles.

"When is your due date?"

"The doctor said November 2nd, but Dad said I came early, so who knows?" She selected some fresh washrags and set them on the cart next to the tub of water. "Thanks so much for this."

She rolls the squeaky cart out the door to wash the tables. I notice some girls in the corner glancing her way and whispering. Pennie was the same age as Mom when she was pregnant with me. Did any girls talk about her and give her a hard time? It must've been hard for her. She told me she had little support from her parents. I wonder if Pennie does?

"Hey, Summer Bummer! You know what today is!" Ryan startles me as he reaches between the students' heads in the cafeteria line and hands me a doughnut.

"Fri-Yay!" I say with as much enthusiasm as my hair net will allow. Despite getting a glare from my cafeteria manager, I quickly take a bite, allowing the chocolate glaze to melt on my tongue. "Thanks! I needed a sugar rush this morning!" I slap another pancake on the tray to hand to the next student in line.

"Hey, do you want to go mudding with me tomorrow? David and I have almost perfected the side yard on my property."

My mind goes blank at creating a good excuse.

"Come on! Just like the good old days." Ryan makes his begging face he has been manipulating me with since he was eight years old.

Another student steps around Ryan to grab his breakfast tray. The side of his lip snarls up in disappointment.

"Just text me later and let me know. Don't forget that Grandma's Pumpkin Carving Party is in a couple of weeks. You and Chad are both invited." Ryan starts walking backwards towards the door. "I'll be looking for you in the stands tonight during the game. You can watch us beat the Dunbar Wildcats. Y'all are coming for pizza again, right?"

"Yeah, I'll see you there! Good luck!" My stomach feels like I'm going to be sick. This is the first time I have ever outright lied to Ryan. I just can't have this conversation right here and right now. In order to prove to Chad that I can do different things, I promised him we wouldn't go to the game tonight. The look on Chad's face told me I had made the right choice.

I just dread the look on Coach Ryan Sheppard's face when he looks into the stands from the sidelines tonight, and I'm not there.

18 Third Option

**End of September
Present Day**

First Week of October
Present Day

I spread my blanket over the bleacher to help provide a little cushion for the long night ahead. Frank, Pennie's dad, walks along at the bottom of the football stands. She runs up to him and gives him a big hug. She told me this morning he was supposed to come watch her tonight. I don't think I have ever seen Pennie smile so big. This will be her last time playing in the band since the baby is due in one month. He hasn't seen her perform in over two years, since his wife died. Frank gives her a big hug and follows her back to sit next to the band section.

Thank you, God, for nudging me to talk to Pennie. What an honor it is to see You work in their lives.

I glance down to the field and see Shep is scanning over the hometown side of the crowded bleachers. *Should I wave to him or not? He might be looking for someone else.* His head stops searching and looks straight towards me. His arm pops in the air with an enthusiastic wave, and I mannerly wave back. I don't want to seem too excited since I friend-zoned him last weekend.

"No, not until after Thanksgiving Break." Macee yanks my arm back down and pulls me to sit.

"We won't date. I've made it very clear to him I just want to be friends." I raise my eyebrows to emphasize the word friends, so that she knows how serious I am. It doesn't seem to faze her.

"That's fine and dandy. Be all the kind of friends that you want to be until Thanksgiving Break. I will win this bet."

"Just how much did you bet on me?" I've thought all along this must be a joke; however, I'm suspecting it is real.

"Twenty dollars."

"Twenty dollars?!" The row of black and gray t-shirts in front of me all turn around, startled by my outburst. "So sorry. I'm sorry." I reassure them I am okay, and they turn their attention back to the field. "You seriously bet twenty dollars on when we would go out? I thought you were joking the whole time."

"Well, the whole thing started as a joke. But the more we watched the two of you, and especially how we have seen how he has changed this year, we decided to actually lay down some serious money on the whole idea." She throws a piece of popcorn in her mouth and chomps on it dramatically to emphasize her confidence on the entire issue. "You know, he's never really dated anyone before. And we definitely have never seen him show as much interest in anyone as he does in you. He has even started wearing cologne at school. He's never done that before, for sure."

"He is pretty cute," David chimes in, wiggling his eyebrows up and down. He goes for some popcorn, and Macee blocks him.

I do like his musky scent as he passes me in the hallway. I glance back down at Shep on the field and admire how he is obviously ramping up the energy in the huddle as he talks to his boys. The football players jump up and down, chanting something. He smacks several of them on top of their helmets one by one and sends them to the field. It is obvious how much they all respect and like him.

"Well, I'm sorry that you are going to lose twenty dollars on my account. There is no way that I'm going out with him, especially not right after Thanksgiving Break."

"Sure, whatever you say." She throws another couple of popcorn kernels into her mouth. "You realize we can see how YOU light up when he comes around too, right? The main thing that you need to understand is that the bet is not IF you will ever go out with him. It is about WHEN you will go out with him. And it doesn't have to be right after Thanksgiving Break. I really think you will hold out until next spring, but I wasn't sure how long you would last after he started wearing cologne."

David tries again for the popcorn. "He does always smell good lately. Thanks for that!"

I swat his hand away and toss some popcorn at both of them. David laughs and opens his mouth to catch some. Suddenly, the crowd around us goes wild. Cowbells ring all over the stadium as fans jump up and cheer. The Panthers scored their first touchdown of the game.

After scoring another point for the kick, the crowd finally settles in.

The loudspeaker erupts, "And that touchdown was for a special Panther friend."

My eyes widen as I stare at the field. The entire line of football players is pointing to the stands in our direction. Shep takes off his hat and folds his arm in front of him, bowing in victory as the crowd goes wild, believing it is all for them.

Feeling my face flush, I look at Macee. She slyly grins as she throws more popcorn kernels into her mouth with her dramatic chomping.

The walls seem to reverberate as more and more football players arrive at Bella's Pizzeria. It was a Panther victory over the Brownwood Lions: 44-16. Thankfully, there were no more displays of touchdown dedications for the rest of the game.

Pennie approaches our booth.

"Hi, Ms. Forte. This is Tony." Pennie puts her arm around his waist as he reaches his hand out to shake mine.

"Hello, Ms. Forte. It's nice to meet you. Pennie sure talks about you a lot." He runs his other hand through his damp hair and gives it a good shake. He must have hurried over after the locker room shower.

"Nice to meet you also, Tony. Pennie talks a lot about you, too."

Tony's face blushes as his weight shifts from one foot to the other.

"Great run tonight, Tony-Pony." Shep walks up behind him with damp hair as well. He looks at Pennie. "You know why we call him Tony-Pony?"

Pennie giggles and shakes her head. Tony's face turns a deeper shade of red.

"Because he struts his stuff out on the field like a prized pony. The other team never knows what is coming." He slaps Tony on the back as they head back to their group in the opposite corner.

Shep slides onto the bench right next to me. "What a game!" He expels a huge sigh. This is probably the first opportunity he has had to relax in the last few hours. "That was a fun one."

He turns to me. "Did you like your special touchdown? It was a very FRIENDLY one for ya."

He smirks as a waft of his freshly sprayed cologne seems to be thrown my way by the turn of his head.

"It was great, but what took you so long? It was two minutes into gameplay." Two can play this game of sarcasm. He's not even aware of the bear he is poking.

"Well, looky there, folks. The prim and proper Miss Jasmine has a fun side. I knew you were in there somewhere underneath all your manners." He takes a long sip of his soda while I let him enjoy his moment. But just temporarily.

"Besides, I almost didn't notice the touchdown because I was too busy watching the cute coach on the other team," I retort, causing Macee to choke on her bite of pizza. We all erupt

124

in laughter as Shep remains speechless, impressed by my sassiness.

"Remember, I grew up with a little brother whom I had to humble many times in his teenage years. I can hold my own when I choose to." I took a victory slurp of my drink, and Macee reached over the table to give me knuckles.

"My, my, my, what many layers you have," Shep nods his head in approval of my quick wit at his expense. "I had no idea and am very pleased at this new side of you."

"Don't get too pleased," Macee jumps into our conversation. "At least not until after Thanksgiving Break."

I wad up my napkin and throw it at her as Shep looks confused. "I'm not even going to ask," he says and engulfs another huge bite of his slice. This time when he winks at me, I don't roll my eyes.

The next afternoon, Macee swings by to pick me up. Shep's grandma, with whom he lives with, has a pumpkin carving party the first Saturday of October every year. I'm not exactly sure how it started, but I know they began it when Shep was a freshman in college and all of Shep's friends come. It's been his family's tradition now for over a decade. I believe Macee's convincing argument was, "Fall doesn't really start around here until Grandma Shep throws her party."

The acreage is stunning. I'm sure even more so in the next month as the leaves turn colors. The yellow farmhouse looks like a typical one on the front of any magazine that relishes that particular style. White painted posts and railing support the porch that wraps around both sides of the house. The steps are decorated with yellow, red, and orange mums, along with a variety of pumpkins leading up the stairs. A large wooden Welcome sign stands tall by the door with a painted orange pumpkin for the "o" in "Welcome."

Two wooden rocking chairs sit to the left of the front door, separated by a small wooden table. Just the right size to set hot coffee on in the winter, or maybe a glass of sweet tea in the hot summer months. Each chair is decorated with orange pillows, making it seem even more inviting.

"Come on. Everyone will be around back." Macee motions me to the side of the house, and I follow her, mesmerized by the way this place makes me feel. I've never felt instantly so welcomed and at home like this. A wave of peace washes over me.

The scent of hot apple cider hits me while I hear laughter and chatter even before we round the corner into the backyard. A lot of planning went into the front porch, yet this area was set up like a magazine photo shoot.

There must be between twenty and thirty people in the backyard. Ages range from some who are apparently Grandma's friends down to little ones who I am guessing are kids of some of Shep's friends. I recognize the little cowboy from the Fourth of July parade and the football games. He is still sporting his cowboy hat and playing a game of tag.

Tables created out of hay bales are scattered across the yard with blankets spread on the ground to sit on next to each one. Two or three people sit in each section, knives in hand, carving pumpkins of all sizes. I never could have imagined that day in July when I first saw Shep that I would stand in his backyard a few months later.

A table of homemade refreshments and drinks sits close to the back porch. Grandma Shep sure can throw a party.

"There they are. Let's go say hi, and then we can pick out a pumpkin to decorate." Macee leads me to where Shep, David, and an older lady that I've seen at the football games are sitting. Shep and David hop up when we approach. Maybe he has some manners deep in there somewhere.

Shep helps his grandma up, and she goes straight in for a hug from Macee. "And you must be the lovely Jasmine I keep hearing about." She politely pushes my stretched-out hand to the side and gives me a hug instead. "We don't shake hands here, honey. It's all about the hugs." Grandma Shep gives me a tight squeeze and holds my shoulders as she backs up to get a good look at me. "Well, aren't you a beautiful one? Those eyes. I've only seen one other person with eyes that color before, but he's not around here anymore. Where did Shep say you moved here from?"

She lets my arms go and offers me a seat at her hay bale table. "I moved here from Fort Worth. I grew up in the Rivercrest area." Her eyes are so kind and set me at ease. "This is such a beautiful place you have here. No wonder Shep still wants to live with you."

Grandma Shep lets out a robust laugh. "Oh, he doesn't live with me, darlin'. He's kind enough to let me live with him. This is his house. I do have to claim that I keep a woman's touch on the whole thing, but everything belongs to him. I earn my keep by keeping everything clean and cooking for him a couple of times a week, but he pays all the bills and does his own laundry."

I glance up at Shep, and I don't think that I have ever seen him blush before. "Let's go pick out our pumpkins," he says, turning away, trying to change the subject.

After a couple of hours of carving, painting, and reveling in some delicious snacks, everyone lines their pumpkins up on the back porch railings. We are all given a sheet of paper numbered one to twenty-seven and told to rank our top five favorites.

Grandma Shep looks to Shep. "Remember, no cheating, Ryan. You can't vote for your own pumpkin." She turns in my direction. "One year we had to disqualify him because his pumpkin ended up with more votes than there were people." Shep dramatically creates a "Who, me?" face. We all laugh and line up to begin our pumpkin inspections.

When we finish, Grandma Shep and her neighbor Annie go into the house to tally the votes.

"Come on, let's go." David and Shep head to the barn.

Macee grabs my arm, pulling me along behind her. "We always go out on the four-wheelers while they are counting the votes. You have to see his land. It is so beautiful."

David hops on a four-wheeler with Shep hopping on the other. There is no more in sight. "So, I guess we just wait for our turn here?" I look at Macee, confused.

"No, that's ridiculous. It's more fun to go together." She hops on behind David and wraps her arms around his waist. "Hurry, or we won't have enough time."

I glance over at Shep, and he has the biggest grin on his face. He scoots up a little further on his seat, showing me he is ready for me to hop on behind him.

"If you wreck with me on the back, I will never let you live it down." I throw my leg over the seat and let my arms hang down to the side.

"You'd better hang on there, Tiger. It will get mighty bumpy in some parts. I promise not to wreck, but you better not fall off." He gases it so that it jerks me enough that I wrap my arms around him and hold him tight before my brain realizes what it is doing. "There you go. A nice and tight, friendly hug." I can feel the back of his rib cage laughing up against the front of me, so I give him a really tight squeeze. He coughs as though I were strong enough to push the air out of him and then laughs again. I choose to let him have the last laugh for now.

"Dave, let's take the path that leads to the creek first. Jazz will really like it there." Both guys take off with David in the lead as we tour around the one hundred acres. We stop momentarily to admire the creek that divides his property from the property next door. Shep explains to me it used to be a four hundred acre farm when he was growing up. After he and his three siblings inherited the land, they all sold their portions, but Shep wanted to keep his and continue to live here.

We head towards the north end of his property, and he explains how he leases out half of it to a rancher down the road who needs a little more space for his herd of cattle occasionally. Shep said he had too many special memories to let it all go. I never expected him to be such a sentimental guy.

"How did you inherit all of this at such a young age? What happened to your parents?" I feel bad yelling such a sensitive question in his ear, but it is hard to have a discussion over the roar of the four-wheeler.

"That will be a story for another time!" he yells back. I don't press the issue since we are pulling back into the barn. It looks like everyone is gathering up to hear who will claim pumpkin carving bragging rights for the next year.

Climbing back into Macee's car at the end of the evening, we both adjust our air conditioner vents to blow directly on our faces. It may be fall, but it still feels like summer. We, along with the boys, helped Grandma Shep clean up everything after everyone left. Grandma Shep hugged every single person and told each one that if she were the judge, his or her pumpkin would have definitely won first place.

None of us was even close to winning with our pumpkins. We talked more than we carved, and some of those attending were downright serious about their carving. Annie, the neighbor next door, crowned her son, Clay, the official winner with a homemade pumpkin crown. His carving was very intricate, spotlighting a haunted house. He had even carved the tiniest bats flying around. Next year, I will have to come up with a plan. *Next year? Who knows whether I will even be here next year? I guess it all depends on what I discover while I am living here.*

"So, do you?" I was so deep in thought about my real reason I moved here that I didn't hear Macee talking to me.

"I'm sorry. What did you say? My mind wandered to my family back home. We never carved pumpkins. Mom always said it was too messy. She would just have the gardener put some pumpkins in our potted flowers." *Ugh... I shouldn't have said that. Please don't pick up on that. Please don't pick .....*

"Gardener? Your family had a gardener? I had a feeling you came from money, but a gardener? Wow, no wonder you could buy such a big house being single and a teacher and all. You know your house was David's childhood home, so I'm aware of how much they sold it for." She turns out of Shep's driveway and heads towards town. We are meeting the guys for an ice cream float. Apparently, they haven't had enough sugar yet.

I sit silently, trying to decide how to respond or if I even should acknowledge her invasive comment.

"Oh, Jazz, I'm so sorry. That was really rude of me. I know you have been a pretty private person since you moved here. Sometimes my big mouth spurts out words before my brain has time to filter them. It gets worse when I'm hot and cranky, too."

I laugh a little to allow her to feel more comfortable. "Really, it's okay. I'm kind of surprised it took you this many months to ask. I had a bet with myself about how long it would take you to interrogate me." We both burst out laughing. "And yes, I want to go with you guys." Hopefully that will be enough to deter any more probing questions into my personal life. I'm just not quite ready to share that yet, if ever. I don't want anyone to feel sorry for me.

We pull into the Tasty Twirls Ice Cream Shoppe. The guys pull in right behind us in Shep's pickup. Macee claims this place has the best root beer floats in the world.

When we walk in, I understand what she means. The menu is written in neon-colored chalk markers on the black chalkboard wall behind the ice cream station. The blenders whir, creating excitement for the children in front of us waiting for their special treat. Every type of sprinkle and add-in is laid out behind the glass countertop that separates us from a major sugar rush. The colorful menu has 21 root beer floats listed along with many other options.

I consider getting a strawberry smoothie but settle on the Chocolate Hot Fudge Root Beer Float. Macee chooses the Chocolate Chip Cookie Root Beer Float. Both boys order the Firecracker Root Beer Float, which is made of three scoops of ice cream: one red, one white, and one blue. It is then topped off with an entire package of Pop Rocks. We probably all need to go run a few laps when finished.

We find a round table on the outside patio under the string of lights and sit silently for the first few minutes of our indulgence. Shep licks a drip off his wrist, not wanting to waste any of it. Macee stops momentarily to bear through the pain of her brain freeze. David shoves a large scoop of pop rocks into his mouth, leaning towards Macee so she can hear the tiny explosions. Shep looks to do the same for me until my raised eyebrows change his mind.

We make small talk about the day and brainstorm different ways to win the pumpkin carving next year. We all leave about half of our ice cream to melt in the bottom of the glass except for Shep. He drinks up the last drips that are left in his striped straw and finishes up with a chef's kiss in the air. "Delizioso!" He then, thankfully, holds in a large burp. Probably caused by gulping down his whole float. We all burst out laughing.

"I think you have your manners mixed up with too many countries," I say. "Burping after a meal is rude in Italy but is expected after a good meal in Egypt."

They all look at me in silence for a minute. David then burps loudly. "My compliments to the chef," he says. I haven't laughed so hard in a few years.

When it is time to go, I notice David and Macee whispering together. We all head out to the parking lot, with the two of them leading the way. David walks straight to the passenger side of Macee's car and opens the door.

"Hey, Macee and I thought that since your house is on the way to Shep's, it would be smarter for him to take you home instead of Macee. She is going to take me home. See you tomorrow at church, Shep! Jasmine, you need to join us one Sunday." He climbs in, shutting the door to the car and to any further discussion of who is riding with whom.

"Hop in. I guess I'm taking you home." Shep opens the passenger door for me, waits until I am all the way inside, and shuts my door. Manners seem to come out of him sporadically.

For the first couple of minutes, we sit in silence listening to the radio. He has it tuned to the local country music station. I wouldn't expect anything different from him.

"So, I guess I can answer your question now about my parents."

Remembering how invasive Macee's inquiry was to me earlier, I suddenly felt embarrassed by my prior probing. "No, really, I should be apologizing to you. I shouldn't be asking you such personal questions. You have nothing to explain to me." I fidget with my circle necklace, understanding how private some memories can be.

"I don't mind at all. We live in a small town, remember? Everyone else knows what happened. I'm just catching you up, that's all." He sits silently for a moment as we round one of the many curves to my house.

"I told you earlier that we had a four hundred acre farm when I was younger. Our big money-maker was cattle. Dad would buy, sell, breed, butcher, you name it. If it had to do with cattle and could make you money, Dad did it. We were very blessed. Anyway, they have a sixteen-day National Western Stock Show in Denver, Colorado, every January. Dad would go up there every couple of years to get a variety of cattle other than what he usually bought at the Fort Worth Stockyards. My grandfather, Grandma Shep's husband, was a retired commercial pilot. He had his own private 210 plane that he had flown for years. He offered to fly Mom and Dad to Denver, drop them off, and return to pick them up at the end of the two weeks." He turns the radio off.

"This was to be Mom's first time going. She had never been because she always had to stay home with us kids. However, I was a senior, and they trusted me to stay home with Grandma Shep checking in on me and bringing me some food every couple of days. I was too busy with basketball season to really do anything stupid like throw a party. Anyway, they had a great time. Mom said she loved being able to spend that time with Dad and she got to go shopping at some different stores. She knew she wouldn't be restricted in how many packages to bring home since they would fly back on Grandpa's private plane. Dad said it made him happy seeing Mom so happy, so it was a win-win for everyone."

Shep pulls into my driveway and shifts his truck into park. We both stare out the front windshield watching a rabbit hopping across my driveway. He stops in the brightness of the headlights, and Shep turns them off.

"Grandpa Shep flew up the night before they were to come home so that Dad could show him all the cattle he had purchased that were to be delivered the next week. That night, a big winter storm came through. My basketball homecoming game was the next night. I was the crowning captain, so Mom really wanted to be there. They almost waited until the next day, but after talking to the local airport, they decided they would be okay to fly out. Grandpa ended up flying into a cloud with an updraft." He takes a minute to stay composed.

"The investigators' best guess is that it was a combination of Grandpa Shep getting confused by the jarring around of the storm and the ice that had accumulated on the plane. He lost altitude because of the extra weight of the ice and could never recover.

"He was trying to make it to the airport in Guymon, Oklahoma, and crashed just short of it. Grandma Shep and I hopped in the truck and headed that way. Dad and Grandpa

Shep were both pronounced dead at the scene. They had been sitting up front. They found Mom at the back of the plane, covered in her packages. She was in the ICU when we arrived. She was never conscious again, but we got to see her and say our goodbyes."

I reach over and put my hand on top of his hand that lies on the seat between us. "I am so sorry. I had no idea. That must have been so hard for you."

"That was the toughest year of my life. Annie's husband, Hawk, next door temporarily took over the ranch. Grandma Shep moved in with me so that I could stay here in Glass and finish out my senior year with as little change as possible. Her having to focus on me helped her with her grief over losing Grandpa Shep. She always says, 'He's just waiting for me up in heaven. I'll see him again one day.' She started this pumpkin carving party idea the first October after the crash. She knew the upcoming holidays were going to be hard, so she tried to throw some fun into it all. And it gave all my friends an excuse to get together. We could talk about how things were going since we all went off in different directions after graduation. It's still a nice way to start off the holiday season, and she has been hosting one ever since. It just seems to get bigger and bigger every year." He sits silently for a minute, allowing grief to fall over his face.

"The grief still hits me out of the blue sometimes. There are the normal times you would expect, like holidays and birthdays and such. Even basketball homecoming when it rolls around every January. These are the times that you expect and can prepare for. You know it's coming. It's all the other times that are so hard. A vintage car drives by, and I picture Grandpa. He loved vintage cars. He always had a story of riding in that particular car, no matter what model it was. He rode in all of them." Shep snickers at his memory as I'm sure he is envisioning his grandfather riding around in one of his treasures.

"I see a cow and think of Dad. Do you realize how many cows there are in Texas?" We both chuckle at this fact.

There are thousands of cows around here. "The ones that get to me the most are the Chick-fil-A commercials. I expect to see cows in all the pastures around here, but the cows in the Chick-fil-A commercials catch me off guard. When I was five, he dressed me up as one of those for Halloween. He wrote 'Eat Mor Chikin' on a posterboard and hung it around my neck. He had bought white sweats and hoodie and then painted some black spots on it to resemble a cow. That was the best Halloween. I won the costume contest in kindergarten." He slowly shakes his head as he fondly shares this sweet memory with me.

"And then there's Mom." He lets out a huff. "There are so many things that remind me of my momma. She used to sing in the kitchen when she was making us anything to eat. Sometimes when I'm really missing her, I will stand in the middle of the kitchen and close my eyes. If I'm really still, I can almost hear her singing her songs. They were always Christian songs. Songs about how much she loved God and how thankful she was to Him for everything He had done for her. She had a rough time growing up with her family, so she worked hard to make sure my brother and sisters and I had a loving home to grow up in. That's why she got along so well with our neighbor, Annie. She had a rough life growing up as well. They would always sit on the porch in the rocking chairs, drinking sweet tea, and talking about everything under the sun."

I squeeze his hand as tears roll down his cheeks. He turns his head to look at me and gives me a little smile. "That was probably more than you bargained for," he jokes as he lifts his shirt collar up to wipe his eyes and nose. "Man. I haven't thought about all three of them at the same time in quite a while. There were a couple of years after the crash where I had a really hard time with God and all. Grandma Shep made sure that we all stayed in church. She made me come home every weekend from college so she could sit by me and prod me awake if I would doze off. I don't know where I'd be without her."

"She is one spunky lady, that's for sure. I want to be like Grandma Shep when I get older." I let go of Shep's hand, shifting my body in the seat to face more towards him. He has opened up so much to me and made himself so vulnerable that I want him to feel how grateful I am for his honesty. I understand grief. My grief came in a different form, but I understand how it can hit you out of the blue. You never really get over it. You just learn how to absorb it into your life. My fingers slide over the circles on my necklace.

"Oh, she's a spunky one, for sure. Since Grandpa Shep was a pilot, she had flown on planes all her life. She didn't want me to be terrified of ever getting on a plane again, so for my 21st birthday, she surprised me with a skydiving trip."

"Seriously? Did she go with you and watch?"

"Watch? She went with me and jumped out first! She said it had always been on her bucket list, and she wanted to check it off with me. Looking back, she did a great job of keeping me in line and making sure I was going to be okay. Because of Grandma Shep forcing me to go to church every Sunday and, I'm sure, because of her countless prayers over my life, I am very confident in who God is and what He has done for me. And I know I will see Mom, Dad, and Grandpa Shep one day again when I join them in heaven."

A soft smile spreads across his face as he finishes bearing all the layers in his life that have made him become the man sitting in front of me today. I return a smile of my own, not yet as confident in God as he is. Sure, I believe in God, and I pray to Him all the time. I'm fantastic at praying for others around me. But Shep has something different in his confidence as he speaks of his relationship with God. A relationship that I'm not so confident God would want to have with someone like me.

20 Summer

Middle of October
Present Day

Ryan is upset with me. Or maybe he's just hurt. It's hard to tell since we both have been avoiding each other. It's been a couple of weeks since I missed Grandma Shep's pumpkin carving party. That was my first one I've missed since she's been hosting them. Mom told me it was a good turnout and lots of great pumpkins this year. She always enjoys attending and helping Grandma Shep with tallying the votes. I told her that if Chad and I are going to make a life together, I've got to make him a priority. I couldn't make Mom understand Chad's reasons, so I made up some lame excuse. Mom passed the message along instead of my telling Ryan myself.

Chad and I haven't been to any more of the football games, either. Ryan and I have been eating pizza after football games since middle school. Start Fridays with doughnuts and end them with pizza. This has been our routine for years. It's been tough, but I keep reminding myself that I'm doing this for Chad and to make him more confident about us. Ryan didn't bring me a doughnut last Friday at the cafeteria. He texted me to say he had a last-minute football coach meeting and didn't have time. *I don't blame him. I wouldn't bring me a doughnut anymore either.* Apparently, Ryan didn't mean what he promised Dad about me the week before the accident. I'm making the right decision with Chad. It's time I put myself first in what I think is best for me.

I glance out my kitchen window to see if Mom is home yet. Without even thinking, I pick up the heart-shaped rock on the windowsill and rub it seven times. It is possible Chad is right. Perhaps I should make room for some new memories by letting go of some of my old memories with Ryan. Moving to Dallas was an idea that he really liked. He began exploring potential job openings and shared the University of Texas in Dallas website with me to apply for school again. It makes me feel good that he's excited about the possibility of my becoming a teacher.

I was concerned about leaving Mom, but Chad said we can come every weekend if I want to. He also said that when we get married, we can get an apartment with an extra bedroom so that Mom can come stay whenever she wants. I put my life on hold for her once before. Now, it's time to put myself first.

I hear Mom's car door shut, so I head out my door and start up to her house. I'll miss living next door.

Chad's car pulls in right behind Mom, and he jumps out to grab the grocery bags from her.

"What a gentleman," Mom says. She lovingly pats him on the cheek and walks up the steps to unlock her door.

"See, that went really well, don't you think?" Chad wraps his arm around my shoulders as we walk back to my house. Chad took this opportunity to tell Mom our plans about moving to Dallas. I wasn't prepared yet to break the news to her, but Chad seemed so excited. Mom acted thrilled for us and made comments about how it was our turn to create a life for ourselves. However, she was blinking a lot as she continually popped jellybeans into her mouth. I've learned the difference between her sincere smile and her fake smile to reassure others around her. Tonight was the fake kind.

"Yeah, it went perfectly." I snuggled up a little closer to him. It appears a cold front moved in today. Or maybe I'm just unsettled about the conversation that we just had with Mom.

We decide to build a fire outside and enjoy some s'mores with the cooler weather. I love sitting outside this time of the year. The air is crisp. Leaves are turning gold, red, and orange. The cicadas play their musical symphony in the trees while the frogs in the creek croak out of tune.

"I almost forgot! I have a surprise for you!" Chad gets up and runs back to his car, which is still sitting in front of Mom's house. He grabs a large box from the back seat and brings it to the firepit.

He pulls a large pumpkin out of the box. "It occurred to me we could start our own pumpkin tradition." He pulls out some paintbrushes and paints. "Let's paint one together."

"I love this! What a sweet idea!" I jump up and give him a big hug. These changes are going to pay off.

"You come up with an idea, and I'll go get a bowl of water for the brushes."

I get my phone to find pumpkin painting ideas. Do we want cute or scary? I search for the cute ones. I can find one to complement my cute fall pillow and sign that I bought at Front Porch Designs. I settle on two ideas. One idea is a large candy corn (Chad's favorite fall candy) and the other is to paint fall leaves all over it. I'll let Chad make the final decision.

Chad finally comes back out of the house but is empty-handed. "Could you not find a bowl? The plastic ones are in the left cabinet."

Chad doesn't answer me. He continues to walk towards me at a determined pace and comes to a quick halt when he reaches my chair.

"Where did you get this rock?" He thrusts his hand at me and opens his fingers up to reveal my heart-shaped rock in his palm.

"I've had that rock for a long time in my kitchen. You know it's the rock that I always pick up and rub when I look out the window."

"Yeah, I know. You rub it seven times. I asked you where did you get it?" I can tell by his demeanor that he somehow already knows the answer, yet I can't bring myself to confess it.

"It's just a stupid rock. What does it matter?" I reach out, and he tightens his fist around it.

"Why won't you answer my question? Where did you get it?" His jaw juts forward, emphasizing his point.

"Ryan gave it to me, okay? It was a long time ago in high school. What difference does that make?"

"It makes all the difference. It must be really special since he has one just like it."

My body stiffens. "How do you know he has one just like it?"

"What does it matter? The fact is that you both are hanging on to heart rocks. Don't you think there is something wrong with that? Do you want to be with me or with him?" He lifts his arm, threatening to send the rock flying.

"What are you doing? Give that back to me!" I jump out of my chair and lunge towards his arm. He swings his arm back and forth like a bully on the playground playing keep-away from his latest victim.

"Chad, give that back. It means nothing. It's just a stupid rock."

"If it's so stupid, then why do you want it so badly?" He chucks it down at my feet and heads towards his car.

I scramble to the ground to pick it up. Snatching it, I hug it close to my pounding heart. *What just happened? How does he know Ryan has one, too? Why would Ryan tell him that?*

21 Third Option

Middle of October
Present Day

22 Jasmine

Middle of October
Present Day

Shep called me earlier this afternoon asking me to go to church tomorrow morning with him. I told him I just couldn't right now but maybe soon. We had a lot of fun eating pizza after the Panthers' victory over the Hillsboro Fighting Eagles last night. So far, the only loss they have had has been the first scrimmage of the season with Glen Rose.

I've been here almost four months and keep putting off what I really came here for. I'm not really sure where to start or what to do, but I need to come up with a plan.

I settle into my desk chair and pick up my papa's pocket-watch from its place of honor on my desk. The chain feels cold as it falls between my fingers. I trace the steam coming from the locomotive embossed on the case cover. Memories of me sitting on his footstool in front of his recliner come flooding back. He would allow me to open the watch and play train conductor as he would pretend to be the fireman shoveling coal for the engine. It was a special time when my brother and I would get to visit an actual train and play on it for a few minutes with him.

He received his pocket-watch at his retirement, working for Union Pacific for thirty years. He passed away when I was in high school and left it to me since I had been so intrigued by it when I was younger. I press the latch release so

I can admire the mother-of-pearl face. The hands are forever stuck at 3:07. He would always say, "Never forget, Jazzy, time waits for no one. If something needs to be done, don't put it off." I've never understood this statement more than I do right now.

"Dear Lord, I work hard not to ask for anything for myself, but I really don't know the right way to pray for this. Please show me what to do with the information that I have." I carefully place the pocket-watch back in its resting spot and pull the large manila envelope out of my top desk drawer. I shouldn't put this off any longer.

My phone buzzes. A weather alert warns of an impending thunderstorm. Rain sure would be nice. I stick the envelope back in its hiding spot. Answers will have to wait a little longer.

Heading out to the backyard, the southwest sky looks dark. I check the pool to make sure everything is put away. Grabbing a couple of decorative lanterns and a small potted plant, I bring them all underneath the patio cover. I need to ask Shep to teach me how to shut my pool down for the season.

Going back into the house, I discover that I have a missed call from Dad. I've tried to keep conversations with my parents at a minimum since I've moved. Especially with Mom. If I am going to uncover any truth here in Glass, I can not be distracted by how my mom feels about it all. I understand she is scared for me. Probably more for herself. But I'm a grown adult now, and this is something I must do. I can deal with her after I find what I'm looking for.

A pull at the base of my neck makes me flinch. When I'm lost in thought, I habitually twirl my hair. Mom would cringe when I was younger when I'd pull hairs from my ponytail to twirl.

I better call Dad back and make sure everything is okay. Hopefully, they won't ask again to come for a visit. I'm not sure how much longer I can put them off.

"Hey, Dad. Did you call?"

"I was just checking on you. A pretty severe storm is headed your way, so I was thinking about you." Dad and I always loved it when storms would come. We would sit together on our back porch and watch them roll in. Sometimes when I was little and if it wasn't lightning, we would dance together in the rain. Dad and I would run through the door laughing, and Mom would get so mad because we would leave a water trail through the kitchen.

"Thanks for checking. The alert just came in on my phone, so I was checking things in the backyard before it hits."

"This one looks pretty bad. I don't want you dancing out there all by yourself, you understand?"

I giggle into the phone. "Yes, Dad. I'll be good and stay inside. This house has a basement, so I'll head down there if the tornado sirens go off. You watch yourself too. Don't make Mom yell at you too much before you come in from the back porch."

Dad agrees, and we say our goodbyes. God sure blessed me with a loving father. I'm so thankful that things are getting back to normal with us, even though we still all disagree with the bigger situation at hand.

Pookie meows, rubbing herself around my ankles. I pick her up and hold her close when she startles as a gust of wind rattles the back windows. She jumps out of my arms onto the couch and buries herself between the cushions. I dig her out as the doorbell rings.

"Shep. What a surprise. Is everything okay?" I widen the door to invite him in.

"Yeah, everything is just fine. Listen, I came over to fetch you and bring you back to my house. I can't relax knowing this storm is rolling in and you are over here by yourself." The wind picks up, and the tree branches switch directions as they follow the wind's lead.

"Oh, that's really sweet, but I'm fine. I have a basement if the sirens go off. I'm not really scared of storms, but thank you anyway." My heart warms knowing that he cares. I notice the branches switch directions once again. "It's really coming in fast, isn't it?"

"Yeah, it is, and that's why we need to hurry. You may not be scared of storms, but Grandma Shep really is. I need to get home to be with her and help her down the cellar steps if the sirens go off. I can't leave you here by yourself. It's supposed to be a bad one. And Grandma Shep would tan my hide if she knew I came back without you. Will you please come with me? Save me from getting in trouble?" His face squishes up as he places his hands together, begging me to come along.

How can I say no to his squishy face? "Okay, but only for Grandma Shep." Relief falls over his face. "Let me unplug my laptop real quick and take care of Pookie." It would be nice to spend some more time with Grandma Shep. I really enjoyed meeting her a couple of weeks ago. It seems like she has been an enormous influence on the man that Shep has become. As I keep discovering more layers of his personality, he seems to be the type of man that I would want by my side for the ups and downs of life. I'm just afraid that I wouldn't be the type of woman that he would want once he finds out about my past and what I've done.

I shut Pookie down in the basement after enticing her with a treat. I quickly make a pass through the house, turning off the lights and grabbing my purse and phone charger.

The wind has picked up and blows me towards Shep's truck as he holds the door open for me. This might be a dreadful storm after all. Nothing good ever comes out of storms.

23 Summer

Middle of October
Present Day

An eerie green color covers the sky as I run up the sidewalk to Mom's house. The dark, ominous cloud looming in the west grows larger as it gets closer. A lightning show in the sky highlights the point of a funnel forming at the bottom of a wall cloud. My hair blows back and forth as the wind can't decide which direction to blow. I find Mom in her living room huddled up in Dad's chair with tears rolling down her cheeks.

"Come on, Mom. Let's head to the cellar." The sirens were blaring as I was pulling into the driveway. I knew Mom would be scared. I am too, but I shove my feelings aside to take care of her. I grab the umbrella by the door as hail hits the roof. The winds are howling, warning us it is not far away. We still have time to get to the cellar. I hope.

I escort Mom out of the doorway, wondering how I am going to get her to the cellar, get the door up, get her down the steps, and pull the door shut and secure it by myself. I should have answered Ryan's messages earlier when he asked if we wanted to come to his cellar. It hadn't looked this bad. Besides, I can't rely on him to keep saving me.

We step out onto the porch, and I see headlights pulling in. It's Chad.

"Look. Mom, Chad is here to help!" My muscles somehow don't feel as tense anymore. We haven't talked for a couple of days since he stormed off the other night. I tried calling him, but he never returned my calls or texts.

"Come on, Ms. Hawksley, let's go." He wraps his arms around Mom and leads us to the cellar. The hail has stopped, but now heavy rain works hard to push us back towards the house. Pulling the cellar door open, he holds the umbrella over us as we ease down the wet steps. A sudden gust of wind turns the umbrella inside out and snatches it away, adding it into the sky along with all the other debris this funnel monster is collecting in its path. The newly captive treasures fall into the choreography created by the howling winds and dance throughout the sky. Chad follows us down the steps and closes the heavy door with a loud bang. He latches the large slide lock and then loops the heavy rope through the metal eye cemented into the floor. Mom made Dad add extra security years ago.

Chad turns his phone flashlight towards us to make sure we are okay. I am so very thankful he showed up for us. He shines his light into the corners of the cellar. It is stocked with everything needed for a week or two. Water bottles, candles, flashlights with extra batteries, and a small transistor radio sit on the shelves along with canned goods and a manual canned food opener. Mom even put in a sealed pot with a roll of toilet paper. She was prepared.

I grab a blanket from the shelf and shake it free of any hidden spiders. I wrap it around Mom's soaked body. After lighting a couple of candles, I drag my chair closer to her and rub her shoulders, trying to help her relax. I catch Chad's attention and mouth the words, "Thank you."

He nods at me and turns to double-check the knot he has put in the rope. We sit in silence listening to the roars above us. Something bounces off the cellar door, causing a loud bang, making Mom whimper a little louder.

As she trembles, I'm positive we are both thinking about the same memory from years earlier. Her fear of tornadoes has always been strong, and now it is more justified than ever. I wrap my arm around her and give her a little squeeze.

She pulls back and looks at me. "Your eyes are just like your dad's. They remind me he's still here with us." I hug her a little closer, and she lays her head on my shoulder.

That's when we hear it. The swirling rocks, twigs, and debris collide with each other, causing a low rumbling train sound. Getting louder and louder, it sounds like a train is rolling over its tracks right above the cellar. The cellar door bangs faster and faster as the wind tunnel tries its best to suck it up and add it to its rotating party. Chad pulls down on the rope as hard as he can. We can hear the heavy snaps of what must be tree trunks breaking in half. Something else hits the door, causing another booming noise. Mom lets out a little yelp, so I squeeze her tighter.

Chad never lets go of the rope, and we all sit in silence listening to the destruction overhead. It seems to go on for the longest time but actually only lasts a couple of minutes. Eventually, the noise reduces to light rain. A few minutes later, we hear the all-clear siren and know that the danger is over.

Untying the knot, Chad slowly pushes open the cellar door and steps out to assure the coast is clear. Mom and I sit in silence, preparing ourselves to handle whatever is to come. He steps back down enough to lower his head into the cellar with us.

"It's safe to come out. Your houses are still standing, but we are going to have some major cleanup to do."

He offers his hand to Mom as she ascends up the stairs and then does the same for me. We slowly take in the damage. Our houses seem untouched, but the yard is littered with odds and ends. It looks as though all the spectators discarded their trash in our yard after the tornado's dance recital was over.

Our eyes lock on the location where our barn once stood. In its place is a pile of twisted metal and broken wood pieces with a large tree lying on top of it. The barn is demolished.

Mom folds her arms across her chest and lets out an enormous sigh. Her hair is dripping from the light rain as a look of relief grows on her face. "Good riddance," she says. She closes her eyes and slowly nods her head up and down as if approving of the annihilation of the barn.

It held so many painful memories. And God wiped it away just like that.

24 Third Option

**Middle of October
Present Day**

25 Jasmine

A Layer From the Middle of September
Nine Months Before the Move
Twenty-six Years Old

"Jazz!" Ice ran through my veins as the familiar voice calls after me over the sound of the street traffic. I quickly attempted to dash into the next store, which was a cute little boutique. I felt a hand wrap around my upper arm, trying to turn me around.

The chills suddenly turned to a flash of anger as I felt his hands on me once again. I pulled my arm free and gave way to the rage washing over me. "How dare you grab me like that!"

The look on Ted's face was instantly remorseful, realizing he had just given me cause to take out a protective order against him. Something his mother had paid me a large lump sum to avoid last year. The agreement was that Ted would never approach me again. Apparently, his parents also made large lump sum donations to someone high up to avoid jail time from the hospital report and any mention of the incident in the paper.

"I'm so sorry. I didn't even think." He shoved his hands in his pockets after he realized I was staring at them. I was sure the flashback could be read all over my face. His sports jacket brought out the brown specks in his eyes. "Look, I just wanted a chance to talk to you for a few minutes. I've been to lots of counseling sessions, and I've come to grips with a lot of things.

I was just wondering if you might be willing to have coffee with me so we can talk." My eyes darted from his hands shoved in his pockets to his face. Surely he was joking. He looked as serious as could be.

His pleas continued, "Or your favorite smoothie shop is right around the corner. Maybe if you had time right now, we could grab one. Is strawberry still your favorite?"

My mind betrayed me and conjured up visions of him walking into our tutoring sessions, carrying two smoothies always with the biggest, most charming smile he could muster. One for me and one for him.

"Are you crazy?" I shoved the memories back down into the depths of my heart where they belonged. I could not do this right now. "Do you really expect me to just say, 'Yeah, that sounds great! Let's go!'? Seriously, Ted?" I stared at his forehead to avoid looking into his eyes. A trick one of my high schoolers taught me when she was forced to look her parents in the eyes when she was in trouble.

"I knew it was a long shot, but, hey, you never know till you ask, right?"

I rolled my eyes at his attempt to make me smile. This was always my phrase to him when I would try to convince him of something I would want to do or a new restaurant I wanted to try.

That was before he utterly destroyed any future we had together.

"It doesn't matter if I have the time. I'm not interested in having any kind of discussion with you. That is what our lawyers are for." Our divorce should be settled in a couple of weeks. It had drug out for almost a year because of one complication or another. "Whatever you feel you need to say, you can tell your lawyer to tell mine."

I turned away as a flash of reflected light caught my eye. He pulled the object completely out of his pocket. My whole body tensed up at the sight of it.

"This was yours before we got married, and I just wanted to get it back to you. It's way too special to get caught up and listed in the divorce settlement." He held the gold pocket watch up by its chain and extended it out towards me.

Tears formed in my eyes as I held my breath. I outstretched my arm so my grandpa's pocket watch could rest softly in my hands as he allowed the chain to swirl gently on top of it in a circle. The fingers on my other hand wrapped protectively around it.

"Thank you so much. I truly appreciate your giving this back." I held the pocket watch close to my heart and tried to wipe my tears off with my shoulders.

"I counted on you still being pretty routine and thought today was the day you did a little shopping in this area."

"Yeah, I always enjoy my shopping days." I slid the pocket watch into my purse. My mind struggled back and forth between the fairytale that my life was supposed to be and the nightmare that it turned into. Why couldn't he have stayed the prince charming that he promised he would be?

I located the spot on his forehead to stare at again so that I was not trapped by his pleading eyes.

"I just wanted personally to see that you received the pocket watch back. I remember it was your grandfather's. The day you gave it to me is the only time in my life I have ever felt the most love and acceptance from a person. Thank you for giving it to me."

I struggled hard to keep my eyes focused on his forehead. I knew I would lose it if our eyes actually connected. At one time, he reminded me of my grandfather, which is why I gave him the pocket watch. All the corny jokes. The way he held the car door open for me. The way he protectively walked on the sidewalk closest to the street.

But my grandfather would never, ever have hit my grandmother.

"I appreciate it. I really need to go now." I stepped off the curb to cross the street for a quick getaway. If I ever needed some retail therapy, it was right then.

"Jasmine, if you don't mind, I would like to say one more thing." I hesitantly pulled my foot back up onto the curb and turned slowly around. Not that I owed him anything at all, but he did go out of his way to get my grandpa's watch back to me.

I found the forehead spot once again and waited without saying a word.

"I'll try to make this as quick and to the point as I can."

I let out a big huff to signal him to hurry.

"I've been going to a counselor twice a week for the past few months, and I've learned so much about myself. I recognize this doesn't make up for anything, but I am truly sorry for what I put you through. I didn't realize I had so much anger shoved down from my childhood, and you definitely weren't the one I was ever angry at. You were the best thing that ever happened to me."

I huffed even bigger and crossed my arms to signal that a little faster pace would be preferable.

"I understand I can't go into all of it right now, but I just wanted to thank you for loving me when I never deserved you in the first place. I apologize for everything. For not being the man that you deserve. For not discussing things with you and letting them fester up inside. For not protecting you. For being the one you needed protection from. I'm so, so sorry."

I allowed my eyes to meet his as tears spilled over his lower eyelids. The sorrow I saw in his eyes was almost too much for me to handle.

"And I'm the sorriest about our baby."

My hand automatically shot up in his face with my finger wagging back and forth so close to his nose that I hit it a couple of times.

"You have absolutely no right to talk about our baby!" I screamed at the top of my lungs. Passersby were stopping to witness the fallout. I glimpsed someone holding up his phone to video the spectacle. I had to get out of here.

I backed up to step off the curb when Ted lunged forward to grab my arm. The look on his face confused me. It wasn't a look of anger like the last time he lunged at me but a look of fear.

"Jasmine, get back!" He grabbed my right upper arm, and I suddenly was back in our lavish kitchen in my dream home on the worst day of my life. Instinct from the self-defense classes that I had taken over the past few months kicked in. My left leg swung around as my right arm quickly circled upwards, lessening his grasp. I grabbed his arm, which was still extended towards me, and slung him back behind me, knocking him off balance as he stumbled off the curb.

The truck didn't even have time to honk its horn before it slammed into Ted, catapulting his body into the intersection. I suddenly realized Ted wasn't grabbing me in anger this time but in an effort to save my life from the truck coming down the street.

I ran to Ted while hearing someone in the crowd claiming to call 911. I kneeled beside him, pleading for him to open his eyes and look at me. Moments before, I had avoided his eyes, and now that was all I wished to see.

I was suddenly flooded with precious memories of falling in love with this man. This man that made me laugh like no other. This man that always let me choose where we ate out. This man that promised to love me forever.

Ted gasped and began coughing. Blood spewed all over my lap. His eyes fluttered open, and he looked like a little boy who had fallen off a merry-go-round and was confused. If only life could be that simple once again.

"Jazz." His face contorted with the pain of his broken body.

I gently lifted his head and softly placed it in my lap.

"Shhhhh, Ted. It's okay. Don't talk." My hands trembled as I attempted to wipe some blood off his chin. His arm slowly came up and laid his hand on top of mine. I moved my hand and carefully placed his hand on his chest. I gently rested my hand on top of his and wrapped my fingers underneath his palm. He curled the ends of his fingers around my fingertips and gave me a little squeeze.

"If I had known this is what I needed to do to get your attention, I would've jumped in front of a truck a long time ago." He attempted a laugh and ended up moaning and spewing more blood over his chin.

"That's not even funny." I wiped the bloody drool away again with his shirt collar and mustered up a little smirk for him.

Tears formed in the corners of his closed eyes and slowly rolled down his cheeks. I remembered a flash of the man who stood at the end of the aisle on our wedding day.

His eyelids slowly opened, inviting me in. This look. This was the man I fell in love with. This was the man who enticed me with his charming smile, gentlemanly manners and strawberry smoothies. This was the man I dreamed of a future with.

I swiped away at a tear trying to escape.

"I'm so sorry I wasn't the man that I promised I would be. Just that. No excuses. I'm just so, so sorry." His voice was barely a whisper as life seeped out of him, flowing towards the nearby drain.

"I know." I stroked his hair into the spiky hairstyle that I had loved so much at one time. The blood acted as a gel to hold it in place.

The sirens screeched louder, signaling they would soon be here to relieve me. A sizable crowd had gathered around us. I leaned down close to his ear so that my words could be heard by him alone.

"I loved the man that you were when we first met. I will always love that version of you."

His eyes fluttered back open. This time with a grateful look.

A single tear rolled down his cheek. Just like it did on our wedding day.

26 Summer

A Layer From the End of March
Five Years Before the Wreck
Twenty-one Years Old

I subconsciously twirled my hair at the base of my neck. Mom does that when she is in deep thought as well. I quickly rubbed my hair back up into the bun that I had thrown up on the way out of the door. I hated waiting rooms. They were way too quiet and allowed my mind to wander too much. I wish I would've at least grabbed my earbuds so I could listen to music. I made a mental note to keep it in my bag.

The sliding glass doors occasionally opened to welcome the next catastrophe. An older man gently guided his wife in with their heads soaked. The storm was really picking up outside. The man spoke too loudly, showing that his hearing had failed him in his old age. After making sure his wife was safely seated, he limped to the counter to check in.

"My wife is having chest pains," he informed the check-in nurse. I glanced at the gray-haired lady as her face turned red. I didn't know if it was from embarrassment at how loudly the nurse was having to talk to be heard by her husband or if she was about to have a heart attack right then and there. I truly didn't believe I was capable of handling any more trauma tonight.

After giving all the necessary information, the older gentleman plopped down in an exhausted huff next to his wife as she put her hand out and pointed to his pants' leg.

"You really should have changed clothes before we came," she scolded as she attempted to brush the dried dirt off onto the floor.

"Oh, there isn't anything wrong with me having a stain on my britches, Woman. That way people know I'm a hardworking man. You just need to worry about yourself right now. They said that they would take you back as soon as they could." He picked her purse off the ground and fished around until he pulled out a pack of gum. He sat the purse on his lap and gently put his arm around her shoulders. Her head leaned to the side, resting in his embrace.

This was how I wanted to be. I wanted to grow old with my best friend always by my side through thick and thin. Someone who always knew exactly what I needed without me having to ask for it. I had that once, but there was no hope of rekindling that relationship. I'm pretty sure that bridge had burned over the past two years from neglect on my part.

I started to drift off in my daydream of maybes when suddenly the old man made eye contact with me and gave me a nod and a smile. Embarrassed to be caught staring, I gave a quick nod back as the check-in nurse slid open her little window.

"Summer Hawksley?"

Grabbing my bag, I jumped up and hurried towards the emergency room doors.

"He is ready for you to come back now." She walked me down the hallway to the last door on the right. The ER seemed to be quite busy tonight for such a small town. The storm must have brought in a lot of accidents. I fought off the flashbacks from being here a couple of years ago. I hoped tonight fares better than that stormy night did.

I heard him before I saw him. His whimpers and moans were making my stomach turn. I didn't know whether I could handle this. Watching him flip his motorcycle earlier on his homemade race track had already been on repeat in my brain. His screams of pain drowned out the sound of twisted metal hitting the old tractor. Perhaps I should wait in the waiting room until he was stitched up or whatever it was they needed to do.

"Summer! Summer!" Clay wailed as soon as he saw me. My big sister's protective instincts kicked in as I ran to grab the hand that was stretching out towards me.

"Clay, you are going to be just fine." I hoped I sounded more convincing than what I was really thinking. Blood was everywhere. His right arm was covered. His hair looked like he was born a redhead instead of his natural light brown. And his face. His sweet little face. Even though he was 15, I still saw that sweet little four-year-old face that would come crying to me for a band-aid when he scraped his knee, or elbow, or whatever body part took a battering for the day. He had always been a stuntman at heart. His stunts were now more dangerous as a teenager. This particular one backfired on him.

I kissed my hand and touched it to his forehead. Mom called this our special love spot. My phone buzzed. I switched hands with Clay and grabbed my phone out of my bag. Hopefully, it was Mom or Dad. Actually, hopefully it was Dad. Mom would blame me. Dad would be more sympathetic. He realized how hardheaded Clay was when he constructed one of his harebrained ideas.

Great. It's Mom.

"Mom? Hey, he's going to be just fine. No, Uncle Tate doesn't need to come. They are cleaning him up right now, and we are waiting for the doctor. Yes, he rode here in the ambulance, and I followed in my car. No, I'm not sure yet. Mom, do you know how hard it is to convince him to come in from the rain? Or to do anything that he doesn't want to do. Yes, Mom, I understand I was the responsible one in charge, but.... Mom....." I gave up trying to defend myself and glanced at Clay. He had gone silent after listening to the phone call. A little smirk started on his bloody lips. *Would the painkillers work this quickly?* "Look, Mom, can we discuss how irresponsible you believe I am later? I'll message you when we hear from the doctor. Love you too. Yes, I'll tell him."

I hung up the phone, and I was positive that the painkillers had now kicked in. Clay started pointing his finger at me. "Yeah, Summer, why did you let me jump that dirt hill in the rain? It's all your fault." He started wagging his blood-stained finger at me. He cocked his head to the side and raised his eyebrows in a "told you so" manner when he suddenly winced. The movement cracked open some dried blood on his forehead where the large gash was. It slowly dripped down the length of his nose again.

"Yeah, Clay, it's all my fault that you have to one-up your friends all the time." I went to squeeze his knee where I knew he was ticklish but stopped short, not knowing exactly where he was hurt. "Mom said to tell you they are catching the first flight back in the morning. Guess your freedom is over now. Mom is going to smother you so badly to ensure that her little baby boy has the best care," I said teasingly.

161

Clay rolled his eyes and fell back on his pillow. "Maybe now she will buy me that video game that I want! And make me her famous pecan pie. I love her pecan pie."

The painkillers had obviously taken full effect. Slurring his words, Clay went on and on about all the things that he would make Mom do for him. And she would. That was one thing I could say about Mom. She had definitely spoiled us. She talked about how she had never been doted on by her parents, so that was her primary goal in life, making sure we felt loved. And she had done a fantastic job of it.

Our nurse finished up the seven stitches on Clay's forehead. I took that as a good sign. Not six or eight, but seven. Clay's x-rays came back normal. The gash was the only injury he'd suffered.

"That should do it." The RN wiped the rest of the blood off of Clay's arm. "The head just bleeds a lot, so that's why there was so much blood everywhere."

I didn't take the opportunity to fill him in on how familiar we were with blood and head injuries.

"And that should leave a little scar once it heals up. That will be great for the girls. They always love a good scar story." He gave a little laugh and turned to wink at me.

"Speaking of girls, I thought nurses were only girls." Clay's pain meds were working pretty well, so I couldn't blame the kid for just saying whatever popped into his injured head.

I glanced at the RN's name tag. Chad. I gave him a little "sorry for that comment" smile and hoped he also would chalk Clay's rudeness up to his current state of mind.

"I actually have been surprised at how many people around here have made that comment. I just moved here from Fort Worth recently, where I worked at Medical City. We saw all kinds of emergency situations there. My mom and little brother moved here a few months ago when she married a rancher in the area. I fell in love with the quiet of the small town and decided to give it a try. This place snatched me up due to all my experience at a bigger facility. I miss all the action at Medical City though. It's not nearly as busy in this ER. That's why I jumped at your case when I saw them roll you in. I hadn't seen that much blood since I moved here." Chad peeled his gloves off his hands and disposed of them. "I think that will do it. I'll bring the doctor in so she can double-check my stitches and, hopefully, you can make it home before the storm gets too bad."

I stood to be closer to Clay after messaging Mom and Dad that Clay was doing just fine. I didn't inform them about the storm rolling in. Mom had enough to worry about tonight already.

We were about one block away from the ER when the tornado sirens went off. Clay and I looked at each other, hoping the other would have a quick solution.

"Let's go back to the ER. I'm sure they have a safe room or something!" Clay yelled. His immediate rush of adrenaline must have overtaken any leftover side effects of his pain meds.

I was already making a U-turn in the middle of the street before he even finished his sentence. I found the closest spot to the front door. I threw a towel over

Clay's head to keep his stitches dry as we ran for the sliding doors.

Chad happened to be standing there, looking outside for any sign of a tornado, and noticed the panicked look on my face.

"Back so soon? Hey, it's okay. You are as pale as a ghost." He put his arm around me and led me inside.

I shrugged his arm off and talked a little louder than I probably should have in a place like this. "You don't understand. WE HAVE TO FIND A SAFE ROOM!" My shrill exclamation caught his attention.

"Okay. Yes. Follow me, please." Chad turned around and led us to an elevator as our wet shoes squeaked against the tile floor. He pushed the B button. "We've taken everyone down here who is able."

His sudden professionalism made me a little guilty that I had yelled at him like I did. He was just trying to console me.

The doors slid open, and Chad led us to what must be a breakroom in the basement. Most of the chairs at the table were taken. I let Chad know we would sit on the floor. He showed us to a quiet corner behind the vending machines. He pulled out his wallet and inserted a dollar bill into the open slot. A bottle of water spits out of the bottom. He repeated this process again and handed the two bottles of water to Clay and me.

"Thank you. Look, I'm sorry that…" He cut me off before I finished.

"No. No. No apology necessary at all. I'm going to go back and check upstairs for anyone else, and I'll come back and check on you two in a few minutes, okay?"

I nodded my approval and watched him as he turned around. He casually checked in with several others misplaced down here. I noticed he checked on the older couple, patted the lady on the back and assured her that everything would be okay. Her husband held her a little tighter as her right hand covered her heart. I tapped the floor with my fingers seven times and repeated this pattern until my heart slowed down to a normal rhythm.

By the time that Chad came back down to give us the all clear, Clay's pain meds were wearing off and he complained of a headache.

"Chad, do you have anything that Clay can take before the pain gets too bad? We can't get to the pharmacy until tomorrow." I studied the man who has come through for us twice so far. Why not go for a third time?

"Sure. Why don't you meet me upstairs in the waiting area, and I'll see what I can gather up for you." He pushed a wheelchair towards the young man in the corner with a cast on his leg. After helping him get seated, Chad directed the wheelchair while also trying to carry the man's crutches and dropped one of them right at the door.

"Here. Let me carry those for you." I darted over to pick them up before he could protest. I gathered he's the type of man to do everything for himself.

"Thanks, but I can get them." He realized I was not giving them up and gave me a charming smile. It's the least I could do after I yelled at him earlier.

After waiting for about fifteen minutes in the waiting room, Clay decided he just wanted to go home. We headed out the door and walked towards our car. The rain had stopped. The storm clouds had moved northeast to terrify the next town. The full moon seemed to light up the sky once again.

"Hey! Wait a minute!"

Turning around, I saw Chad running towards us across the parking lot with a sack in his hand.

"Sorry that took so long. I grabbed some clean bandages and a sample of that antibiotic ointment that you can put on after a couple of days. If he is a normal teenager, I'm sure he will not keep it as clean as we like." He handed the bag over to me. "I also grabbed a couple of samples of the pain meds that the doctor prescribed. That should tide you over until you can get to the pharmacy."

His blue eyes twinkled in the moonlight. *Why didn't I notice the color before? Oh yeah, I thought we were going to die.*

"Did you just put some cologne on?" The words fell out of my mouth before I realized what I was saying.

Chad's face lit up with pride instead of embarrassment. "Yes. My shift was over during the tornado, and I'm headed to meet up with some friends in Glen Rose. They always complain that I smell like hospital rooms and that it scares all the potential girls away." His confidence brought out the blue in his eyes even more.

Chad opened the car door for Clay while his hand hovered protectively over the repair job he had performed earlier on his forehead. He shut the door and turned back to me.

"I'd like to explain my freakout earlier."

Chad shoved his hands in his jeans pockets. "Really? You don't have to explain anything."

"Please let me explain. I know myself, and I won't be able to sleep tonight beating myself up about how rude I was to you earlier." I switched the bag of medical goodies from one hand to another. "There was

166

a terrible tornado that came through here two years ago. Two years ago next month, actually. Clay and my other little brother, Dusty, were following our parents out to the cellar when Dusty's little dog got scared and jumped out of his arms. He was only eleven years old. Old enough to be stubborn to run after the dog, but young enough not to think things through."

My fingernails dig into the soft skin of my palm to force the tears to stay back.

"Dad had run ahead of everyone to get the cellar door open. Once Clay got to the cellar stairs, Dad asked where Dusty was. They both ran back towards the house to see if he had fallen or something. That's when the tornado ripped over the top of the barn. Dad sent Clay back to the cellar and kept looking for Dusty. He finally found him in the barn. A piece of sheet metal that was still stuck there had hit him in the head. The dog was whimpering, snuggled up against his side. By the time the ambulance finally reached us and then drove back to the hospital, Dusty barely had a heartbeat. He lasted only another couple of hours."

I wiped the tears off my cheeks that had escaped. "I was finishing up my freshman year at the University of Texas in Dallas, so as soon as I got the phone call, my friend and I headed home in the middle of the night. Mom ended up having a breakdown after watching her youngest son die. I dropped out of college a couple of weeks before the end of the semester and moved back home."

He just stared at me. I was suddenly mortified that I had just spilled my guts to this stranger in the ER parking lot.

"I'm so sorry that I just laid all that on you." I shifted the bag back to my other hand. "Anyway, that's why the mixture of the one brother that I have left at the ER during a tornado kinda sent me over the edge." I stared at him, waited for some kind of response, or expected him to just turn and run as far away from me as possible.

Chad took his hands out of his pockets and moved three steps towards me. He wrapped his arms around me, and suddenly all the tears that I had worked so hard to keep back burst out all over his chest. It's been a long time since I allowed anyone to fully see my true self. His embrace tightened around me as I emptied my sorrow from the last two years under the full moon.

When I crawled into bed later that night, the smell of his cologne still lingered on my forearms. I closed my eyes as I took in his scent. Maybe it was time to try something different. I had never allowed myself to look at anyone else but Ryan, and that chapter was obviously closed. Maybe it's time for a new chapter. A new book even. Maybe tonight I could finally have peaceful dreams.

27 Third Option

**Middle of April
Five Years Ago**

28 Jasmine

Middle of October
Present Day

When we emerge from the cellar, it looks as though we have entered a parallel universe. I recognize Shep's house, but his yard is unrecognizable. Pieces of wood are littered all over. The ground is blanketed with leaves resembling snow, as if a giant passed by and shook the trees, making them all drop. Branches were strung about. Grandma Shep's pumpkins were smashed far away from their original spot on the porch steps.

I follow behind Grandma Shep as she surveys the yard. She shakes her head slowly, shocked by the sight. Her neighbor, Annie, comes up the steps behind us. She made sure to extinguish all the candles in the cellar.

"Oh, Ry, what a mess." Annie walks over to observe a sliver of wood that is stuck upright in the yard. She walks in a circle around it, eyes squinting. "This wood looks like it might be from my barn. See the faded red paint on this side?"

Shep walks over and pulls it out of the ground. He glances towards the creek that lies between the two houses and notices several more pieces of wood. "Let me get Grandma settled in the house and check my windows. Then I'll take you back home, Annie."

Annie gives Grandma Shep a big hug. "Thank you so much for sending Ryan after me. You know how terrified I am of tornadoes. I was so thankful not to be alone in this one. I'll call Clay at college and make sure he takes cover. Looks like it is headed his way." Annie walks towards Shep's truck and pulls out her phone.

"Jasmine, I'll be right back." He tosses me his keys. "Start the truck if you don't mind."

Catching the keys, I head over to the truck, trying not to interrupt Annie's phone call.

"Yes, me too. Ryan will take me home soon, and I'll update you after we check for any damage. I'm sure he will help me look around." *It is so odd hearing his family call him Ryan. Everyone at school has always referred to him as Shep. I keep thinking they are talking about a different person.*

We both climb up into the truck to wait. His truck is lifted so high that he really could use an extra sidestep on the railing. An awkward silence hangs in the air between us. "I want to apologize ahead of time for any reaction I may have when we pull up to my house." Annie lets out a little laugh. "I feel like I am holding my breath until I can determine whether there is any damage. Tornadoes and I don't mix very well." She fidgets with her necklace. Her fingers wrap around a butterfly charm that looks like a locket. *Who does she treasure in there?* My hand goes to my circle charm necklace. My finger traces over the big circle and then the smaller circle.

Shep jumps in the truck, informing us that everything appears fine except that the electricity is still out. He said he helped his grandma light some candles and found her a flashlight so she could walk around. We are on the road only for a few seconds before we pull into Annie's driveway next door. As we pull up, I can hear her gasp in the backseat. Shep gives me a sideways glance as I return it with a reassuring smile.

By the time we pull to a stop in front of Annie's house, she is in full-blown crying mode. Our headlights shine on a large tree that has fallen over and flattened whatever structure that was standing there just an hour ago.

"Thank you, dear Lord, thank you," Annie murmurs in repetition in between her sobs. I'm a little confused about what she would be thankful for. Shep nodded my way, giving me the go-ahead to get out with them to check everything.

Annie walks straight to the pile and shouts, "Thank you, God. You KNOW I hated that barn!" Her sobs become laughter, and her laughter becomes sobs. She turns to me and grabs my hands. A solemn look falls over her face. "My son died in that barn seven years ago in a tornado. I've hated looking at it every single day since. I've been praying for the past couple of months, telling God I just don't know if I can stay here anymore. The house feels so empty." She looks back at where the barn once stood. "And I told Him I couldn't stand looking at that barn one more day. I guess I got my answer!" The biggest smile spreads across her face. She lets go of my hands and walks towards Shep to give him a big hug.

We follow her into her house so that Shep can inspect all her windows and make sure there are not any urgent repairs necessary. She points out a couple of flower paintings she made in an art class she attended with her longtime friend Liza before she follows Shep down the hallway. I stay in the living room to stay out of the way. I shine my phone flashlight around the shelves to look at her framed photos. A happy family stands in the foreground of what must be the Paluxy River: Annie, her husband, and two boys. Annie has her arms wrapped around the oldest boy while the youngest one is on his dad's back. The photographer captured a priceless moment of the happy family of four.

My eyes pan over to the next frame. My lungs hold my breath hostage with the shock of it. The overstuffed chair behind me provides support as I stumble back and sit on its armrest. Pressure builds up in my ears until they feel like they are going to explode. Not being able to take my eyes off it, I try to compose myself.

My handwriting on a receipt from my first night in Glass stares back at me, surrounded by an ornate gold frame.

"Those were my husband's last dying words." I turn to face Annie, who was standing on the other side of the room. "He died a few months back. God had sent someone who drove by at just the right time to be with him. I'm so very thankful he didn't die alone." Tears streamed down Annie's face. "I need to go to the sheriff's office to look at the report so I can find out who it was and thank them, but I don't want to see all the other details yet. Apparently, a deer ran out in front of him. I was supposed to be with him that day but was too tired to go. I've always wondered if I should've gone with him. Maybe he would still be alive. Maybe I would've seen the deer coming. Hawk was always racing around those curves."

She sits on the couch. I notice a tissue box on the side table next to a bowl of jellybeans and hand one to her. My mind goes back and forth. *Should I let her know it was me who stopped that night? Would she hate me for not saving his life?* Something urges me to confess.

I sit down on the couch next to her and grab her hands in mine. "Annie, I was the person who stopped on the side of the road to help your husband. It was my first night in Glass. I tried to do everything I could to help him, but I just didn't know what else to do. I didn't realize until now that it was your husband." Annie pulls her hands away from me, and I'm afraid she is going to yell at me. *Why didn't I just keep my mouth shut?*

"You? It was you that stopped?" Her voice is so soft I can barely hear her. "You are the one who wrapped a belt around his leg?"

I stand up to create some distance between us. She promptly stands up and takes a step forward to close the gap. I step backwards once again. "Yes, I'm so sorry. I didn't know what else to do."

She springs forward at me, and instantly, her arms are wrapped tightly around my waist as she begins to sob. I enclose her in my arms as she empties her sorrow and gratitude in the form of tears.

"Thank you so much for stopping for him. Thank you! Thank you!" We stand there for a minute while she cries some more. My heart begins to melt for this woman. I can see Shep out of the corner of my eye as he dabs at his own with the collar of his shirt.

173

"Please sit down and tell me all about everything he said. The one thing I was so thankful for was that he didn't die alone." She scoots as close as possible to me after we sit and clasps my hands so hard it is almost painful. I recount everything I can remember from that night as tears run down her cheeks, soaking in every word that I say.

The ride home with Shep is quieter than usual. I suppose we are both in shock from the chain of events of the night. The electricity came back on during the hour we visited in Annie's living room. She had told me all about Devin, her husband, and what a great man he was. Shep inserted his own fond memories of Devin taking him fishing when he was younger after they moved in next door. He also really stepped up to help Shep around his own farm after Shep's parents died. They had even gone fishing the week before the wreck. Shep said he was always a quick phone call away, and if he didn't have the answers, he would help Shep figure them out somehow.

It was getting late, so we had to end the conversation so Shep could take me home and get back to Grandma Shep. I really wanted to ask about the daughter Devin mentioned to me as he lay dying in my lap that night, but it will have to wait for another day. I had a feeling it might be a touchy subject, since I didn't see any pictures of her with all the other photos.

Besides being amped up from the activities from this evening, there is something else that I know will keep me up all night. I noticed something sitting on the side of Annie's house that looked very familiar to me.

Shep followed me inside my house and made a quick round to ensure everything was still intact. After seeing all was good and after loving on Pookie, he excused himself, saying he would call me tomorrow. We plan to go back to Annie's to start a cleanup plan around her house. Her son should come back into town, and she informed me he would want to meet me as well.

I refill Pookie's food and water bowls and head to my desk. In my office chair, I take a deep breath. Pulling the envelope from the drawer, I offer a brief prayer for answers.

The photograph slides out onto the desktop, and I'm overwhelmed with how many prayers may have been answered tonight with the tornado that just blew through town.

29 Summer

Middle of October
Present Day

My eyes stretch open as wide as possible. Rubbing my face, I work hard to get the circulation going as my mouth falls into another yawn. Although my head feels like it is going to explode, so does my heart.

Chad ended up staying with me until about three in the morning. We ate chocolate chip cookie dough ice cream and had a very long talk. He started off with an apology for overreacting about the heart rock. I was honest with him and told him I had put it back on the windowsill. I explained to him that even though Ryan gave it to me; it represents that love will come to me in my life at some point. I told him I believe the "forever love" that I have been waiting for all my life is him.

By the time he left, I felt all our puzzle pieces were falling into place. I can't wait until the day he doesn't have to leave. I promised Dad once I would never spend the night with anyone until I was married to them. It's been hard, especially last night, but there is no way I can break that promise to Dad now since he's no longer here. Chad has been so respectful and patient with my wishes.

I can hear people gathering outside. It must be noon already. Ryan quickly organized a cleanup crew and recruited more at church this morning, I'm sure, to get as much done as possible before the work week starts back tomorrow. Luckily, there wasn't much damage in town, so multiple people are available.

By the time I get dressed and head outside, it is half past noon. There are several trucks and trailers gathered around. Uncle Tate and Mom are passing out sandwiches and cups of lemonade to anyone who will take one. She waves me over to help pass them out.

"Here, take this to Ryan. He's been working so hard and won't come get anything to eat." I don't want to inform her that we aren't really talking. I grab the sandwich and drink and head towards where she has pointed me.

Ryan glances up at me and then quickly looks back down, grabbing more pieces of the demolished barn to throw on his trailer.

"Mom told me to bring this over to you." I hold the sandwich and cup up towards him.

He glances in Mom's direction and sees that she is watching. He takes them out of my hand and holds them in the air.

"Thank you, Ms. Hawksley!" He takes an obligatory bite of the sandwich and gulps half the lemonade. He sets them on the tire well of the trailer and gets back to work. My head throbs a little harder.

As I turn to walk away, Chad pulls into the driveway. I run to greet him as he steps out of the car. Wrapping his arms around me, he twirls me in the air. I lean forward as he gives me a quick peck on the forehead and takes hold of my hand. He leads me to the cellar and holds my hand up, suggesting that I stand on top of it. He steps up after me and goes down immediately on one knee. You can hear the hush sweep over all the workers in the yard, and Mom lets out a loud gasp.

"Summer, the night I met you, we bonded over a tornado. Last night, the tornado reminded me of that first time when I held you under the stars. I can't imagine my life without you, and I hope I never have to. Will you do me the honor of being by my side through all the tornadoes of life?" He turns his palm over, revealing a ring box he had hidden in his hand. He opens the top of the box as I am already nodding my head.

"Yes! Yes! I will!" My hands fly up to my mouth as I jump up and down. He grabs my hand, forcing me to be still so that he can place the ring on my finger.

"I want to be the 'forever love' that you have always dreamed of," he whispers in my ear as he twirls me around on top of the storm cellar.

Whoops and hollers erupt all over the yard from everyone but one person. Ryan doesn't look happy at all. He throws his work gloves onto the ground and walks off toward the creek between our houses.

30 Third Option

Middle of October
Present Day

31 Jasmine

A Layer From the Middle of November
Seven Months Before the Move
Twenty-six Years Old

"Do you have your forms filled out already?" Her hand reached toward me as her eyes stayed glued to her computer screen.

"Yes ma'am. Here you go."

I sat and waited with my fingerprint cards ready to hand over as the clerk entered my information. Her desk was littered with paper piles and leftover coffee cups. The Social Security office buzzed with a low hum of workers helping others get their life's information updated.

I felt such a sense of relief finally getting this accomplished. Changing my last name was the last step in cutting all ties in my life to Ted Bertarelli. I was going back to my maiden name, back to the path that I should have been on, reclaiming who I truly was. I watched her fingers fly over the keyboard as they probably did several hours of the day. Suddenly, they stopped as she flipped back over my printed forms I had given her.

Her eyebrows knitted together as she pushed her face closer to the computer screen, scrunching her nose like something didn't make sense.

"I think you just forgot to fill one of these blanks out right here." She shoved the form back at me with a pen.

"Section Three under the letter i. You are supposed to list all your previous names."

I reviewed my form, puzzled by her comments. "Yes, I have Jasmine Dawn Forte, my maiden name, which I want to use again, and my current married name, Jasmine Dawn Bertarelli. Well, I'm not married anymore, so that's why I want to change it back." I handed the form back to her so she could finish.

"I'm sorry, but your social security number is showing a third name. Actually, it must be your birth name because it looks like it changed for the first time in June, right after you were born. You must've been just a couple of months old. You are required to list all your previous legal names on the forms." She grabbed a pen and filled out my form for me.

As she laid it down, I glanced at what she wrote.

Summer Dawn Hawksley.

Summer Dawn Hawksley? Who was that? "I'm sorry, ma'am. There must be some kind of mistake. My name has never been Summer. And my last name is not Hawksley." My mind swirled, trying to figure out what was going on.

The lady looked at me as if I were the crazy one. "Have your parents never told you they adopted you?"

And right then, that was when my world turned upside down.

Again.

I drove straight to my childhood home to find out from my parents what was going on. *Was I really adopted? This surely was a mistake. Why wouldn't they tell me? Was this why I was the only brunette in the family?* I've always colored my hair to match Mom's blonde hair. It had always bothered me that mine differed from everyone else's. And my eyes. They all had green eyes. Mine were brown. *Was this the reason I've always had a nagging feeling that something was missing?*

I could never put my finger on it, but I have always felt that I never quite fit in. I had always attributed my perfectionist qualities to my attempt to make myself feel complete.

Intrusive thoughts and unanswered questions quickly took over my brain. My hands were trembling so violently that I turned off the highway and found the back roads to my parents' house. I cranked the air conditioner to full blast as my vision begun to blur.

Breathe in.

Breathe out.

Breathe in.

Breathe out.

I signaled the blinker to turn on Rose Road. Memories of my dad flooded my mind. He would always tease any guy that came to take me out, claiming they must present me with a rose. He said our street name demanded it. Dad always had the corniest jokes for any situation. I couldn't see any way that he could make a joke out of this tonight.

I pulled into the driveway like I've done thousands of times before.

Barging in with all my girlfriends for a last-minute slumber party after a football game. Mom always kept our cabinets full and ready with the best snacks.

When I got my first speeding ticket and was so scared to let them down. Dad paid for it without question when I promised I would never speed again.

Pulling into a homemade car wash that my brother had set up to make some extra money. He wanted to buy some new boxing gloves.

Coming home from college with Ted to surprise them with our engagement. They were both so elated for us. Mom ugly-cried, of course.

Pulling in from the hospital after picking me up from my latest beating from Ted. All three of us sat on the couch, holding one another, grieving the loss of my baby and their first grandchild.

I grew up in this home. All my lifetime memories existed within these safe walls. My lifetime refuge was about to come crumbling down.

Hours later, I drove away and headed back to my house, mentally exhausted. I had more questions now than when I first confronted them around the dinner table. They looked as blindsided as I felt.

Tears were shed. Explanations were attempted. After some failed apologies, multiple heated discussions, and a pounding headache, I finally decided that I needed to walk away.

As I pulled to the stop sign at the end of Rose Road, the streetlight shone down on the photograph in the passenger seat. The lady who gave birth to me stared back at me. But she was not a lady in the picture. She looked to be about six or seven years old, with brown hair like me. Innocent of what life had in store for her, she sat in the back of a red truck parked before an old red barn. Her smile turned up at the left corner of her mouth, just like mine.

This was what my birth mother wanted me to have. Life and this picture of her.

My parents never knew her name, but it accidentally slipped to them she was in high school in Glass, Texas, at the time of my birth.

I turned my blinker on and turned off Rose Road. Even though I had driven this road hundreds of times, it all felt unfamiliar. I suddenly didn't belong here anymore. My perfect life was now a total lie. A sinking feeling developed in my gut, and I had never felt so alone and so betrayed.

What else could be yanked out from under me? How many more things would I suffer a loss from before I found my footing again? I needed some solid ground underneath me, and it wasn't here in Fort Worth anymore.

Summer Dawn Hawksley?
How different would my life have been if I had lived as Summer?
Why did they keep me for two months and then give me up?
What kind of person would I be?
Who would I have fallen in love with?
Is that where my perfect life would have been?
I need answers.

32 Summer

A Layer From the End of April
Seven Years Before the Wreck
Twenty Years Old

"I did it again." Ryan's smile worked hard to charm his way in.

"Seriously, Ry? How did you even survive without me here last year?" I opened the door wider to my suite. He gave me a quick peck on the cheek and grabbed his extra truck keys off the hook by the door.

"Return those extra keys when we head back to Glass tonight. I'll need them the next time you leave your keys somewhere." I slugged him in the arm, and he immediately reached to tousle my hair, which needed little help in the first place.

"Thanks, Summer Bummer!" He darted back out the door and headed down the hall to the elevator. Freezing in his tracks, he turned around and ran back towards me.

"What did you forget now?" I really didn't know how he made it here last year at the University of Texas in Dallas while I wrapped up my senior year.

"This." Ryan wrapped his arm around my shoulder and his other arm around my waist. He dipped me backwards, causing my bare toes to barely touch the ground. He slowly and softly placed his lips on mine.

I returned the favor and wrapped my arms around his chest. This chest I had grown so fond of leaning on while watching a movie together. This chest that I laid my cheek on under the stars by The Fountain so I could hear his heartbeat.

This chest that held the heart that I had finally allowed myself to fall in love with.

He set me back up straight and tousled my hair one more time. "I'll pick you up at seven tonight when I get off work. Don't forget to bring some gummy worms for the drive!" He disappeared into the elevator.

I was sure he would be late for work after riding his bicycle back across campus to where his truck was parked. My head shook either in admiration of how he survived day to day or in disbelief that he had survived this long.

I shut the door and headed back to my bedroom. The suite was quiet, with my roommates both gone for the weekend. Working at a daycare, I thankfully always had my weekends free.

The reflection in the hall mirror caught my eye. I'm always surprised by the smile on my face. These past few months have taken my life in a whole new direction. I finally gave "us" a chance, and I'm so glad I did.

I climbed back into bed and pulled the covers up to my chin. What a whirlwind the past few months had been. When I first came here, I was so overwhelmed by the size of it I almost dropped out after the first month. This place was much larger than our hometown of Glass. I finally gave in to letting Ryan introduce me to some of his friends.

I started riding back with him to Glass every Saturday night because Grandma Shep made him come back to church every Sunday for the first semester. Eventually, she agreed he didn't have to drive back every weekend as long as we took a picture of us in a church on Sunday mornings here in Dallas to prove that we were going. She said she only allowed that because she trusted me to keep him in line. It was during those many car rides that long discussions happened, and we both laid out what we wanted out of life and discussed the future together.

My favorite discussion was on our way home for Christmas break. Ryan told me that his favorite Christmas was the one before I was born. After slugging him in the arm for what I thought was another dig at me, he had the most serious look on his face. "I'm serious, Summer. That's the Christmas your parents got married in high school and decided to keep you and not put you up for adoption. What if they had given you away to some stranger? What if you hadn't grown up here? What if we had never known each other?" He reached out to grab my hand. "What if you had fallen in love with someone else? I don't know how I would have functioned in life without you by my side."

Similar thoughts occasionally ran through my mind. *What would life have been like if Mom hadn't stood up to her mother? How would it have been like if I had been adopted and had different parents? How would I have survived without Ryan in my life?*

That was the moment that I knew I was absolutely, without a doubt, in love with Ryan Sheppard. He made me feel so seen. This was exactly where I belonged. In his arms.

If everything went according to plan, he would propose sometime this summer, and we would get married in the following year. When we celebrated my birthday last week, he hinted again at coming up with a proposal plan. I would be halfway finished with my courses, and he would only have one year left.

After his parents died a couple of years ago, Ryan had a really hard time with God. Thanks to Grandma Shep, he felt like he was on the right course. He felt like we should both move back to Glass and teach there. Sounded like a grand plan to me! Life couldn't get much better.

Rolling over in bed, I reached for my phone to check the time. I would get up in seven minutes.

I grabbed the heart rock from my bedside table. Holding it above my face, I turned it and studied the mix of colors God used to create it. For years and years, sediment had settled in just the right shape for this rock to look like a heart. It was incredible to think about.

How many pieces of God's handiwork have I overlooked in my life? Sometimes, God has worked for years putting situations together in just the right way for me, and I don't even realize it. I needed to be more intentional in looking at the circumstances in my life that God was using for my good. He shaped the pieces of my life together even more purposefully than He did this rock.

A smile spread across my face, remembering the end of the summer picnic when Ryan gave it to me. I had wanted this relationship to happen between us since he first placed my hands on his shoulders, trying to learn how to dance at campsite number seven that one summer. I had always been too scared to really give it a good try. Now, one of my favorite things was when he twirled me dancing in the kitchen at Mom and Dad's farmhouse.

He told me one day we would dance with our children in that same kitchen with Dad playing the guitar and Mom singing one of her silly songs. My parents would be the only grandparents our kids would have since his had passed in the plane crash. He wanted to get married young because he said that life was too short to wait for something that you know is right.

I wholeheartedly agreed.

My phone buzzed with a text from Ryan.

> Change of plans grandma just called and her and your dad decided we shouldn't drive back tonight. Some storm is coming in. Looks like movie night for us. I still want gummy worms. I'll pick up some pizza on the way home 🍕

I hope it is not a bad storm. Mom hates them so much.

33 Third Option

**End of January
Two Years Ago**

34 Jasmine

Middle of October
Present Day

By the time that Shep picked me up the next day after church to go help with the cleanup at Annie's house, I've about worked myself into a panic attack. I keep changing my mind about whether to go. He showed up when I was on the 'yes, I'll go' side of the fence.

I climb into the truck, envelope in hand, and hand Shep the bottle of water that he asked for. I pat my pocket to ensure the chocolate candies that I like to snack on when I get nervous are there.

"What's that?" He nods at the envelope as he gulps down half of the water before putting the truck in drive.

"Nothing important." I reach up and slide it safely in between the roof and the visor.

"I brought you some extra work gloves. Thanks so much for offering to come today. Clay will not come in until next weekend after all. He couldn't take off work. I assured him we have it covered. There will still be plenty for him to do later." He tosses the work gloves into my lap.

I easily shove my hand into one. "Thanks. They are kind of big, though." I wiggle my fingers down into them as far as I can. "Hey, you never told me Annie's last name."

"Hawksley. Annie and Devin Hawksley. My parents were great friends with them from the very moment that they

191

moved in next door. Annie and my mom were really close. They both came from tough situations and bonded over that."

He turns onto the road that will hopefully lead me to what I've been searching for. My insides are trembling, bouncing back and forth from fear to excitement.

Shep continues, "They had just gotten married when they moved to the farm next door, but I'm pretty sure that they had dated in high school years before. I overheard her on the porch one time telling my mom that she had gotten pregnant in high school, and they broke up shortly after that. I'm not sure what happened to the baby, but their two boys aren't old enough for it to be one of them."

I know what happened to her.

Shep pulled into Annie's driveway and drove in a circle in the yard so that his trailer ends up close to what used to be the barn.

I glance up at the envelope. "Do you mind leaving your truck unlocked, please?"

"Sure! Who is going to steal it out here?" Shep laughs and steps out of the truck. I am fully aware that the next time I climb back in, life as I know it will be different.

Time passes by quickly, and I'm amazed at how many people have shown up to help. Annie's brother Tate brought in some equipment from his lumberyard. Trailer after trailer is filled, taken to someone's own personal landfill for a future bonfire, and then comes back for more. After a few hours the yard starts to return to normal. There are still items left in a pile that were in the barn, but Shep explained that a lot of those items are salvageable and one of the local farmers will come by this week to examine them.

Annie has continually handed out peanut butter and jelly sandwiches (she said they are her favorite, so she had plenty of supplies on hand) and has made gallons of lemonade to quench everyone's thirst.

I catch myself throughout the day wanting to stop and watch her. She handed out each sandwich and drink with a smile. I wanted to offer to help her with the sandwiches, but I was afraid that I would be too awkward. She wore an old Texas Rangers baseball hat with her brown ponytail hanging from the back. When she was sure that everyone was fed, she pulled on some gloves and rain boots and buzzed around from one trailer to another, helping to clean up all the scattered debris.

With the workload dwindling, I decide now would be a good time to take a break. I walk around the side of the house to get a closer examination of what I had caught a glimpse of last night.

I wipe my hand along the red hood, knocking off some twigs and leaves. Faded graduation tassels hang from the rearview mirror. Running my hand along the side, reality sets in by touching the details committed to memory from staring at the photograph for the past year. My hands dip in and out of the grooves and dents along the side.

I round the corner at the tailgate and see Annie looking at me. She slowly walks my way. My stomach turns, and my breathing picks up pace. I remove my hand from the truck, and it immediately heads for the comfort of my necklace.

"I'm so glad that wasn't in the barn. My grandpa gave me this truck when I turned sixteen. Well, I say he gave it to me. I had to work all summer to earn money for the parts to make it run again. I sure have some great memories in it." She stops at the driver's side window to peer inside, going into a momentary trance.

"I remember when my grandad would use it around this very farm when I was a little girl. He would let me ride in the bed of it with the hay. Sometimes when my mom and dad weren't around, he would even let me drive it." A soft smile forms on her face. "I once had a picture of me sitting in the back of the truck, and I would keep it right here in the dash panel so that I could see it and remember fond memories of my childhood. All my best memories from when I was young happened on this farm. I was so grateful when Grandpa allowed Hawk and me to buy this place when he couldn't farm anymore. I loved being able to raise my babies here."

That last comment stabs at me a little bit. "What did you do with that picture? Do you still have it?"

Annie looks down as sadness takes over her face. I can tell she works hard not to cry. "No, I don't. I gave it to someone quite special many years ago." She wipes away the tears that escaped despite her efforts to avoid them.

"I'll be right back. Will you wait right here for me, please?" She agrees, so I start my last walk before I get the answers I came for.

How do I do this? Hand her the envelope? Take it out and hold it up in front of her face? Throw it at her and run away? What if she gave me away because she didn't want me in her life? What if all I am is a terrible memory for her? My breathing gets heavier and heavier. *No, not now. I can not experience a panic attack right now.* My chest is heavy, and my ears throb. My choice right now is to control my breathing or allow myself to succumb to my fears to avoid the possibility of rejection. I choose to breathe.

Arriving at Shep's truck, I glance over at him, and he waves my way, smiling that charming smile of his. My eyes avert to Annie, noticing that she has climbed into the cab of the truck.

I scan around the house and towards the creek in between Annie and Shep's houses. *What would my life have been like if she had decided to keep me? Which bedroom window would be mine? Would my little brother still be alive? Would Devin still be alive? Would Shep and I have grown up together? Would we have played in the creek together and collected those rocks he always talks about? So many possibilities taken away by one decision.*

I stare at the envelope. I know that once I present it to her, my life changes forever. And not just my life, but so many others as well.

If I don't do this right now, I'll regret it. This is the exact reason I moved to Glass. This is the answer I have been desperate for. This is the day that I have been looking forward to and putting off all at the same time.

I grab the envelope and shut the door to Shep's truck. I walk towards my new life, hoping it is better than my old one has been lately.

By the time I get back to the red truck on the side of the house, Annie is still sitting inside the driver's door. I climb in on the passenger side, thinking this might give us some privacy.

"There was a day a long time ago that I believed this truck would take me away from Glass, Texas. Take me to a dream-filled life that only exists in a teenager's head." She fondly rubs her hand back and forth over the top of the black steering wheel and swipes at the dust on the cracked dashboard. "I never imagined that I would end up living on my grandpa's farm with this same red truck."

Not knowing what to say, I offer the envelope for her to take.

"For me? What is it?"

Will she still smile after she opens it? I'm positive she can hear my pulse surging right now.

She pulls the photograph out and turns it over to inspect it. I'm curious about her thoughts as her smile disappears. Her hand raises to cover her mouth as she takes a large gulp of air. Her head turns, and her wide eyes look at me.

She looks back and forth between my face and the photograph. Her eyes finally settle on my face as they take in every detail. She looks away and places the photograph behind the steering wheel on the dash panel in its old resting place.

"You have Hawk's eyes. I couldn't stop staring at them last night. I thought I would never see eyes like his again. Those honey-brown eyes were always one of my favorite things." She reaches her hand up and cups my cheek. "We have always loved

195

you so very much." I lean my face deeper into her hand and feel her warmth as my eyes well with tears of relief. My heartbeat slows down at her touch. "My little Summer Dawn. Our only girl. We were so sad that we missed out on your life."

The words of the man dying in my lap on my first night in Glass come rushing back. "So you don't have another daughter? Was he talking about me?" The tears spill over, realizing that the man that died in my lap that night was my daddy. *He was talking about me. He missed me. He loved me. Thank you, God, that I got to meet him as well.*

We hold each other for a few minutes until our crying subsides. Her hands exploring my head and back as if to make sure I was real.

We end up sitting there for hours as she shares her story with me about how they tried to keep me. Her parents weren't supportive at all. Her grandparents had offered to let the two of them live in a camper on the farm, but Devin's parents disapproved. They thought he would be throwing his life away. They ended up breaking up a couple of months after I was born, and then her mom talked her into giving me up for adoption.

She then explained how she and Devin had run into each other a few years later and ended up getting married after all. They deeply regretted their decision to give me up. All they could do was pray for me every day that I was loved and safe.

I shared the highlights of my life from childhood to growing up. I held back the details of why Ted and I had separated, but I did tell her of Ted's tragic death and how that eventually led me here to find her.

Twice I saw Shep peeking around the corner of the house, checking on us. Thankfully, he left us alone, and the trailers disappeared one by one until Shep was the only one left.

Long after dark, Annie and I walk into the house holding hands and find Shep snoozing on the couch.

"The two of you are about the same age. I bet you would have been the best of friends growing up next to each other. He's grown into such a fine young man. I still see him as a little kid when he gets that goofy grin on his face."

I nod in agreement. I know the grin.

"He always seemed like he was missing something and was a loner. Don't get me wrong, Ryan has always had tons of friends and is the life of the party, but it was like he knew something was missing. I've always thought it was you." She squeezes my hand as we both watch Shep sleep. "And look what God did. He made sure the two of you found each other. He makes everything beautiful in its time." She gives me another hug as her comments sink in.

All the different layers of my life and how God has had to orchestrate them to get me standing in the living room where, in an alternate life, would have been my home, engulf me. My spine shivers. Shep stirs awake and sees us both staring at him.

"What? Am I drooling?" We both giggle as he swipes at his mouth. I've never wanted to kiss that mouth more than I do right now.

35 Summer

End of October
Present Day

I hold my left hand up so that the sun reflects off the diamond in my engagement ring. I've worn it for over a week now, and I am still startled when it catches my eye. It is proof to everyone that I am someone's priority. Maybe real life can be like the storybook movies after all. I just needed to be a little patient.

Chad has been so attentive lately, and it's been exciting to dream about our future life together. We will marry early next summer, move to Dallas where I will start back to school, and he will return to work at Medical City. This will give us time to find an apartment and get everything in order.

Mom has already ordered a wedding planner online and has a stack of wedding magazines she has been collecting. This will be a great distraction for her. She has smiled more this past week than she has in the last few months. I'm glad I could help put a smile back on her face.

I've always dreamed of a wedding in Mom and Dad's backyard. We would repeat our vows to each other in front of our loved ones with the creek in the background. I always pictured it happening with Ryan and dreamed Dad would walk me down the aisle.

Neither of those is a possibility anymore.

When Ryan drove me home from school the night my brother died in the tornado, we sat in silence for the entire drive. I prayed to God the whole way to save my brother. We made it to the hospital before he passed away. I was thankful I got to say goodbye, but God not allowing my brother to live really knocked my family off track.

I refused to spend time alone with Ryan after Mom had her breakdown. I felt so guilty and selfish doing things that made me happy when she was so sad. I was afraid to leave my family after that. It had always been my job to follow my brothers and make sure they made it to the cellar during a tornado. If I had been home where I belonged and followed my brothers that night, my younger brother would be alive.

The porch swing creaks as I move back and forth, waiting for Chad to come pick us up. I got up extra early to make sure I wasn't running late. Chad says it makes a good impression when one arrives early somewhere. I hope Mom is ready by the time he gets here.

Mom has convinced us that, since we are starting a new life together, we would all be better off if we went back to church. Our old church has a widow's group that has been reaching out to Mom, but she doesn't want to show up by herself. Chad volunteered us to go along with her. I told him she could sit by her friend Liza, but he said it would be good for us, too. I'm not looking forward to going. Hopefully, I can convince Chad to sit in the back row. It will be easier to avoid Ryan back there.

Two butterflies hover over Mom's hanging basket of lantana. One chooses a bloom to land on while the other heads in my direction. It flutters in front of my face as I sit frozen. Landing on the armrest of the swing, it faces my direction. A memory invades my mind from a couple of months ago, sitting in this very spot and listening to Mom talk about her dream of her and Dad sitting in church together.

"Okay, Dad." The butterfly continues to stare at me. "Maybe this will be a good thing." The butterfly takes off and joins its friend on a nearby bloom.

Chad pulls into the driveway, so I get up and head to Mom's front door. Pulling the screen door open, I stick my head inside. "He's here, Mom. I'll be in the car."

Chad purchased a new red Prius a couple of days ago. This is my first time I've seen it in person. He claims it will be so much better for us with the gas mileage once we move to Dallas in a few months. I head to the car, watching Chad talk to someone on his phone. He doesn't look thrilled. He hangs up as I open the door.

"Who was that? Everything okay?" I lean over so he can kiss my forehead.

"Yeah, it was my younger brother. He needs me to come over this afternoon and help with his truck. So, what do you think?" He wipes at the dash as though there are specks of dust on it.

"It's beautiful! I love it! When do I get to drive it?"

Chad scoffs and steps out of the car when Mom approaches so he can open the door for her. He gets back in and starts the car back up. When he does, his phone connects to the car display, and its information pops up on the screen. His recent calls are listed, and his brother's name is not the last phone call. The screen reveals it was Laney.

A video begins as the church sanctuary lights fade. Tied to a center stake, a donkey pulls a board behind him and walks round and round in circles, trampling on wheat on the threshing floor underneath him. The video changes to someone beating stacks of wheat with a large club. It changes once more to someone holding a large bundle of wheat and beating it on a large rock.

Chad leans towards me and whispers in my ear. "I wasn't aware that church was so violent." My hand flies up to slug him in the arm. I stop when I remember how much he hates that. I don't want to ruin the good streak we have enjoyed for the past week. I glance across the aisle as Grandma Shep gives me a smile and a little wave. Ryan sits next to her, staring straight ahead.

"Threshing is the process of separating the grain from its husk." Pastor Alan speaks as the video continues. "It is a two-step process. First, it must have some type of friction or struggle to cause the grain to separate from its surroundings. Second, the wind is used to separate the now worthless chaff from the heavier grain."

The video shifts; a man now shovels grain, flinging it skyward.

"The weighty grain, the part that has all the substance, falls straight down to the ground. It's the good stuff. This is what you want. This is the goal. This is why you go through all the hard work, to get to the important stuff on the inside. All the extra particles that are no longer needed fly away with the wind. Being weightless, it can be effortlessly taken away, leaving the most valuable part of the crop exposed and ready for collection."

We watch the video as it portrays exactly what Pastor Alan has said. I find it intriguing to watch the large dust cloud fly off into the wind. It reminds me of the smoke after a firework goes off. It slowly dissipates; what was used to help develop the grain is no longer significant.

"God allows threshing in our lives in a variety of ways: struggles, trials, difficulties. It can be through people or situations. The situations can arise through our choices or someone else's choices. The possibilities are endless; however, the result is always the same. God wants to restore you back to Him. He wants a relationship with you. God loves you and pursues you. Occasionally, we require help in letting go of unnecessary baggage to help restore that relationship."

Pastor Alan pauses, looking around the congregation to confirm everyone's focus is on him. "Always remember that God is in control of the wind in your life. What is God threshing out of your life that you are still trying to hold on to?"

Mom sniffles as she sits beside me and wipes a tear away. God knew Mom needed that barn blown away like the chaff that was no longer needed. It symbolized a hole in her life that she couldn't get past by looking at it every day. She was still holding onto the hurt that it represented. I reach my hand over and pat her knee. She tilts her head my way and tightens her lips to hold back her emotions. I give her a knowing smile and give her knee a slight squeeze.

I turn my head to include Chad in our exchange and see that he is scrolling through social media on his phone. My stomach drops with disappointment that he is choosing not to get anything out of the sermon when it was his idea to come. I quickly glance across the aisle. Ryan averts his gaze away from me. He leans forward, and I notice Tony and Pennie are sitting next to him. Tony puts his arm around Pennie as she wipes her eyes. Good for Ryan for bringing them to church. I'm not surprised at all.

I turn my focus back to Pastor Alan as he continues to go over examples of threshing and reads different verses from the Bible, applying them to an assortment of struggles that many can relate to. I get lost in thought over the medley of struggles that I've had in my lifetime.

Have I fallen back on God from each one or allowed myself to be blown around in the wind? Where did I get sidetracked? When did I lower my expectations for where I felt God was leading me when I was younger? Better yet, what in my life needs to be threshed?

I feel Ryan's eyes on me once again. I turn towards him, and this time he doesn't avert his gaze.

36 Third Option

**End of October
Present Day**

37 Jasmine

End of October
Present Day

The past week has been a whirlwind of emotions. I ate supper at Annie's every night. We have so much life to catch up on and always struggle to say goodbye. Clay skipped classes and called into work on Monday so that he could come home and meet me. He was the male version of me, except he had Annie's eyes. It's a unique feeling when you recognize yourself in someone else's face.

The three of us laughed and cried. Photo albums were strung across the kitchen table. Memories filled the air, along with regrets. Regrets of missed experiences on both sides. I realized that even though I hated missing out on growing up with my biological family, I would never trade the memories I had with my adopted family. I was flooded with my own childhood adventures as I shared them. My family means the world to me. I've been too hard on Mom. Annie helped me realize that. She shared she has prayed not only for me but also for my parents all these years. She is so grateful to them for giving me the life that they did. Clay left at two in the morning to drive back to school. He knew he'd likely fail the test scheduled for the next day; however, he decided this was a good excuse.

Yesterday, Annie and I drove into Glen Rose to eat and do some shopping. I informed her I wanted to show her something. When we stepped into Front Porch Designs, I grabbed some more of the specialty jelly jars and then led Annie to the prayer journal on the counter.

Macee and I had stopped in here on our shopping trip in August. I flipped back a couple of pages, scanning each one for my handwriting. My finger directed Annie to read my prayer request. One simple word. "Answers." My heart filled with overwhelming gratitude for all that God had answered for me over the past few days.

The owner, Traci, took a picture of Annie and me pointing to my prayer request on the page. She thanked us for stopping by and sharing our story with her. Hearing about granted prayer requests fueled her to do even more. She was considering the idea of creating a Prayer and Praise Wall where others could be inspired with stories just like ours.

I give Pookie one last rub on her head before I shut the door to head to my car. Annie invited me to sit with her in church today. She always sits with Grandma Shep and would love to have me by her side.

I open the visor mirror to check my makeup one last time. My eyes appear brighter as they dance around in my reflection. A much better version than I saw in the storefront window shopping with Colleen over a month ago. I know there is still a burden hidden back there. Multiple burdens. Some that will never subside. I am slowly learning to integrate some of them into my life. But there is one burden I can eliminate. I vow to make a phone call to Mom this afternoon.

My shoulder brushes against Annie's as we sit back down in the pew after singing a couple of songs. I'm squished between her and Shep as Grandma Shep insisted that we young people needed to sit by each other.

Tony, Pennie, and Frank, Pennie's dad, sit on the other side of Shep. Pennie gave me a hug when they walked in, sharing this was the first time her dad had come with them to church since before her mom passed away. Sitting between the two most important people in her life, her face radiates.

Ryan seems to be exhausted after his drive back from the football team's loss to the Gatesville Hornets last night. The shortage of referees for Friday night pushed the away game to Saturday. The fact that his star running back was injured during the game made it a very long night. This next week is the Glen Rose game that the team has been gearing up for all season. Maybe I could do something for him this week. I'm sure he will be stressed.

My eyes blink a few times as the lights come back on after a video demonstrating the threshing process. Pastor Alan shares his interpretation after reading some verses and tying them to what we just witnessed.

"Sometimes in life, it feels as though God is punishing us." My chin raises. It is as though he is talking straight to me. "Life layers us with dirt. At times, we feel buried beneath it, wondering where God is. I need to tell you today that treasure is hidden underneath those layers of dirt and chaff. Sometimes we are forced to dig through those layers to recognize what was there all along. God meets you there on the threshing floor. He has been there all along. Even the times when you feel life has beaten you down. The floor is where the most valuable part is waiting to be collected."

He walks across the stage to engage the youth sitting on the other side of the church. "Life will not be what you think it is. Life is hard. What will come out of you when life squeezes you? When you are being threshed and crushed on the threshing floor? I promise you it's coming. Students, you need to have a plan now on how you will react when life doesn't go your way. Will you dig through those layers to find how God can use the hard stuff in your life, or are you going to allow yourself to be swayed with whichever way the wind is blowing? Making that decision today will make a tremendous impact on your future life."

I notice Frank slide his arm around his little girl as she lays her head on his shoulder. He leans over to kiss the top of her head as she places her hands on her growing tummy.

How different would my life have been if Annie's dad had been as supportive? What would it have been like to grow up here in Glass? I've had some hard blows, but I realize God has been there with me the entire time. Directing me in the softest ways. He led me to Glass to add to my family, not to replace them. I don't believe He caused me to lose my baby, but I do believe He used the situation to help get me here where I am today.

Annie reaches over to grab my hand. I draw it onto my lap and place my other hand over hers to give it a squeeze. Life has turned out differently than my expectations when I was younger, but I'm thankful for the path it has led me on.

Pookie is excited to see me when I walk back in the door. I reluctantly declined joining everyone for their Sunday ritual at Spicy Sombrero. This phone call needs to happen today. The pile of letters from Mom on the counter pulls at my attention. I place them in chronological order according to the postmark. There are five of them. One written for each month I've spent here.

As I read through them, it hits me how selfish I have been. I avoided conversations with Mom, not understanding how scared and hurt she was as well. She agreed in her first letter that she would not bring the subject up with me again, other than in the letters, until I was ready to discuss it with her. I've wasted so much time avoiding her in fear of a confrontation.

The second letter describes how she will be forever grateful to my birth mom for allowing her the opportunity to raise such a wonderful daughter as me. Although she admitted she's afraid of losing me to her.

The third letter talks about what a wonderful time she had raising Nathaniel and me. She explained she chose both of our names for their meanings. They both mean "gift of God." She was truly thankful for the gifts that God gave her through us. She always believed my extraordinary purpose for coming into her life was to enable her to experience God's love for her. She had never shared that with me before.

The fourth letter began with an apology of another kind. She realized she had been too hard on my brother and me growing up. Perfection was always expected in our household. Believing God had given her a special gift through us, she was afraid of ruining us. With her infertility issues, she considered she wasn't good enough to be a mom. She was in such a dark place before they adopted me. In order to show her appreciation for the children God gave her, she did not take her role as a parent lightly. She realized now that it had cost her many experiences with us. She would stand at the window and be jealous of Dad and me dancing in the rain. She wished she had joined us. If only she could go back and redo some things with the wisdom that she has now.

Pookie crawls up in my lap and lies on the pile of tissues collecting there. I open the last letter. It is the shortest of all the others. This is the one Frank handed me one week ago, the day of the tornado. Talk about a mother's intuition. The letter informs me she has said all that is on her heart, except for one last thing. This was something she had been arguing with God about and had finally surrendered to what she knew was the right thing to do. She gave me her blessing to love my birth mom. She understood she really had no right to say one way or another, but she also knew that deep inside, I needed to hear that. I've always been a people pleaser and, above all, I hate to disappoint my parents.

Pookie wakes up as I shift to grab another tissue. My head throbs from all the emotions running around in it. I've been extra hard on Mom. Perhaps because I expected her to be perfect, just like she always had been all my life. It rocked my entire existence when I found out she had kept my adoption from me. The letters helped explain her reasoning without my interruption.

I pick up my phone and open my frequent contacts. Her miniature picture circle sits right beside "Momma" with four pink hearts. She insisted I put four — one for each of us in the family. She always said we were a package deal. I tap on her name to start the call that is way overdue.

"You ready?" Shep meets me at the door as soon as I walk up his steps. He is keyed up for the game tomorrow night against Glen Rose, and I'm stressed about my parents coming Saturday to meet Annie. With the rain this week, he decided today was the perfect day to go mudding after football practice. I normally would have turned him down on a school night; however, I haven't been able to talk to him very much one on one in the past couple of weeks. Maybe I have subconsciously been avoiding him.

"Let's go muddying!"

He turns and laughs at me. "Muddying? It's mudding. You have to at least pronounce it correctly before you get in the truck."

I roll my eyes and climb in as he holds the door open for me. He throws a few large blocks of wood and a shovel in the back and hops in on his side. The engine revs a few times as I click my seatbelt.

We drive down the street a short distance when he pulls over to open a gate. His mudding area is on the far side of his property. A circle of small consecutive pits of mud appears as we drive to the top of the hill.

"David and I worked hard to get this mud track just right. We've nearly perfected it." He sits up a little taller as he scans his muddy creation below. "The rain has filled the holes really well. Are you ready?" He revs the engine a few times so that the truck lurches back and forth.

I double-check my seat belt and reach for the grab handle above the door window. "Ready as ever, I guess."

With that, he shifts into gear and starts down the hill towards the first mud hole. My grip tightens as the front of his truck makes contact. Brown liquid fans along both sides of the truck as we travel through the first large pit. He slowly approaches each one, continuing along the circle.

My grip loosens from the grab handle, realizing this isn't so bad after all. Shep laughs at me as he carries on his conversation, trying to explain the process of getting the best terrain. We stop at the top of the first hill once we complete the circle.

"That wasn't so bad." My head nods up and down, not really understanding what all the fuss is about mudding. Shep revs the engine again.

"That was a practice round to make sure everything is still good with all the mud pits. We haven't really started yet." The truck rocks back and forth like an angry dog being held back by its owner. "You sure you are ready for this?" He raises his eyebrows as he continues to lurch the truck forward.

The bottle of water I drank earlier sloshes around in my stomach. I sit up straight, placing one hand on the dash and the other clutching the grab handle once again. "Let's do this thing."

Shep lets off the brake as we speed down the hill towards the mud. My body bounces up and down in the seat as we traverse through the muddy pits. Shep turns on his wipers, but they only smear it all around. The truck follows the muddy ruts along the track, causing it to sling in the air with every turn. I look out the back windshield and watch as the once soupy-looking water now looks to be thick and slimy.

We top the starter hill as he admires the chaos he has created below.

"Do you want to try?"

My eyes fly wide open. "No way. I will stay right where I am. Thank you very much." I tug on my seat belt, already knowing this next round will be even rougher.

We complete the circle a few more times as the mud gets thicker each time we plow through. Our tires spin as we dig ourselves deeper into the muck. Shep alternates between forward and reverse to work our way out a couple of times when we get stuck. He assures me he has a winch on the front if the rocking doesn't work.

We come to a stop once again. Our sides hurt from laughing so much.

"This is just what I needed. Thank you so much for bringing me out here."

"Welcome! I'm glad it finally rained enough for me to show you what it's all about." His windshield fluid has run dry, so Shep pours the remaining water from his bottle over the front windshield to clear a spot to see.

We head back towards the road to drive to the front of his house. "I'm going to run my truck through the car wash in town. Want to go with me? We could grab a bite to eat if you want."

My face shows hesitation before I realize what it is doing.

"Never mind. I just thought since it was getting late, you might not have any plans." He pulls into his driveway and heads towards my car.

"Only on one condition."

His face perks up, surprised by my response. "What's that?"

"There is no way I'm helping you at the car wash. I might break a nail." I flash my pink nails in his face and wiggle them around.

"Deal!" He shifts into reverse and heads towards town.

"So, what are your thoughts on this weekend?" He offers me another French fry as the conveyor pulls us through the tunnel, rinsing away our stress relief from earlier.

I draw a deep breath, unsure how to put into words what I am feeling.

"I think I'm okay." A sense of relief comes over me as I realize this is the truth. "My mom and I had a great conversation on Sunday and worked through a lot of issues. She's very excited to meet the person who gave me life." My brain can't even comprehend having my adopted mom and birth mom in the same room. It will be surreal.

"Good! I'm looking forward to meeting them." Shep has offered to grill burgers at Annie's house so we can all concentrate on talking. He holds the last of the French fries my way, and I push them back.

"I am stuffed. I ate that burger way too fast." My finger slides along my waistline to readjust my leggings and give me a little relief. "Are you ready for your game against Glen Rose tomorrow? All the kids are so hyped up this week. Oh, I meant to tell you, my family is coming in tomorrow because they want to come watch the game. My mom even said they will go eat pizza afterwards with us. That's a big statement coming from her. You and my brother will really hit it off. I told him how fun you are to watch on the sidelines." I imitate the different facial expressions Shep makes according to the calls the referees make on the field.

Shep laughs at his own expense. "Don't forget this one." He juts his chin forward with a shocked look on his face. His hands jerk back with his palms facing upwards. "The refs love that one." He poured the last of the fries into his mouth.

"The boys have been playing really hard, and I think we might get an excellent shot this year." He looks my way, hesitating before he says what comes out of his mouth next. "Maybe you are our good luck charm." He smiles really big, knowing that this comment will make my eyes roll to the back of my head. If he only knew what it really does to the inside of me.

"Hey, I did want to tell you something. I know you are going to be there on Saturday when the families collide. I'm not sure what all is going to come up in conversation that you might hear, but I wanted some information to come from me." I readjust in my seat, looking out the front windshield. Luckily, the truck is finished with the wash, so he is forced to look forward as well.

"Sure. What's up?" He turns on his blinker as we head back out of town towards his place.

I roll my window down, causing a cool fall breeze to stir around my face. My brain backpedals, unsure of how much information about my past I really want to divulge to him. Things are good with him right now, and I don't want to scare him away. He's been such a good friend.

"Never mind. I'm not really sure where I was going with that." I fidget with the seat belt, suddenly feeling like it was tightening on me.

"Sure, Jasmine. You don't worry about me. I'll just be a quiet little chef preparing all your food. You won't even know I am there." He squeezes in his shoulders, attempting to shrink as small as he can.

My phone buzzes. It's my brother Nathaniel.

Almost there. Two minutes

It's about time! It's almost halftime already.

Sorry got held up at work

I put the phone down and look over at Annie. She came, since this was the big rival game. It will be awkward with her and my parents meeting here for the first time, but Macee thinks maybe this is for the best. It's not like they can get into deep conversations here at the game.

I glance down at the field as the players wrap up a timeout and head back to the forty-yard line. If they can make this touchdown, we will be tied going into halftime. Shep looks in my direction and makes one of his famous faces at me. It makes me laugh. *How does he always know when I need to smile?*

My phone buzzes again.

> Headed to the ER
> Dad has chest
> pains

I don't even take the time to respond. I tell Macee and Annie I need to go and that I will message them later.

We monopolize a corner of the waiting room, causing a steady buzz in the otherwise vacant area. Mom is the only one allowed in the ER room with Dad, so the rest of us are sitting and waiting to hear something while they finish running more tests. Annie and Macee came right after I texted them what was happening. My brother charms them with his quick wit. He's so much like my dad. He can make friends anywhere.

David and Shep walk in. The game must be over. I give Shep a questioning look, and he shakes his head, letting me know they didn't win their game. He had told me earlier that since they had done so well this year, they would be in the playoffs starting next week no matter what the outcome was tonight.

They inquire about Dad. Nathaniel shares with them we are waiting to hear more information. They want to keep him as calm as possible, so no one else is allowed back there right now. Shep disappears momentarily and comes back, secretly dropping a bag of chocolate candy in my lap from the vending machine around the corner. *How did he remember I need to snack when I'm nervous?*

The candy keeps me occupied while everyone makes small talk around me. I sit quietly, trying to focus on the conversation but having a hard time. I can't lose my dad. I've lost so much so far in life. A nurse enters the waiting room and heads our way.

"Are you the Forte family?" We stand expectantly and nod for him to carry on. "Hello, I am Chad, the RN in charge of Mr. Forte's case. We are still waiting for the results from one final test, but so far, it looks like everything is just fine. We recommend he follow up with his cardiologist on Monday morning. From the tests that we ran, he is not in any immediate danger."

Without thinking, I lunge forward and hug him out of relief. He stands frozen until I step away. His chin juts forward to exert confidence, but in my line of work, I know that it typically covers up insecurity.

"He has requested that his two children come to see him. You are clear to follow me back there."

I tell everyone thank you for coming. Quick hugs are passed around as we all gather our belongings. Shep sits down and informs me he will stay in case we need help with anything else. *Why does this not surprise me?* I give him a thankful nod as my brother and I follow Chad through the doors that lead me to my daddy.

38 Summer

Middle of November
Present Day

Tonight, I will get some answers. It's been a couple of weeks since Laney's name popped up on Chad's recent call list, and he lied to me about who he was talking to. I decided to remain observant and not press him about it. My dad always taught me never to jump to conclusions. It's better to wait and see if you were wrong or if you can collect undisputed evidence.

I've only seen Laney twice since Chad and I became engaged. It's been one excuse or another, but now I'm thinking she is avoiding us. I've been watching for additional warning signs. So far, I have noticed no others. Maybe she was just helping him plan a surprise for me to celebrate our engagement.

At least that's what I hope they were talking about.

Both will join me for pizza this evening, each ignorant of the other's invitation. This is the only way to get the three of us together to talk about the wedding. If she is going to be my maid of honor, I want her involved from the beginning so that she is aware of all the details.

It's early afternoon, so the restaurant isn't very busy. Eighties music, which has been changed into elevator style, plays on the speakers. An older couple sits in the corner booth, adding words to the music. I'm thankful for the minimal distractions.

"Hey!" Laney slides onto the opposite bench and sets a notebook down on the tabletop. "I brought a notebook to make notes in for all our ideas." She is smiling, and it relaxes me. I guess she's not mad at me after all.

"Yay! I can't wait!" I dump Mom's collection of wedding magazines on the table and retrieve some scissors and tape out of the bag. "Let's get started. I already ordered our pizza."

Flipping through the magazine pages, we show off details that catch our eye. It gets cut out and taped into Laney's notebook. Mom has already dog-eared several pages and circled some of her favorites. I keep an eye on the door after about twenty minutes. I staggered the times I told each of them so they wouldn't run into each other in the parking lot.

Laney's phone buzzes. She picks it up, smiles, and responds. Then my phone buzzes. It is Chad informing me he is pulling up.

I intentionally sat on this side of the booth so I can see Chad enter. He spots us and heads our way. Interestingly enough, he doesn't seem surprised Laney is there.

"Hey!" He leans down to kiss my forehead. "You two are looking busy. Do you have it all planned out yet?" He slides into the booth next to me and puts his arm around my shoulders. I slide a little closer to him and look up at Laney. She has a forced smile and directs her attention down to the happy paper brides in front of her.

The intercom announces our number, so Chad slides back out to retrieve our pizza.

"Sorry, I didn't tell you Chad was coming. I was afraid you wouldn't come if you knew."

"Why would you think that?" She flips through the pages, not even taking time to view what is on each page.

"I just feel you have been avoiding us. I'm sure it is just me being weird about it all." I reach over to grab the scissors to cut out an example of a magnificent table setting.

"Guess so." She selects another magazine to inspect.

Chad comes back to the table carrying our pizza, and a young worker follows him with plates and a pitcher of soda.

"I knew I recognized you," the worker says. His eyes widen as he addresses Chad and points to Laney. "I delivered pizza to your girlfriend's house the other night. You pulled in as I was walking back to my car. Sorry again that I forgot the pepper flakes you asked for."

Examining Laney, her face flushes like she has been under the sun for hours. Her eyes dart between Chad and me.

"Thanks, man." Chad grabs the pitcher and plates from the guy. "But you must be mistaken. That's not my girlfriend, and it wasn't me over there." Chad slides into the booth once again, putting his arm tight around my shoulders.

"Sure it was. You mentioned how that afternoon you had just bought the cool red Prius you pulled up in."

39 Third Option

End of November
Present Day

40 Jasmine

First Week of December
Present Day

It's been a Monday. The three weeks of teaching between Thanksgiving and Christmas are always so long. And this week is Spirit Week to prepare for the first round of playoff games.

I grab a folder from my passenger seat. Pennie has been out of school for three weeks now since her baby boy was born. She called in for her schoolwork, and I volunteered to take it to her. She and Tony married at the courthouse right before the baby was born and are currently living with her dad. I had heard the marriage was a stipulation for living under the same roof.

I notice movement at the window as I allow myself a minute for composure before I step out of the car. This is the first baby I have been around since I lost mine.

I step over the broken pieces of sidewalk. Their house is a modest, older home with a large front porch. Overgrown vines and weeds have taken over the flowerbeds, with hints of a woman's touch left over from years ago. A faded welcome sign lies on its back behind a large potted plant in desperate need of some water. Frank opens the door before I even have time to knock.

"Ms. Forte! So nice to see you again." His face is alive with fresh energy. "Come on in. Perfect timing. He just finished his bottle."

221

I step immediately into the living room and find Pennie burping the baby on her shoulder. She looks exhausted but manages a smile.

"Oh, Pennie, he's so tiny." I move a package of diapers so that I can sit on the couch next to her.

"Sorry about that. We are all walking zombies right now." Placing her hand on the back of his head, Pennie gently brings him down to lie in her lap after he gives up an impressive burp.

"It looks like you are doing a tremendous job so far."

"Thanks. Babies are cute and all, but they sure are a lot of work." She wraps the green muslin blanket around his torso, swaddling him snugly.

"Looks like you have that down pretty well."

A flash of pride comes across her tired face. She stands up and turns to face me.

"Here, hold him while I go put his bottle up." She stretches out her arms, not giving me the opportunity to say no.

I glide his little head to rest on my shoulder after Pennie places a burp rag on me. She walks out of the room, and I suddenly realize I am alone. My body instinctively rocks back and forth slowly as I begin to hum. I don't even know what tune I am humming; it just naturally comes. My eyes close as I allow myself to imagine what could have been.

Peace settles over me with the assurance that I will get to experience this with my own child one day. I am confident that I will be able to look into the eyes of a tiny human and see myself in there.

"You look like a natural."

My eyes pop open and see Frank standing in front of me. A rush of heat flushes over my face.

"He is so sweet and tiny. Can you believe we were all this little at one point?" It hits me that Annie held me when I was this little for two entire months. *How bad must it have been for her to hand me over to a stranger?* She must not have had any support at all.

222

"He is pretty special." Frank sits down in the rocking chair next to me. "I am only getting to enjoy my grandson, thanks to you."

I startle the baby as my body jerks out of shock. "Me? I don't understand. What did I have to do with it?" I rub little circles on his back as he relaxes once again on my shoulder.

"Remember our conversation at your mailbox? I had told you Pennie had left me a note, and we ended up having a discussion."

I nodded my head, remembering how drained he had looked a couple of months ago. It's a big contrast to his demeanor today.

"One thing I left out was that Pennie had laid out an ultimatum to me. She claimed that she and Tony had plans to get married and raise this baby whether or not I wanted to be involved. It was my choice to be a grandpa, or I could continue to live in the past and miss out." His chest puffs out a little, showing how proud he is of the choice that he made. "That conversation wouldn't have happened without you. They had plans to move her in with Tony's family that weekend. And I probably wouldn't have said a word about it."

Pennie walks into the room and moves next to her dad. She sits on the arm of the rocker and reaches around to hug him. Pride washes over his face as he swipes quickly at his eyes.

"And he probably wouldn't be named after you, either." She pulls back and turns towards me. "His name is Wade Franklin."

Frank's throat catches as he swipes at his eyes again. What a beautiful beginning this baby has. He is surrounded by others who love him and want the best for him. More proof that good things can come out of hard times.

I thought Friday would never get here. Every day has been a dress-up day. Today is Panther Pride Day, so I gladly pulled on a Panther sweatshirt along with my jeans. I turn into the parking lot, and it looks like everyone else is having a difficult time getting here early as well at the end of this crazy week. I grab my schoolbag and paper sack and head across the pavement to school. I wish I could just pause my mind for one day to give my brain a break.

There are so many different puzzle pieces up in the air right now. Mom has Dad on a new diet and exercise regimen, so he is on his way to feeling better. However, it made me realize that I'm not sure if I want to live so far away from them. Annie and I ended up driving to Fort Worth for Thanksgiving last week so that we could finally have our delayed meeting of the parents. That way, Dad could avoid another trip so soon. I sent Clay the address, and he drove in from work and met us there.

Conversation was easy. Mom pulled out all the photo albums and shared stories as Annie traced her fingers over each picture, soaking in all that she had missed out on. They both hugged and cried. Mom and Annie couldn't thank each other enough. Mom was thankful for the opportunity to raise me, and Annie was thankful that Mom kept me safe and loved me. She gave Mom a painting of sunflowers she had painted in her art class.

Annie shared that she loved that I was a teacher. She revealed that she had always wanted to be one when she was younger. It was also very special to Annie when she found out that Mom and Dad kept my original middle name. Jasmine Dawn. It felt good to sit around the dining room table again and laugh. It had been too long.

Nathaniel took Clay out to the garage, where he hung up his old punching bag and taught him a couple of combinations of quick punches. Clay ended up having to put an ice bag on his hand after trying to keep up with Nathaniel. I have two little brothers now. It saddens me that I missed out on meeting the third.

I thought that finding the answers of where I came from would help me understand where I belonged. I'm even more confused now because of it. *Do I stay in Glass to continue life here and see where it leads me? Or do I move back to Fort Worth, where I grew up and can be close to the parents that raised me?* I am feeling pulled in two different directions, and I am undecided about what to do.

I walk into Shep's dark classroom and set the paper sack on his desk. Tonight, we meet up with Glen Rose again in the quarterfinals bracket. Shep seems to be optimistic about the game, but they already lost to them twice this season with the scrimmage and the regular game. His extra keyring, which he is always losing, sits on top of his gradebook. He is going to be a lot to keep up with for someone one day.

Grabbing a sticky note, I scribble "Good luck" and place it on the sack. I suspect he might enjoy a doughnut to start off this special Friday.

David and Macee invited me to ride with them to the game in Glen Rose. Painted tigers and paw prints are plastered in every store window. The parking lot is filled with decorated cars. I believed we were getting here early, but the lot is full already.

We find a spot and climb out of the car with our matching t-shirts on underneath our coats. Macee ran with my joke from the first game and had t-shirts made. People bought them like crazy. "Battle of the Jungle Cats" is written across the front in two lines. In between them, a tiger is caught in a snare hanging from a tree with a panther flexing its muscles standing next to him. Macee gave me mine for free as thanks for the idea.

Making pleasantries as we weave our way through the crowd, we finally settle in a spot on the forty-yard line. Shep spots us and gives us a wave. He asked earlier if I was coming. He tried hard to hide his smile when I said yes. He has claimed before that he believes I am his lucky charm. I surprised myself with how much I liked his reaction. I'm not sure what to do with these feelings, though.

The stands are bursting at the seams on both sides of the field, yet more and more people crowd in. The Glen Rose Tiger Pride Band forms a solid clump of red in the stands. When the band finishes playing "Eye of the Tiger," their student section starts a chant that our student section enthusiastically returns. Our drumline begins a cadence to get the Panthers riled up and ready. The bleachers vibrate with the excitement of the crowd as the showdown on the field begins.

A commotion starts by the band when I notice Pennie is there. I'm sure she came to watch Tony play. Her dad, Frank, protectively holds the baby while the students ooh and aah over him.

Feelings stir within me. *Did my mom show me off at school events before she gave me up? What would it have been like to grow up here?* I push the questions back down. They do me no good. All they do is muddle up the confusion that already resides in my head. I must focus on the here and now and decide what to do. *Where do I belong? What future do I want for myself?*

The crowd erupts as the Panthers score their first touchdown. Cowbells ring out as grown men jump up and down in the stands in front of us. High schoolers run across the end zone with large black flags in celebration.

When the crowd settles back down, I can spot Shep on the field. He looks my way and blows a chef's kiss in the air in my direction. My face heats up despite the cool breeze. This decision to stay can be really easy or really hard.

The crowd explodes with a loud roar as the final buzzer sounds. Looking like an army of ants, the students swarm over the fence and onto the field. The Glass Panthers won with a field goal kick at the end of the second overtime. Football players huddle up, pouncing on one another in celebration. The battle was long and hard-fought on both sides. Timing was on the side of the Panthers tonight.

I hang back with David and Macee while the crowd in the bleachers dissipates. We know it will be a few minutes before Shep is available to talk.

"So, Jasmine, what do you think of small town football?" David, who jumped up and down a few times himself, starts collecting trash around us.

I pick up my empty popcorn bag. "There is nothing quite like it, huh?" A warm, comforting feeling courses through me, forcing me to realize that Glass might be where I belong. This confuses me even more.

Macee laughs and follows us down the stairs towards the field.

We wind our way through the maze of celebratory families. Everyone is taking pictures and patting the players on their backs. We head towards the goalpost, which is always our meeting point with Shep. He is there posing for pictures with some of his players.

I watch as he interacts with them and see the admiration that his players hold for him. A father shakes Shep's hand, thanking him for being such an outstanding role model for his son. Shep humbly nods and turns it right back to praising the father for raising such a great young man.

I bet Shep would make a great father. He's grounded. He's got his act together. He loves God. Of course, knowing Shep, he might misplace the kid somewhere, but he would be a great dad.

I shove the thoughts back down, surprised they even came to the surface.

"Fun game!" David pulls Shep into a congratulatory hug. Shep doesn't take his eyes off me.

"Thanks! I'm glad my friendly good-luck charm was here tonight for the complete game this time." He gives me a wink, and my face flushes again. I really need to decide what direction I want this relationship to take.

227

Shep asks a cheerleader nearby to take a picture of the four of us before we part. Macee and I stand in the middle of the guys. Some students point and giggle at the four of us. Somehow, this time, I don't mind as much.

The orange and yellow flames sway back and forth according to the cool night air that blows through occasionally. I pull the throw blanket tighter around my shoulders as I snuggle deeper into the chair. Growing up, we always had a firepit in our backyard, but there is something different about one in the country. Flyaway sparks dance around the flames before they float into the sky. Closing my eyes, the crackles and pops soothe me. My lungs fill with the smell of burning wood as my breath slows down. It would be so easy to fall asleep.

A large pop makes me jump. I open my eyes and see Shep standing there quietly.

"I thought maybe you fell asleep." He pulls a chair to the opposite side of the fire and settles in. He had walked Grandma Shep back up to the house after David and Macee left. Grandma Shep had insisted on s'mores tonight with all of us to celebrate the Panther victory last night. That had been a family celebration for years on any occasion they deemed worthy. He had asked me to stay afterwards, claiming he wanted to talk to me about something.

Shep placed another log on the fire and moved it around with a large stick.

"I don't think I will ever tire of looking at the nighttime sky out here in the country. Every single star shines so brightly." I lean my head back, wishing I would've paid closer attention to the lessons in astronomy class.

"It sure is a beautiful sight, isn't it?"

I look over at Shep. He is not looking into the sky. I squirm in my seat and sit up a little straighter.

"So, you said you wanted to talk about something? Is everything okay?" I reach to grab my hot chocolate and slowly take a sip.

"Were you aware I ate doughnuts every Friday morning growing up?"

"I knew you liked doughnuts, but I didn't realize they were a dangerous habit for you."

Shep laughed at my attempt to keep the mood light.

"Once I got my driver's license, I would always stop on Friday mornings on the way to school to get a doughnut. I had forgotten about that until you dropped off that sack on my desk yesterday." He picks up the long stick and pokes the fire some more. "It just brought back some memories of lacking something when I was younger. I don't really know how to explain it. Anyway, it was a nice surprise to find on my desk. Thanks for thinking of me."

Shadows dance on his face as he stares into the fire. He seems to be lost in thought.

"You wanted me to stay so you could thank me for the doughnut?"

Shep looks up. Even in the shadows, I can see his face turn red.

"No, I mean, yes…. I don't know. It's just stupid. Never mind." He gets up to choose another log, even though the fire doesn't really need one just yet.

"What's on your mind, Shep?"

He lets out a big sigh as he attempts to squeeze another log onto the teepee he has created out of the previous logs. He gives up and lays it to the side of the pit and sits back down.

"I understand you've had a lot to deal with lately with finding Annie and all. I can't even imagine discovering that I have a whole other family out there that I knew nothing about. So, I promise I'm not trying to make it about me. Because there is no way I could ever comprehend what you are dealing with." He pauses as he polishes off the rest of his hot chocolate and throws the paper cup into the fire. It shrinks right away.

229

"It has been a lot, but it's been good. When I discovered another family existed, I never envisioned they would be as wonderful as Annie and Clay have proved to be. I do wonder how different I might be if I could've grown up here in Glass."

His head pops up. "That's exactly what I've been wondering!" He leans forward in his chair as his eyes grow bigger. "Like, would we have hung out together or played at the creek? Maybe you would have ridden with me to school and gotten doughnuts every Friday morning." He leans back and takes a deep breath. "Would we have ever dated, or maybe we would have hated each other?"

I finish my hot chocolate and throw my cup at him. "Oh, I definitely would have hated you."

He catches my cup and tosses it right back. "You think so?" He laughs and settles back into his chair. "I've just had a lot of thoughts running around in my head. I almost feel like I also missed out on something not knowing you when you were younger."

Our eyes lock momentarily. A life I never knew flashes through my mind. The endless possibilities are overwhelming.

"Who knows? But I'm guessing we would've been good friends."

He smiles at my confession. "I think so too. Which means we've got a lot of catching up to do."

41 Summer

First Week of December
Present Day

It must be close to midnight now. I roll over, facing the empty side of my bed. My hand glides over the pillow next to me. *My husband's head should be on that pillow. I've lost two potential ones. One I pushed away and one that wasn't worthy of me.* I struggle back and forth about whether to be thankful I found out about Chad and Laney before it was too late or just be mad at the fact that my life is not at all what I expected it to be at this point.

As if the holidays will not be hard enough with Dad being gone, they will be even worse now. Not too long ago, I thought all the trying times were behind me. In the past six months, I've lost my dad, my future husband, my best friend, and my lifelong friend Ryan will probably never talk to me again.

This is exactly why I sank into my shell a few years ago when my brother died. My heart can not survive another abandonment. I don't understand what I have done to deserve this misery. I want to go back to being invisible again.

I half expected Ryan to show up and bring me a doughnut this morning, but he didn't. Surely, he has heard that Chad and I are no longer together. He hasn't eaten in the school cafeteria since Chad proposed to me. Maybe I should quit and go to work for Uncle Tate at the lumberyard.

I don't know what I've done to make God so mad at me. I should be married with kids and happily teaching at my hometown high school. Instead, I'm all alone, live on my parent's land, and wear a hairnet to work.

Chad tried to tell me he loved me, and that Laney meant nothing to him. The easiest decision would have been to forgive him and carry on with our plans we had already made for our lives together. I realized that I would have had to lower my standards to continue to allow him into my life. It's not that I expect more of him, but I expect more for myself. And there is that promise I made to Dad the week before he died.

Chad wanted nothing to do with Laney after I broke up with him, so he moved back to Dallas last weekend. Laney ended up apologizing to me and told me I could do better than Chad. The fact is, I knew that all along. The only other one that I would want, ironically, now wants nothing to do with me.

Pastor Alan's words echo in my mind. "God allows threshing in our lives." Maybe God was threshing Chad out of my life because He knew Chad wasn't needed anymore. He blew away with the wind, straight back to Dallas.

I determine sleep will not happen anytime soon, so I get up to fetch some ice cream to bring back to bed with me.

As I shut the freezer door, the heart rock in my kitchen window catches my eye. I pick it up and rub it seven times. *Why do I even do this? I have no luck in my corner. What good has this rock brought into my life? None.*

Adult life is not at all what you think it will be when you are younger, full of hope and dreams. It is full of heartache and bills. Day in and day out.

I spot my reflection in the kitchen window. Her head tilts as she takes me in.

"Remember, this is the life you chose for yourself. What are you going to do about it now?" My reflection stares back at me as I have no response.

I throw the rock into the trash and put the ice cream back in the freezer.

Pulling on some sweatpants and a hoodie, I slide on my rain boots. It's time for a change. I grab my flashlight and head outside.

Walking towards the creek on the side of Mom's house, I follow what was a worn path years ago. The place where I spent hours upon hours creating memories and dreaming about my future. It's time for fresh memories and new dreams.

"God, I know You and I haven't been on the same page in quite a while. I'm at rock bottom here, and I don't know what else to do. If You care for me at all, please show me what to do now."

I stop at the bridge Dad built for me so many years ago. My hand slides back and forth over the handrail. Flashes from countless times in the past that I have crossed over and grabbed it for support flood my memories. It occurs to me the meticulous detail Dad put into crafting that bridge. It didn't need a handrail. The bridge itself is low to the water, and the water is only ankle deep in this spot. Yet he added a handrail to keep me extra safe for all the times that I have run wildly back and forth over it through the years.

A thought intruded on my memories. *God has kept me safe from countless things without me ever realizing I was in danger. Invisible handrails at different times in my life protecting me from falling over the edge. Maybe God's not finished with me yet.*

I step off the bridge onto Ryan's side of the creek and head to our favorite spot where the water falls over some bigger rocks. The sound has always soothed me. It has been my escape many times in my life.

Dead leaves crunch under my feet as I walk the familiar, worn path. I realize I didn't bring a big stick to kill any copperheads or a blanket to sit on once I reach my spot. "God, it is up to You to protect me now or send a snake to end my misery." I continue along, too emotionally drained to even care about how dangerous this might be this late at night.

When I finally reach my destination, I find a large rock to stand on overlooking the creek. My eyes slowly close as I lose myself in the familiar sounds of the trickling water.

I expect the quiet to calm me as it normally does. Instead, it has the opposite effect. My throat tightens as the lull of the water causes an itching in my inner waterworks to flow. Warm tears stream down my cheeks as my lungs work hard to keep my shaky breath under control. Moans of so much pain I have collected over the years scramble to be let out in the darkness of the world around me.

Hatred towards Chad. Missing my dad. Laney's betrayal. Feeling tied down to take care of Mom. Guilt from my brother Dusty's death. Confusion of God and His supposed plan for my life. Loss of Ryan's friendship.

Anger builds, and I need to scream. My fingers coil into tight balls. A quiet moan begins in my throat and builds to a loud shrill as I force years of pain out through my open mouth. My fists raise towards the heavens and shake as a guttural wail empties out of me. Years of emotions that I have stuffed down at my own expense overflow and refuse to stay hidden anymore.

What if I hadn't pushed Ryan away when my brother died?

Why did I ever lower my expectations and allow Chad into my life?

What if Mom were equipped to handle her own emotions?

Why do I feel all the responsibility rests on my shoulders to take care of everyone else?

I scream until I can't scream anymore.

As the misery escapes out of my body, the tension slowly subsides into mournful sobbing. I collapse to the ground as my head drops to my knees. My defeated body feels the liberation of the release that has been building up for what seems like years.

"Summer? Is that you? Are you okay?" The light from Ryan's flashlight bounces everywhere as he runs up the pathway.

I don't move. I'm too exhausted to even care.

His footsteps slow down as he realizes there is no immediate danger. I sense his presence hovering over me once he reaches where I am. His breath is labored from running so fast. I ignore him, being too deep in my own regrets to acknowledge why he is here. After a few minutes of standing there, he quietly sits down next to me and allows me to continue to cry.

I must have fallen asleep because my head quickly snaps up, and I'm not sure where I am at first. Startled by my sudden movement, Ryan sits up a little straighter. His hoodie, which must've been draped over my back, slides down to the ground. I look at him under the moonlight. He has his arms pulled into his t-shirt to keep them warm.

"Here, put your hoodie back on. Grandma Shep doesn't need you getting sick." He takes his hoodie back and slides it over his head. "Thanks though. That was really sweet of you."

He forces a slight smile and nods his head. I've known him long enough to know his facial expression is one of confusion. He's not sure whether to talk or to get up and leave.

"Thanks for sitting with me."

"Sure. You shouldn't be out here by yourself." He picks up a couple of rocks and nervously rubs them together in his hand.

"How did you even know I was out here? You were here too quick for it to be from my scream."

"Grandma Shep woke me up because she saw a flashlight over this way when she was getting a drink of water in the kitchen. She assumed it was you and wanted me to make sure you were okay."

"Tell her I said thanks for caring." I pick up a stick and draw random circles in the dirt.

"So, are you?" He tilts his head and looks at me. "Are you okay?"

"No, I'm not okay."

We sit in silence. I continue to trace circles while he tosses a few rocks into the water.

"So, what can we do to make you okay?" The sincerity in his voice somehow rubs me the wrong way.

"We? There is no we anymore." I toss the stick into the water and watch it disappear into the darkness. "You stopped talking to me a couple of months ago." Resentment wells up inside.

"Because Chad told me to."

236

My head pops up at his attempt at an excuse. "What do you mean, he told you to?"

"A couple of weeks before he proposed to you, he came over and we had a long talk. He told me that because of the history between you and me, there was no way you could be happy if I was around all the time. He said that you were constantly reminded of me all over town. It made you miserable, and you wanted to move to Dallas to get away from me. He said he just dropped by out of respect to give me a heads up that you didn't want me around anymore. So, I backed off."

I stared at him, trying to process everything he had just divulged. Chad is the one who told him to stop talking to me. Chad is the one who tried to erase the parts of me that have always made me feel safe. Chad took away my handrails.

"He also saw my heart rock I keep by my recliner in the living room and commented you used to have one like that, but he wasn't sure what happened to it. I think that hurt the most." His head drops and hangs out over the top of his chest. The chest I used to love resting my head on while listening to the rhythm of his heartbeat.

"Well, we all know now that Chad is a big liar, don't we?" I make a mental note to grab the rock out of the trash when I get back to my house. *What was I thinking throwing it away?* "I can't believe he told you to stop talking to me. Why would you even listen to him?"

Ryan looks up at me with his eyebrows scrunched together. "Because all I've ever wanted in life is for you to be happy. And if stepping out of your way leads to your happiness, I'll step back."

A flood of emotions claws their way to be the dominant one for what I say next.

Anger wants to yell about how stupid that is.

Revenge wants to get back at Chad for trying to control me.

Confusion doesn't understand how Ryan would ever have believed such a far-fetched idea.

And then there is the feeling I haven't felt in a long, long time. Probably about seven years. The last day I felt this way was when he dipped me at my door and kissed me with the softest kiss before he left for work. The day he lost his keys. The day the tornado took my brother's life. I stuffed this feeling way down deep to take care of Mom. I put myself, my dreams, my future underneath all my pain and piled on the responsibility of making sure Mom was going to be okay. The day I made myself invisible.

Seven years ago. Seven. How ironic.

Instead of saying anything, I reach out and slug his arm.

"Ow!" He places his hand over his bicep, pretending it hurts.

"Chad always hated it when I would hit his arm like that." *I should've hit him more often and harder.*

"Well, Chad is a sissy baby."

"A sissy baby? That's the best you can come up with?" We laugh and joke about picturing Chad in a diaper crying for his pacifier. Laughter feels good. I haven't laughed like this in months.

Ryan stands up and offers his hand to help me up. "Let's go. It's getting cold out here."

"Awww.... Does little sissy baby want to get home to his blankie?" I stand up, ignoring the offer of his hand, and brush off the back of my pants. I'm afraid of what will awaken in me if our hands touch right now.

I grab my flashlight and quietly follow Ryan down the path that he has led me down for two decades. Memories flood my brain of all our times together at this creek. Our numerous picnics. Hiding out here from our parents to avoid our chores. Our rock hunting contests.

Long talks ranging from who has the best jokes to what we wanted our future to look like.

We walk silently back towards the bridge. *Is he having the same flashbacks? Or is he thinking of the future memories that he wants to make with me? Or have I messed that up so badly it is off the table forever?*

Ryan crosses the bridge, and I instinctively know he will walk me to my door. He is too much of a gentleman to let me walk the rest of the way by myself.

I stop on the bridge, rubbing my hand along the handrail once again. I remember the talk I had with God at this very spot a couple of hours ago. Look at all the answers I have now. A sliver of hope shines at the end of a very long and dark tunnel that I have formed around myself.

Thank you, God, for sending Ryan out to me tonight. I really needed a reminder of what life could look like if I allowed myself to feel seen again.

I snuggle back in bed as a sense of peace washes over me. My mind hasn't felt this silent in years. It's as though this is how it was meant to be all along.

As soon as I walked in earlier, I fished the heart rock out of the trash. Holding it tight to my chest, I close my eyes. I inhale deeply and slowly exhale. My phone buzzes; I pick it up to see who it could be this late.

It's Ryan.

> sweet dreams
> summer bummer

I had forgotten what it feels like to be giddy. It's been so long. Seven years, to be exact. I can't stop the smile forming on my face. Before I can overthink it, I hit send with the first response that comes to my head.

> Congrats on your win tonight over the tigers. Bring me doughnuts in the morning to celebrate
> ○ ○ ○ ○ ○ ○ ○

I stare at the three little dots informing me he is responding. *Maybe that was too forward. Maybe that was expecting too much too soon. What if he isn't feeling the same way? I wouldn't blame him.*

His response finally comes through.

> Ill be there 7 sharp

My smile widens even more. I'm never going to get to sleep now.

42 Third Option

First Week of December
Present Day

43 Jasmine

A Layer From the Middle of June
One Week Before the Move
Twenty-seven Years Old

After I smoothed down the packing tape on the last box, completing my final school year in Fort Worth, I glanced around at the blank walls. These walls have witnessed the craziness of my life over the past three years.

I managed to keep it together while my students continuously entered and exited my classroom, unaware of the personal turmoil I was experiencing. I gave myself a high five for at least holding all of it together in front of them.

The most challenging time was after school hours. I would avoid home at all costs. Initially, Ted's unpredictable moods at home were a factor. After we separated, it was because the large house was so empty and lonely.

This classroom became a sanctuary for me. Tears were shed. Things were thrown. Meltdowns were had. Lots of prayers were seemingly unanswered.

Until now. Things seemed to be finally clicking into place.

I loaded up my last box onto the dolly and pushed it through the doorway. I paused, then glanced back one last time.

"Thank you. Thank you for being my source of happiness for the last three years. I pray for blessings on this classroom, the new teacher, and the lives she will impact in the upcoming school year."

I switched out the light and shut the door to my past.

As I drove to the house to finish packing my belongings, I glanced down at my phone as it buzzed. I hit ignore once again.

My brother Nathaniel wanted to talk. I, however, had nothing new to say. I'm not changing my mind about seeking my birth family. He believed that moving to an unfamiliar town was causing more problems. He would never understand.

The blood that coursed through his veins was the same blood as the ones that raised us. There were two people out there who created me and shared my bloodline. What if each of them had other kids? Or even had more kids together? I could easily have siblings somewhere that shared some of my characteristics or mannerisms. Eyes that I could see myself in.

I needed to know.

I saw Nathaniel's car was in front of my house as I turned the corner onto the street. Speeding on by would be too rude, so I pulled into my driveway.

"Hey, Jazzy!" He ran to my car door and opened it up for me. He's always a gentleman, just as our dad taught him. His hand ran through his blond hair while his charming smile spread across his face.

"Hey! This is a surprise." I held my breath, waiting to see where the conversation would lead.

"Yeah, I've been trying to get hold of you. Mom and Dad said that the moving truck was coming in a few days, so I wanted to see what I could help you with. I understand Dad's back is tweaked again, so I figured you might need my muscles." He pulled both shirtsleeves up to his shoulders and bared his tanned and bulging muscles. "Welcome to the …."

He looked at me, his eyebrows arched at their highest point. His head tilted and eyes opened wide, ready for me to complete his favorite phrase since he was probably eight years old.

"Come on, J! Don't let me down. Let's try it again. Welcome to the …."

I turned around, trying hard to imitate an annoyed teenage sneer, and mumbled the words, "Gun Show."

He pretended to double punch me in the gut like he playfully had for almost two decades now. As soon as his second fist barely made contact, his face suddenly gasped, and he pulled back as fast as he could.

The laughter that I was trying to hold back disappeared as I realized why he had suddenly turned white as a ghost.

"It's okay. Really. We have been playfully teasing each other for years. Don't worry about it." I turned to walk to the trunk and hoped to avoid the looming conversation that I knew was coming.

"I really wish you had given me permission to knock his block off. What kind of coward hits a woman? Especially one he claims to be the love of his life. All I needed was one round in the boxing ring with him." Nathaniel nudged me to the side as he grabbed the heavier boxes from the trunk before I could get them out.

He didn't even know about the loss of the baby. My parents and I had downplayed it as much as we could with him for fear that Nathaniel would have ended up in jail if he ever knew the whole truth. That layer would need to be buried forever.

We finished unloading the boxes into the garage and stepped inside for some ice water. Summer weather skipped the cooler spring weather in Texas. I intended to stay inside for the rest of the day, enjoying the air conditioning while packing. I was thankful for the extra help.

Nathaniel began unloading my bookshelf into the designated boxes. A map I had drawn of my new house lay on the dining room table, each room color coded to match labels for the boxes. I threw some red labels at him, so the movers would know which room to unload the book boxes into. The house that I have purchased in Glass has many extra rooms, so I'm planning on creating a library in one of them. I'll need to find someone to build some bookshelves for me.

When Ted died trying to save me from the truck, I was still the listed beneficiary for the life insurance policy. The amount astounded me. I told Ted's parents that I would take out of it what was needed for funeral expenses and donate the rest back to them, but his mom wouldn't have it. She said she loved her son very much, but that I deserved every penny.

I noticed when she wiped her tears, some makeup came off on her napkin. That little swipe allowed a hint of yellow bruising to show on her left upper cheek. My heart broke for her and all that she still endured.

With the money, I could easily afford a farmhouse-style home on a few acres in the town where I hoped to find some answers and some peace. I had plenty of money to start my life over and to remodel some aspects of the house.

When I started looking into the Glass community, I found that there was an opening at the high school for a math teacher. The school had an excellent reputation, and its football team was supposed to be one of the best. I was sure Friday nights would be an experience like no other. I prayed continuously to God for direction in managing everything life had thrown at me over the past couple of years. This job and house fell so easily into place that I felt very confident that this was the path I needed to take to seek God's will for my life. And hopefully find some answers.

After I confronted my parents in the spring of last year when finding out I was adopted, my mom suggested that we all go to counseling. Despite my initial shock that they thought it was okay not to inform me, we eventually decided to disagree and put the issue aside temporarily. Mom and Dad had feared

I would start seeing myself as not part of the family or as being different, and they never wanted that for me. They just kept thinking, "Maybe next year we will tell her." And next year never came.

Until it did. Agree to disagree. That's the best we could do for now.

The doorbell rang as I taped up another box in my bedroom closet. Pizza aroma floated in from the hallway. Nathaniel must've gotten hungry. I placed a pink sticker on the box to show its future destination and headed towards the kitchen.

Nathaniel already had paper towels laid out and the pizza boxes opened.

"You remembered my favorite!" I grabbed a slice of stuffed-crust pepperoni with olives as the melted cheese stretched out across the tabletop. "Thanks! I didn't even realize how hungry I was." The steaming pasta sauce burned my tongue, but that did not stop me.

Nathaniel laughed and grabbed a slice from his pizza box. Pieces of sausage and bell pepper fell back onto the box as he shoved the first bite into his mouth.

A small package in the middle of the table caught my eye. "What's that?" I set my slice down and reached for it.

"That's for you." He set his slice of pizza down and wiped at the corners of his mouth.

"For me? Is it a going away present?" I held the tiny box up to my ear and playfully shook it.

"Jazz, I know about the baby you lost."

The air expelled from my lungs. Flashbacks of me lying on my kitchen floor came rushing back. How many times had I wanted to confide in him but did not know where to begin? I felt my eyes burn as I tried hard not to cry.

"I felt powerless and wanted to help, so I bought that for you."

I unwrapped the gift and found a small black jewelry box. I lifted the lid. Two silver circles were interlocked. One big circle. One little circle. A silver chain connected on each side to complete the necklace.

"The jeweler said they are called eternity circles. It's a little something to symbolize the unbreakable connection between you and your baby."

I carefully loosened the necklace from the backing of the box. I held it up and watched the light bounce off the silver circles. "This is the most thoughtful present anyone has ever given me."

Unhooking the clasp, I handed the necklace over to Nathaniel. I turned so that he could place it around my neck. My finger traced the big circle and then the little circle as tears silently rolled down my cheeks.

"I understand it may not seem like much, but I wanted to acknowledge your loss. I can not even begin to understand the pain you must feel."

"It's absolutely perfect." I turned to face my little brother. My built-in best friend. We were only fifteen months apart and were inseparable when we were younger. He's always known exactly what I needed, even when I didn't understand myself. I wrapped my arms around his chest and nestled my head under his chin. He held me in his protective embrace while I soaked the front of his shirt.

I finally pulled away and sat back down at the table. "I'm sorry that I never told you." I met his eyes with my own as my breath caught once again.

"J, don't worry about it. You don't owe me any explanation. I'm certain that if I had known back then, I would be in jail now." He picks his pizza slice back up.

"That's exactly what Mom and I thought!" I felt a slight smile forming as I was thankful my loss was no longer a secret between us.

A comfortable silence settled as we continued to eat our lunch. I've missed him over the past few years and the relationship we developed when we were younger. Maybe this will be a new start for us.

"I remember getting pizza being such a treat growing up." Nathaniel finished his second slice in four bites and reached for another.

"Yes, Mom was such a stickler for having home-cooked meals around the dinner table with all the food groups covered. Dad worked hard convincing her that a slice of pizza could easily cover all the food groups as well." Dad would bring home pizza occasionally on a Saturday afternoon, and we would eat it on the back deck. Mom said the dinner table was not made for pizza boxes.

Nathaniel stopped eating and looked straight at me. "You know, Jazz, we had a great childhood growing up. I know Mom and Dad aren't perfect, but there wasn't one time that I ever felt unloved or in their way. We really had it pretty good with them."

"I agree. And I've said nothing contrary to that." I put the crust back in the box because I knew the repeated conversation that was coming.

"Then why do you feel the need to replace them? I just don't get it." Nathaniel wiped the crumbs off his mouth that had escaped being eaten.

"That's what I keep trying to get you to understand. I don't want to replace Mom and Dad. That thought never even entered my mind. I just need to know where I came from. I want to know why she chose to give me up. In fact, the more I think about it, the more I want the opportunity to thank her."

"Thank her? Thank her for what?"

"Thank her for letting me live. Apparently, for whatever reason, she couldn't keep me or didn't want to keep me. I don't know. But she had a third option." I looked down and wiped the crumbs off the tabletop into my hand and dumped them back into the pizza box. "She didn't have to let me live."

I let this sink into Nathaniel's brain while I grabbed a fresh bottle of water.

"I can't even imagine my life without you. Who would have had the constant job of keeping me in line?" He grabbed another slice, finishing half of his pizza.

"Who knows? Perhaps a different adopted sister would've annoyed you even more than I have." I stood in the kitchen doorway, ready to get back to packing for my next chapter.

"No way. No one could ever top your annoying habits." Nathaniel took another sip of his drink, signaling me to wait. Seriousness fell over his face. "Seriously, Jazz, the best advice my manager gives me each time I'm about to enter the ring is this: 'Do not let your emotions dictate your actions.' I haven't agreed with your pursuing this, and I still don't understand, but you must promise me one thing. No matter what happens, keep your ultimate goal in mind. That takes priority over everything else. I just don't want you to get hurt." A hint of helplessness came across his face.

The corners of my mouth turned up as a thank you to my built-in best friend. "I promise." Turning fully to face him, my back stiffened as I drew in a big breath. "I will never apologize for going after answers that I am feeling drawn to, no matter how hurt Mom is and even though you don't understand. I can't explain. This is just something that I have to do for me."

He nodded, showing me he agreed to disagree.

"There is one thing I need from you, though."

His head perked up. "Tell me. I'll do anything for you, Sis."

"Get your Gun Show arms back to work. You've got lots of packing to do."

He attempted to throw his wadded-up paper towel my way as I scurried down the hallway. I knew he was not happy with my decision. There was no way he could understand why I didn't feel like I belonged here anymore. And he really didn't understand why I needed to pursue my questions. I was just thankful to God that I could.

249

44 Summer

A Layer From the Middle of June
One Week Before the Wreck
Twenty-seven Years Old

The minnows swam around in the bucket, unaware their brief life would be over soon in exchange for something bigger. My fingers reach into the cold water and snatch one to put on Chad's hook for him again.

"Chad, if you plan on staying around in this family, you have to learn how to bait your own line." Dad playfully patted Chad on the shoulder as Chad grimaced, watching me stab the little fish on the small gold hook.

"Sir, I've been fishing plenty of times, but we always used lures. I've never used live bait before." Chad threw his pole over his shoulder, preparing to cast into the river.

Ryan quickly ducked as Chad unknowingly barely missed snagging his ear. I tried hard not to laugh as Ryan, eyes opened wide, mouthed, "Good luck with that one." Clay takes a step to the side, giving himself an extra cushion of space between Chad's pole and himself.

Today will go down as one of my favorite days. I could already tell. My four favorite men at one of my favorite spots were doing one of my favorite things. Life didn't get much better than this.

The slow-moving current caused the sun's reflection to bounce back and forth across the surface of the water. I closed my eyes and took a slow, deep breath in order to soak it all in. A strong fish smell passes by as the breeze picks up. What a great day to escape reality for a few hours.

Taking a couple of steps back, I watched the four guys pointing and discussing where the next best place was to throw in a line. I held my phone up to take a picture to remember this moment. This perfect moment. Here, in front of me, represented my foundation, my past, present, and future. I whispered a rare statement of thanks to God for always taking care of me in all my situations, even when I didn't realize He was working behind the scenes.

"Hey, Summer, did you say you brought some food? It's about lunchtime." Chad pulled in his pole as Clay was the one this time, narrowly escaping the carelessness.

"Yes, I even made some no-bake cookies."

"I've told you before, I don't like those." Chad shook his head in disappointment.

"Well, it's not all about you, Chad." I giggled at my quick wit but saw Chad didn't appreciate the comment. I forget to reel in my sassiness around him sometimes. "I need some help, though. I packed some chairs as well."

Clay and Chad volunteered to go back to the car with me to help carry everything. We parked as close as we could get, but it was still a few minutes' walk.

Once we reached the car, I realized Dad still had the keys in his jeans pocket. "Y'all stay here. I'll run back and get them really quick." I started a brisk jog back to the fishing spot where I had left Dad and Ryan.

Seeing the two of them were in a serious discussion, I slowly approached and stood behind a tree.

"I just always assumed the two of you would end up together." Dad reeled in his line and started replacing the minnow that had escaped.

"Me too," Ryan responded. "I still believe she is the one for me. I'm just waiting patiently for her to remember what we had before her world was turned upside down when you all lost Dusty. I understand it was difficult for her. She feels guilty, like it was her fault."

Stepping back behind a tree trunk, I felt bad for eavesdropping but was desperate to hear this conversation. *Would Dad possibly agree?*

"There is no way what happened to her brother was her fault. It's apparent she and her mom have endured a great struggle, blaming themselves and questioning God. But it just happened. Sometimes things in life just happen. Believe me, I firmly believe that Dusty is far better off than any of us here on Earth. We will join him in heaven one day, and he can show us all around." He threw his pole back in as they both silently stared at their lines, waiting for any movement.

"I'm aware you stepped in for her when her brother died and took care of things at school when she didn't go back. I trust you to understand how much her mom and I appreciated your speaking to her professors to arrange special exam times and for packing up her apartment. Her mom and I also watched her ignore you while she helped us get back on our feet. It never crossed our minds that the two of you wouldn't immediately continue where you both left off.

"There is one thing I am compelled to tell you." Dad reels his line back in once again. "Like I was saying before, I always thought the two of you would end up together. I just want you to understand I've always considered you my bonus son. You have been a part of

252

this family through our ups and downs. You yourself have also had some ups and downs in your life."

Ryan's head drops to his chest. I know that the memories of his parents still hit him hard.

"What I'm trying to say is, life is hard. We have good times and hard times. Sometimes it feels like we are thriving, and sometimes it feels like we are only surviving. No matter what times you are going through, it is always best to have someone by your side. Someone who gets you. Someone who knows what is best for you. Someone who will take care of you when you can't take care of yourself. Someone who will constantly point you to God. You are that person for Summer. I have no questions about the matter."

Ryan's head quickly turns towards Dad, surprised to hear him confess his feelings on the subject. "Thank you, Sir. It boosts my confidence to know that you feel the same way."

Dad set his pole down on the ground. Grabbing Ryan's shoulders, he faced him towards himself.

"Please know you have my blessing to take care of Summer for the rest of her life. You are the one I know can step up and be the man she needs. Please promise me if I'm ever not around for any reason, you will watch out for her."

Ryan nodded his head. "Yes, Sir. I would be honored."

Dad patted him on the shoulders and gave one big nod of appreciation. And just like that, they decided what was best for me. My mind shifted between the sensation of being treasured and the sensation of being manipulated. *Of course, Ryan will always be there. But I don't need him to take care of me. Does Dad not think Chad will be around to be with me? Would he rather I be with Ryan instead of Chad?* I took a step back, and a fallen branch cracked under my foot. Dad and Ryan both turned and spotted me behind the tree.

"I just came back for the keys, Dad. You guys catch anything yet?" I took a couple of quick steps towards them as I noticed Ryan's face flush.

Dad took his keys out of his pocket and tossed them to Ryan. "Why don't you go help the boys, Ryan."

"Yes, Sir." Ryan caught the keys mid-air and took off jogging towards the car.

I stepped closer to Dad on the riverbank as he cast another try into the water. The minnow attempted to swim away, unaware it was only attracting its own demise.

"Dad, I heard part of your conversation with Ryan."

Dad held his stare on his bobber, unaffected by my confession. "There is nothing I would say about you to anyone that I wouldn't say straight to your face." The bobber bobbed under once, then remained calm on the surface. "Do you have anything to add to what I said?"

I shifted my weight and contemplated how to voice what I wanted to say. "I'm with Chad. Things did not work out with Ryan and me. Now, I'm with Chad. I would appreciate it if you accepted that and did not talk to Ryan like that. I'm not his responsibility."

Dad placed his rod in his rod holder and turned towards me.

"You are my responsibility, Flutterfly. No matter how old you get. No matter where you are. You will always be my responsibility for as long as I live. And if there ever comes a day when I'm not around, I need to know there is a man in your life who will make you his number one priority. Promise me you will choose someone who chooses you. Undoubtedly, you must be his number one priority. Otherwise, you are setting yourself up for heartache."

Dad held his arms out to me, and I fell into them. I closed my eyes. Taking in his familiar scent, I could feel his heartbeat against my cheek. I had always felt safe and loved in my daddy's arms. He wanted what was best for me; I was aware of that. How did I discern what that was though?

"You promise?"

"Yes, Daddy. I promise."

The boys came up the pathway with arms loaded. Chad set the food basket on the ground and unfolded his chair. He planted himself in it with an exhausted huff and pulled a bottle of water out of the cooler. "What kind of food did you pack, Summer?"

I started for the basket to pull out the sandwiches Mom and I had made earlier in the day. Ryan stepped in front of me.

"Let me. You were nice enough to make us something to eat. The least we can do is serve you." Ryan grabbed a chair and unfolded it next to Chad. "Here, Summer, have a seat."

I thanked Ryan and sat down. My eyes cut over to Dad's face. His head nodded just slightly with a small smirk forming on the side of his smile. His wink told me everything that I didn't want to know.

45 Third Option

Middle of June
One Week Before the Move and the Wreck

46 Jasmine

April 23
Present Day

I pull the car over to the side of the road and place it in park. The white cross Clay made to mark the place of our dad's last moments is donned with faded flowers and ribbon. Grabbing the bag next to me, I step out of my car.

A whiff of cedar brings me back to that night. I close my eyes and see him looking back at me. It was the last thing he said that I have held onto for all these months. It was as if he somehow recognized I was his daughter. Even though I only had a few minutes with him, I'm so glad I did.

Sitting on the ground next to the cross, I take a Sharpie out of the bag. I read over the comments that Annie, Clay, and Ryan have left on the cross. I add a little heart, wanting to add something but not knowing what to say. Even though he didn't raise me, he is the one who gave me life, and I will forever be grateful for that.

"Happy birthday to me, Dad. Thanks so much for giving me your honey eyes and parts of you that help make me who I am. Clay says you were a math whiz like me." I pull a package of jellybeans out of the bag. "Brought you some of these. Annie said they were your favorite."

I set the jellybeans at the base of the memorial. Ryan, Annie, and Clay have continued to tell me stories about Hawk, as his close friends called him. Stories that are hard to attach to someone I've never really known. I'm confident we will be reunited in heaven one day, but it sure would've been nice to spend time with him in the here and now.

My alarm goes off, reminding me I need to get to my next destination.

"Bye, Daddy. I'm so glad I got to be there to comfort you in your last moments here on earth." I kiss my fingertips and gently touch the top of the cross.

I head towards Riverhouse Grill in Glen Rose to meet Annie at 11:30 for lunch. She has mentioned it several times as one of her favorites and wants to treat me. So much has happened in the twelve months since my last birthday. I felt so out of place at the time. I felt like I didn't fit in anywhere. Now, everyday I sense more and more this is where I need to be.

I'm realizing that I still feel part of my adoptive family too. We've been able to work through a lot of the hurt we all caused each other. I now know it's my choice to feel like I belong or not. Dad's heart is doing so much better, and we make sure we all get together at least once a month. Mom almost seems like a different person. She even told me last night that she had danced in the rain with Dad earlier that day.

My phone rings. It's Mom.

"Happy birthday to you! Happy birthday to you! Happy birthday, dear Jasmine. Happy birthday to you!" My parents' voices echo throughout the car speakers.

"Thank you so much! That was great harmony. I'm impressed."

"Well, I guess these voice lessons are paying off then." Mom is definitely enjoying her empty nest. With voice and art lessons, she is constantly sending videos or pictures of her latest accomplishments. She is much more carefree and fun. I can see now why Dad fell in love with her so many years ago.

"We love you, Jazzy. We hate not seeing you on your birthday, but we understand this one is a little different." Dad's voice drops off as I can hear Mom in the background telling him not to make me feel guilty. A playful argument ensues as I clear my throat to remind them that they are still on the phone with me.

"Thanks, Dad. I will miss seeing you both today, too. While we are on the subject, I want to take this opportunity to tell you both thank you so much for the life you provided for me. I can't imagine growing up with better parents than the two of you." Mom sniffles into the phone. "I'm glad God picked the two of you for me."

I give them a silent moment, as I know they are trying to stay composed. We have been able to have so many healing conversations over the past few months. It's such a relief to be truthful with them.

"Like I told you before, Jazz, God knew I needed you in my life. I prayed for you long before you were ever conceived in Annie's womb. And I will continue to pray for you until the day I die. Your extraordinary reason for living was to save me from myself, and I will always be grateful to your biological mother for that. Will you pass that along for me, please?" Mom sniffles again as her footsteps echo down the hallway, probably looking for a tissue.

"Yes, I'll be happy to do that. In fact, I just pulled into the parking lot, and she is waiting for me on the steps of the restaurant's front porch." I give a wave to Annie as she stands and brushes off her pants.

"Your mom and I are going to let you go. Call us later to tell us all about your day."

"Yes, Daddy, I will." We exchange goodbyes and end the call.

Pushing my plate to the side of the table, I hope the server collects it soon. I'm trying to save room for their famous key lime pie, but I can't stop picking more bites out of the grilled chicken breast with the special Dr. Pepper BBQ sauce. I need to bring Mom and Dad here next time they come for a visit.

"Thank you so much for taking me out for my birthday lunch. This was pretty special."

Annie looks up at me with a soft smile. "Hawk and I had a tradition on your birthday every year. He would bring home a single cupcake from the grocery store bakery. We would put a candle in it and sing Happy Birthday to you."

My vision becomes blurry; I wipe at my eyes.

"Then we would discuss what we believed your past year was like. By the way, in our made-up world, you were the president of a large corporation and had three kids."

I burst out laughing and quickly grab the napkin to wipe my mouth. "Wow! Sorry to disappoint you."

She reaches her hand out to cover mine. Her warm hand in mine feels so natural. "I couldn't be prouder." Her eyes filled to the brim as she allowed the tears to fall freely down her face. "You have far exceeded anything we ever dreamed about who you were. We constantly prayed for you, especially on your birthdays."

She pulls a gift bag onto the table. "I thought today was the perfect time to give this to you." She slides the bag over to me. "I bought you a birthday card every year. In each one, I would share my prayers and dreams for you. I would also update you on what was going on in our lives. I've kept them all these years, hoping that one day, I could give them to you."

I peek inside and see an array of colored envelopes.

"Clay and Dusty were always aware of your existence out in the world somewhere. There are even some cards and pictures in there from both of them."

I pull out a yellowed piece of paper and unfold it. A little boy with a stick body is holding hands with a taller girl with long brown hair. They are wearing red and blue party hats.

Balloons of all colors float around the edges of the picture. A little yellow duck wearing a party hat sits at the feet of the little stick boy. The number nineteen is scribbled in the corner.

"That one is from Dusty. That was the last one he ever made." She dabs at her eyes with her cloth napkin. "He loved ducks so much. I've always wondered if we would've let him have a pet duck instead of a dog, if he would still be alive today. He never would've chased it in the tornado."

I get up from my chair to go hug her. "This is the most special gift I have ever received from anyone. Thank you for loving me all my life."

She squeezes me extra hard as we both hold each other. I am so thankful that God led me here. He knew exactly what I needed all along.

Pookie snuggles with me as I sit on the couch waiting for Shep to come pick me up. She has grown so much since I first brought her home. My hand glides over the top of her head as her purring gets louder. What a comfort she has been to me over the past few months.

The framed photograph of Macee, David, Shep, and me at the Glen Rose football game sits on top of the buffet under my television. What a year this has been. It has not turned out as I thought it would. It has far exceeded my expectations.

Nothing has been further from my initial assumptions than my recent feelings for Shep. He has patiently waited in the friend zone I had slammed him into those first couple of months. He has withstood all the boundaries, conditions, and situations that I have made him endure. I can confidently say that he has become one of the best friends I have ever had. And lately, my feelings for him have grown even more so.

Glass is such an appropriate name for this town to me. I understand it is named after the family that initially settled in this area; however, it has been a significant name for another reason.

We watched a video one year in science class about how glass is made. They mix sand with other raw materials, bringing the mixture to an extremely high temperature that melts all the ingredients, changing the molecular structure that eventually results in transparency. It then goes through a long cooling process and can be shaped during this time.

Thinking back over my life to my hard times, the high temperatures of my life, I recall disappointments, betrayals, frightening moments, and times I felt out of control. Each of those times, I came out a different person. Sometimes I came out weaker, and sometimes I came out stronger. I was reshaped in a new way. Similar experiences happen to everyone. Shep's parents dying. Pennie faced the unknown in choosing to keep her pregnancy. Annie's loss of what she thought her future family would be like. Everyone has experienced the high temperatures of life.

If everyone could be as transparent as glass in their own life, how much more grace would they have for each other? How much more would they understand the reasons people are how they are? How much easier would life be if we realized everyone hurts at one time or another?

Pookie's ears perk up as she hears Shep's truck before I do. She follows me into the hall bath to check my reflection. I readjust my face to help cover up some of the giddiness. But the main thing I notice on my face is peace. I'm sure more hard times are to come into my life, but right now, everything is peaceful. Not perfect, just peaceful.

I eagerly walk to the door to greet Shep as he saunters up the sidewalk carrying an enormous bouquet of wildflowers. Earlier he informed me he has a surprise to take me to. He seems to be pretty good at this birthday stuff so far.

We walk towards his barn after having a quick conversation with Grandma Shep. She wished me a happy birthday and made me some of her famous chocolate chip cookies with walnuts.

"So, is the surprise in the barn?"

Shep switches the basket he is carrying from one hand to the other. "Nope, but our transportation is."

"Are we going mudding on your four-wheeler, because I'm not really dressed for it?"

"Relax, Jazz. Do you trust me or not?"

I like the new nickname. "I'm not sure. The jury is still out on that one."

He sets the basket on the back of the four-wheeler and wraps a bungee cord around it. He swings his long leg over the side and scoots forward.

"Let's go, Tiger." He pats the seat behind him.

I sit behind him, wrapping my arms around his waist. I give him a good squeeze for old times' sake. He fake coughs as he takes off, almost throwing me off the back.

Spring is my favorite time of the year. Shep's pastures are greening up. Spots of color are sprinkled throughout as clumps of wildflowers bloom. The trees' branches are filling in with new life and remind me of all the new situations blooming in my life.

My lungs expand as I fill them with the fresh spring air. I close my eyes, tilting my head up, and enjoy the sun on my face. I couldn't have asked for a prettier day.

The ride ends before I am ready. Shep helps me off and grabs the basket.

"I've been working on something for the past month. It's for your birthday, but you can't take it home."

"What kind of present is that? Is this a present for you or for me?"

"You will just have to see."

I follow him along a path that leads beside a creek that runs on the edge of his property. He carries a big stick in case we run into any copperheads, swishing it back and forth when we come to a cluster of twigs or weeds.

He finally stops and turns to me, blocking my view with his large frame. "Close your eyes for just a minute."

I gladly submit, closing my eyes while my smile grows wider. I inhale deeply, filling my lungs with fresh air. Birds sing in the trees next to me as the leaves rustle in the cool breeze. His steps eventually sound closer.

"Open your eyes."

My eyes squint momentarily, readjusting to the rays of light coming in through the trees. My jaw drops at what is before me.

"Oh, Shep, did you build this? It's beautiful!" I walk forward in order to step onto the cedar deck. Two Adirondack chairs sit next to each other, facing the creek with a small table in between them. "Wow, I'm so impressed! Is this the spot you are always talking about?"

I move to the edge of the deck that hangs over the slowly moving creek underneath it. The front edge is lined with baseball-sized river rocks. The back part of the deck meets against a couple of cedar trees.

"This is the spot. I've spent a lot of time right here over the years. Who knows if we would've spent time together here if you had grown up next door?"

"Oh, I definitely would have. It is such a pretty area." I walk back to sit in one chair, and Shep sits in the other.

The creek babbles as the water continually flows from one set of rocks to another. A green leaf slowly spins as it travels downstream and eventually disappears around the curve. I lean my head back to take in the calming sounds. My breathing slows as the sounds carry my thoughts away, just like the leaf.

"I could sit out here every day."

"That could easily be arranged."

I can sense his smile without even looking at him.

"I'm sure you would like that, wouldn't you?" I don't hide the smile forming on my face.

"More than you know."

I sit up and see how serious his face has turned. My thoughts suddenly start sounding alarms in my head. *Am I ready for this? Is this what I want?*

"Jazz, there was something that sparked in me the moment I saw you at the Fourth of July parade. I can't explain it, and I've stopped trying to rationalize it. I've held it off for as long as I can, and I'll force it down for longer if you aren't ready. But, man, it won't go away." His head slowly shakes back and forth. "And then, when it was you that opened the door at the Walsh house the next week …. My insides felt like they were going to explode."

The side of my mouth turns up as I now understand his constant babbling on our first meeting. He was like a wind-up toy. I was so fixated on his lack of proper etiquette at the time that I overlooked all his thoughtful intentions that have endeared him to me ever since.

He stands up and walks to the edge of the deck. Shoving his hands into his pockets, he turns to face me.

"If you want me to stop, tell me now. I'll gladly jump back over to the friend zone." His eyes plead for me to give him direction on which way to go from here.

My life flashes before me. My past. My hopeful future.

This is the fork. This is the fork in the road that comes once or twice in a lifetime. Left or right? The decision at this fork marks the direction of the consequences I will face. Good or bad? Left or right?

"Go on."

His head begins nodding, gearing himself up for the next level of his reasoning.

"I've lost count of how many times I've come to this very spot for discussions with God. I've talked. I've yelled. I've laughed. I've cried. Especially after I lost Mom and Dad. Grandma Shep would let me bring a sleeping bag out here. She would pack some food and water for me. And I always had a walkie-talkie. She made sure she could check on me at any time during the night. She would put extra batteries in a baggie, so I would have no excuse." His eyes drop to the water as his face floods with past memories.

"There was always an underlying plea in all my imploring to God. I needed someone. I knew I had God by my side, and Grandma Shep was always there, but I needed someone. I just always felt like someone was missing. The day I saw you at the parade, the hole in my heart filled up. I couldn't even explain it. I didn't understand. All I knew was that I felt like God had finally answered my prayers and sent you to me." He reaches up to swipe at his eyes, never taking them off me.

"I'm scared to death right now because I don't know if you are going to run away screaming or if you can understand what I'm trying to explain." His eyes widen as his jaw grinds back and forth.

Left or right? Which direction do I take? Which way is good for me? I give him a slight nod to continue.

"You were born to be by my side. I believe that with everything that I am. God knew I needed you, and He made sure you ended up here in Glass. I realize I'm coming on really strong right now, but I have waited for you all my life. I have prayed for you at this very spot for years. This is where I allowed myself to wonder about you. All before you ever walked into my life. Something was always missing. I knew you existed somewhere."

He stops for a minute to catch his breath. He holds his arms out, alluding to the surrounding area. "This is why I built this deck. For you. It's always been about you."

My eyes well up and spill over the edges. *This direction. This is where I want to go. This is the direction I have been fighting against since I moved here. What more do I need him to prove to me? I want someone transparent. It doesn't get much more transparent than this proclamation.*

When I was truthful with him about my past, he still accepted me. He cried with me over the loss of my baby and comforted me over my guilt of Ted's death. That was so healing for me to feel accepted, just as I am.

I stand up and walk to meet him face to face. He reaches down and gently takes hold of my hands. My head tilts up towards him as the breath I've been holding escapes from my lungs. He lifts his hand and rubs his thumb along the side of my cheek, wiping away my tear. His hand slides to the back of my neck as his head leans down towards mine, brushing my lips ever so lightly.

When he pulls away, his face lights up as relief fills the crinkles in the corners of his eyes. He steps back and pulls something out of his pocket.

"I have something else for your birthday. I wasn't sure if I was going to give it to you, but I believe now would be a good time."

"Oh, you weren't going to give me my present?" My hand goes to my necklace. I'm feeling more confident that this is the direction that I need to go.

"Well, it's not a new present. I actually picked it out eleven years ago when I was here by the creek in one of my discussions with God. I've carried it around for years to represent the belief that He had someone special for me that would show up one day in my life." He opens his fist to show me what is inside.

A heart-shaped rock lies in his palm. I reach in to grab it, and he closes his fist over it.

"Even though this heart is rock solid, it will break very easily. Will you take good care of it?" His eyes tell me more than he realizes.

My heart feels more at home than it has ever felt before. I belong here. Ryan far exceeds any perfect expectations I thought I wanted in my life. God knows exactly who I need, and he is standing before me, welcoming me home. I have found more than what I came looking for in Glass, Texas, and it couldn't be more perfect.

A smile spreads across his face as this time I am the one who pulls his head down for another perfect kiss.

47 Summer

April 23
Present Day

My finger slides over my mouth, wiping away the excess lip gloss that has smeared past the outline of my lips. I take a moment to evaluate my reflection in the mirror. Her eyes appear dreamy, almost dancing as she looks back at me. Tiny crinkles form at the outer edges, showing genuine happiness. With a fresh glow, her soft skin resembles that of a lovesick teenager. My eyes glide down to her mouth. A smile beams back at me. I take in this new version of myself.

Gone are the layers of guilt.

Gone are the layers of expectations.

Gone are the layers of invisibility.

"Welcome back," I say, giving my reflection a wink. I turn to grab my tennis shoes out of the closet because Ryan will be here soon.

My head is reeling with all that has happened in the past few months. Ryan and I had several talks with one another and then with Mom. She agreed we were better together and couldn't imagine it any other way. She told Ryan that she and his mom used to watch us play when we were younger and dream about the day that we would realize we were meant to be together. Mom was so relieved the day was finally here.

It was a little awkward at first, but we finally found our rhythm again. I've never been so happy. I remember the day we spent fishing with my dad just a week before his accident. I'm grateful for his advice that day. Ryan always makes me feel like I am his number one priority. I will never be invisible again, whether it be by my choosing or someone else's.

A knock causes me to move a little faster. Running to answer it, I throw open the door and see a huge wildflower bouquet instead of a head.

"Ryan, those are beautiful!" Shifting them to the side, he meets my gaze with those enchanting blue eyes that I have always enjoyed getting lost in.

"Happy birthday, Summer Bummer!" He pulls me in for a kiss, and I place my palm on his chest to push him away.

"You really have to come up with a new nickname for me." I tilt my head to the side, challenging him to defy the birthday girl's wishes.

He pulls me in even closer. Our lips are so near that I can sense his minty breath bouncing off my lip gloss. His lips graze over mine ever so softly, and my knees go weak.

"Okay, you can call me whatever you want as long as you always kiss me like that." I return the kiss as he pulls me in tighter.

Suddenly, his lips break free from mine, and he slides past me. "Let's put these in some water so that we can go. We've got some birthday celebrating to do."

"You still haven't told me what we are doing." I grab a large vase from under the sink and fill it with water. The scent of the flowers has already filled the room.

"Don't worry your pretty little head about it. You know I will always take care of you, right?" He takes the vase from me and sets it in the middle of the table.

I slug him in the arm like I've done for two decades now. "You'd better, because you are stuck with me now." He pulls me in for another quick kiss.

"Let's go. We've got places to go and things to do." We head outside, and he steps in front of me to open the passenger door. "No peeking in the backseat," he warns as he shuts the door, watching me to make sure I oblige.

I quickly glance towards the back and notice a blanket covering whatever it is he is hiding back there.

"I knew you couldn't resist, so I took precautions." He laughs at my disappointed glance and shrugs his shoulders as he slides into the seat, shutting his door. "You will just have to wait and see."

We head up the highway towards Glen Rose. "Are you taking me to eat at Riverhouse Grill? We might make it if we hurry." I glance at my watch and see that my favorite restaurant's lunch hours close in forty-five minutes. "You should have picked me up a little earlier."

Ryan continues to smile without saying a word as he drives us toward our destination. I sit back, knowing full well that he won't budge on telling me where we are going.

As we pass over the Paluxy River and are about to enter the town of Glen Rose, Ryan turns on his left blinker. My mind wanders over the possibilities of where our destination is. I sit silently as we drive along the curves leading us away from Glen Rose. The cedar trees melt into each other as we speed down the highway. My body finds the familiar curves of the road relaxing, as I have traveled it many times in the past. After a few minutes, Dinosaur World comes into view. This is the spot where we not only had birthday parties but also worked together during a couple of summers in high school.

This will be fun. He told me to wear tennis shoes. It must be because of all the walking we will do around the grounds.

"Dinosaur World! I'm so excited!" I look at Ryan as he continues to stare out the windshield, and then passes the parking lot with a smirk on his face.

I huff and lean my head back against the headrest. *Where is he taking me?*

Not too much further up the road, I lean forward to get a better view of what is coming up. Dinosaur Valley State Park.

"Are we going camping? I didn't bring any clothes or food or…" Ryan smiles and shoots a look at me with raised eyebrows. Getting the message, I withhold my excitement and lean back once more on the headrest, eager to discover what he has in store.

After paying our way into the park, we drive past the large dinosaur sculptures and wind our way around the road. I sit in silence, taking it all in. Memories flood over me as I always loved coming here as a child, whether it was with my family or on a school field trip. I reach over towards Ryan, and he puts his hand out to hold mine. The trees are budding, and there are green patches of grass along the way, signaling that the darkness of winter is over and new things are coming.

We drive through the camping area, past a few campsites. Ryan pulls into one, and I notice a tablecloth spread out over the picnic table.

"I don't think we can park here. It looks like someone is already at this spot."

Ryan looks at me once again with raised eyebrows and opens his truck door. He jogs around the front of the truck to let me out, like the gentleman that he is. That always makes me feel incredibly valued by him. After grabbing the secret items from the back seat, he turns to go past me.

I wait by the side of the truck while he walks to the table to set down the bags. Once he returns, he grabs my hand and leads me back towards the road. I start to ask him if we could go the other way and head towards the river but remember that I am trying hard to work on trusting him to lead me. The crunching gravel underneath my feet reminds me of our racing bicycles through the campground, what seems to be a lifetime ago.

We stop at the wooden post at the front of the campsite as he turns to face me. Reaching into his pocket, he pulls out his old iPod with the earbuds attached to it. Memories of the night that we practiced how to dance here at the park come rushing back. As one specific memory comes to mind, I turn to the wooden post and reach out my hand to trace my fingers along the number seven.

"This was the exact spot that I knew I was in love with you. You have always been a part of everything that I have accomplished in my life." He placed one earbud in his ear and the other gently in my ear. Keith Urban's "Kiss A Girl" came on.

"I remember…." His finger raises to my lips to shush me. He places my hands on his shoulders and rests his hands on my hips while we sway back and forth for a few beats. Both of us are much more confident in our dance moves than we were way back then.

I close my eyes and lay my head on his chest. My favorite spot. His heart beats against my cheek. This heart that has always loved me. My sunny side and my dark side. The only time he wasn't there for me was when he thought I was happier without him.

I offer a silent prayer to God, thanking Him for guiding me back to where I should be. Ryan hugs me tight as we gently sway together for the entire song.

Once the song is over, Ryan places his finger under my chin and gently raises it towards him. He tilts his head down to meet mine, and our lips touch. He pulls away and gently places his finger near my lips to remind me to stay silent. Placing my arm through his, he leads me back towards the picnic table.

I have a hard time slowing down my breathing. My insides are turning, and a lump forms in my throat. The last time I was this happy with Ryan, my brother died. When I was happy with Chad, my dad died. Maybe this isn't a good thing. My mom and brother are all I have left. What if my happiness causes something bad to happen to one of them, too?

Pastor Alan's words from his sermon a couple of weeks ago come to mind. He cautioned against viewing life solely through the layers of our past hurts. God doesn't cause hurt in our life but can use it to help restore us to Him if we allow Him to do so.

Past sorrows run quickly through my mind like a movie on fast forward. I can also see how each one allowed me to grow into the woman that I am today. God never promised us a life without trials. But He did promise that He will sit with us in our pain and wait patiently for us. He will never leave us.

I pull Ry a little tighter to my side. He looks down at me, and I can sense the tenderness in his eyes. I've never felt as seen as I do with him by my side.

We reach the table, and I notice Ryan has placed rocks in the middle of the tablecloth to hold it secure from the wind. On closer examination, I notice the rocks are placed so that they form a heart. A closer look reveals that each rock is heart-shaped, like the one in my kitchen window.

"There are eleven of them. Eleven years ago, I handed you the first heart-shaped rock at our creek, confessing my wish never to be without you. It's always been about you, Summer. I've collected one heart rock a year, reminding myself of our conversation. I thought it would only be appropriate that I included these for today."

He reaches into his pocket and pulls out one more rock. I recognize it right away. It's the heart-shaped rock from my kitchen window. The rock that I rub seven times. Seven because that's how old I was when I met Ryan. Seven, because that marks the campsite number where we first danced. Seven. It's always been all about Ryan.

He places my rock directly in the middle of the large heart shape on the table.

"You have always belonged here and always will. Right in the middle of my existence. I am so thankful to have you in all my life memories. I never want to be without you by my side. In the week before your dad's accident, he asked me to always watch over you, and I promised him I would."

Ryan reaches into his other pants pocket and pulls out what must be another rock. It's just one of a different kind.

He goes down on one knee and places the tiny box in his outstretched hand. My hands go to my mouth, not believing what is happening before my eyes.

"Summer Dawn, will you marry me?" A glimpse of fear quickly passes over his face, as though I might say no.

My feet move with excitement, jogging in place, while my hands flap up and down. "Yes! Yes! Yes!" I turn in circles, unable to contain my excitement at this moment that I once thought was lost forever.

Ryan stands to his feet and grabs my hand to force me to be momentarily still. He lets out a laugh as he places the stunning ring on my finger. I immediately hold it up to admire it. Slowly waving my hand back and forth, I allow the sun to glisten off the solitaire diamond. I never expected this today on my birthday. I look at Ryan, and his face is beaming. God knew I needed to lose Ryan temporarily to make me realize how much I truly wanted him in my life.

I hear a gasp behind me and turn around. Mom, Clay, and Grandma Shep step out from behind the trees. Mom wipes tears away from her face while Grandma Shep continually claps her hands. I run to show off the ring, and Clay steps up to Ryan to shake his hand and pat him on the back. Ryan pulls him into a hug.

Mom holds me tight with tears running down her face. She pulls back and places her hands on both sides of my cheeks.

"Summer Dawn, what a privilege it has been to have you in my life and watch you grow into the beautiful young woman God has made you to be. I am so excited to witness this next chapter for you."

I pull her in for another hug. "Me too, Momma. Me too."

Once we all have time to compose ourselves and let the new reality set in, Ryan guides us back to the picnic table. He reaches into the bag and pulls out a box of doughnuts.

"One of my favorite things I always looked forward to when we were younger was eating doughnuts with you every Friday morning before school. Returning to school this year and having you down the hall in the cafeteria has been a dream come true. I have loved being able to bring you one each week. This occasion wouldn't be the same without some doughnuts to celebrate."

He pointed to the box, showing me I needed to open it. A monarch butterfly hovered over the nearby rocks laid out on the table. A memory of the promise I made to Dad the week before he died settles in my mind. Dad would be so proud of the choice I have made.

I raised the box lid and found seven doughnuts inside. Each one shaped into letters of the alphabet that spell "Marry Me." Mom and Grandma Shep murmur in approval of the thoughtful sentiment.

I grab a doughnut and step closer to Ryan. I gaze up at his smiling face before taking a big bite from the bottom of the M.

"It's about time!" I slug him in his arm for old time's sake. This arm that will forever hold me close. This arm that will protect me. This arm that will make sure I will never feel invisible again.

48 Third Option

April 23rd
Present Day

Epilogue Annie

April 23rd
Present Day

The date I've been dreading for months has finally arrived. For every single year for the past twenty-eight years, this date throws me into a funk that I just can't shake. What would my life be like if I would've made a different decision? I had three choices before me at the time I got pregnant: adoption, keep the baby, or terminate the pregnancy.

My intuition tells me it would've been a baby girl. I could've even chosen to give her up for adoption. She may have been the answer to someone's prayer for their family to be complete. She could have been raised by a great family and made a difference in this world.

Or what if I had told Hawk that I was pregnant, and we had gotten married and kept the baby to raise? Life probably would have been tough. But we would have made it work. I know we would've been better parents than what was modeled for me. And I'm sure we would've had more kids. I wonder if she would've had my eyes or Hawk's eyes? Or maybe my brother's dimples? Would she have loved chocolate chip cookie dough and gagged on pickles like I do?

But I chose the third option. She never existed. Just like blank chapters in a book, there are no stories to tell about her life. No memories to dwell on. No impact on the world around her.

I subconsciously twirl my hair at the base of my neck and wiggle uncomfortably in the overstuffed chair. My arm causes the leather to make a squeaking noise, breaking the deafening silence of the room. My counselor just stares at me, waiting patiently for me to answer her question.

"Annie, are you sure you want to be here today?"

Nodding my head, I'm still unable to produce any words.

"After months of dedicated work, today is finally here, and you've done an amazing job getting ready."

I drop my head as it bobs up and down in agreement. Closing my eyes, I inhale deeply, counting to four. I hold my breath, counting to four and then slowly exhale, counting to four.

"Box breathing is a great tool to use for your anxiety. Do you use it often?" I open my eyes to seek reassurance and strength from this kind soul that I have spent multiple hours with over the past few months.

"I've used it more and more lately, as this date has been creeping up." I close my eyes and start the breathing technique again.

I open my eyes when I am more in control of my body, and Carole, my counselor, waits patiently for me to face the conversation that is looming.

"Take your time. I've blocked off a couple of hours for you, so don't feel rushed. Did you remember to bring the photograph?"

I reach down to my bag and pull the photograph out of the side pocket. This is just the beginning of many tears I'm sure to shed. I feel a mix of emotions looking at the little girl smiling in the back of the red pickup. It is the picture that I always go to, wondering what my baby would've looked like.

I hand Carole the photograph and intentionally stop my hand from darting for the back of my neck again. Instead, I grab the sequined pillow next to me and hug it tight. My hand rubs the sequins one way and then the other in a slow rhythm. She calls it her calming pillow. It doesn't seem to work because I am so nervous about what questions she will probe me with.

Carole smiles at the photograph in her hand. "You sure were a cutie. What happened?"

A sudden laugh burst out of my mouth. I appreciate her attempt to lighten the mood before she digs into my soul a little more.

"So, today would've been the due date if you had kept the pregnancy?"

I nod my head as the tears begin to flow. I try to start my breathing technique again, but it's hard to hold back sobs at the same time.

Carole hands the picture back, and I hold it to my chest. Even though it is me in the picture, I've pretended it was my daughter for years.

"Summer. I always thought Summer would be a great name for her because that was when she was conceived." My fingers caress the face in the photograph. "That was the best summer of my life."

The fingers on my other hand trace over the butterfly locket necklace from Hawk. I thought it was appropriate for me to wear it today. Earlier, I stopped by the wildflower patch by the Paluxy River to watch the butterflies. This is the spot where I go to talk to Summer when I miss her. I visit her every year there on what would have been her birthday.

"I want to schedule an appointment with you with Devin Hawksley's one-year death date coming up soon. I understand it's been difficult for you not being able to talk to him about this since you began working with me, since he died in that car wreck." Carole makes a quick note in her notebook.

Probably scheduling my next breakdown.

"Yeah, I had so many things that I wanted to say to him about our past. Hawk never even knew that I was pregnant. He would've been a great dad, too. I know it would've been so hard with me being a junior and him a senior, but we could've made it work. I never even allowed us to have that chance. As soon as I found out I was pregnant, I freaked out and stopped talking to him. He never even knew what could have been." I have a hard time catching my breath.

"Let's talk about that. What could have been. Let's get to the point of what haunts you about this day." I notice Carole gripping her pen, getting ready to write in her little notebook.

Does each of her clients have his or her own notebook? Does she color-code them depending on the degree of help that each client needs? Green is easy-going conversation. Yellow means watch out. Red is no hope. What color would my notebook cover be?

I look at her, knowing it is my choice to delve into this or not. Just like I made it my choice to do what I did years ago. This skeleton that I have worked so hard to shove deep down within the depths of me won't stay buried anymore. It breaks out of its box and climbs to the top of my regret pile every year around this time. And lately it has refused to climb back into its hiding spot.

"I guess besides the surface thinking of what her physical characteristics would have been, I wonder what impact she would have made on others? What would she have been when she got older? Would she have been a teacher like me?" My eyes dart around the ceiling as I ponder all the endless possibilities. "There is a young man who is an assistant football coach at the high school who is still single. He grew up next to my grandpa's farm. Would they have grown up as best friends? Maybe they were meant for each other? Would she have made me a grandma?"

My throat catches at this last confession. I could never have kids after the abortion, so I will never have the privilege of being a mother or grandmother of someone that carries my DNA. That fact has ruined more than a few potential relationships.

"I also think about what her life would've been like if I had gone through with the pregnancy and given her up for adoption. She could have completed someone else's family whose arms ached for a child to hold. I found out a few years ago that a co-worker is adopted. She said that she's always been grateful to her birth mom for giving her a chance at life. That's when I really started to regret what I had done. I hadn't really thought about the potential life that my baby could have had. This co-worker is one of the best people I have ever known in my life. I couldn't imagine this world without her and the impact she has on everyone around her. What did I deprive the world of by not letting my baby live?" The sobs can't be held back anymore. Carole hands me a box of tissues that is never too far away.

She lets me cry for a couple of minutes as I let years of regret and anger and hurt pour out of my eyes. My grandfather's wisdom about how one choice can dramatically alter one's life continues to haunt me. I eventually slow my sobs and use the tissues to wipe away years of hidden regrets.

I glance up and see Carole looking at me. But she doesn't look judgmental or shocked at this display of years of unforgiveness of myself. She looks at me with compassion. She looks at me with patience. She looks at me almost as if she understands.

"I know I'm not really supposed to talk about myself in these sessions, but I'm going to make an exception this time if it's okay with you."

I slowly nod my head, not having a clue what she would have to say that would relate to my blubbering.

"I also had an abortion. I was twenty-three and in a terrible marriage. I had already decided that I was going to leave him after he sent me to the hospital with a couple of broken ribs. I found out during that hospital visit that I was six weeks pregnant. I knew that there would be no way that I could cut all ties with him if there was a baby involved. Roe vs Wade had just made abortion laws to be unconstitutional a couple of years before, so I could take care of it easily without him ever knowing it." Carole now shifts in her chair, looking as uncomfortable as I felt at the beginning of our session.

"I did the best that I felt like I could do at the time that I was forced to make a decision. If the same scenario were to happen today with the wisdom I have, my decision would be much different." She paused with a slight smile. "And it would totally be a miracle, given my age and all." She flips her palms toward the ceiling, and I laugh at her attempt once again to lighten the mood.

"Seriously though," her face begins to exude the compassion that it contained earlier. "Sometimes, in order to forgive ourselves, we have to give ourselves grace to realize the person who we are today is not the person we were at the time of our past regrets. We have grown. We have learned things. We expect more from ourselves. But we are not the same person who we were back then. I can speak only for myself in my situation. I was a broken person who was in a desperate situation. I couldn't think past the current state I was in, and I saw no other way out. I now know that I could have had other options, but at the time, I didn't know any better.

Instead of being so hard on ourselves for things we regret in the past, we need to have compassion for the person we were at the time and be thankful for the person who we have grown into. Remember, don't judge yesterday's decisions by today's wisdom."

I began to understand what she was saying.

Carole continues, "That experience led me to seek counseling and eventually become a counselor to help others who need healing of some kind. God is so good at using the bad experiences in our lives to create pathways that lead to good happenings that align with His will if we allow Him to do so."

I know Carole well enough that when she pauses like she is right now, she's really wanting me to soak in what she just said. I let it seep into my skeleton pile.

"You've told me about how neglectful your parents were to you and your brothers because of your mom's depression issues that you learned about after you moved out. I've heard you say that you felt you were like a parent to your brothers. That just tells me that you felt like you had no support that you could see."

Carole gives me time to let that also sink in. "I'm definitely not trying to make up excuses for you, but these are the facts of your situation, correct?"

My head bobs in agreement. Flashes of my mom convincing me not to ruin my life with a baby still haunt me. She was pregnant as a teenager with me and berated me with that fact for as long as I could remember. She blamed me for being stuck in her depressed life. At one time, she hoped to escape the small town of Glass and never turn back. She always let me know that I was the heavy chain that held her down. I never wanted my child to feel any resentment from me, so I made the choice that I did.

Today, I am almost able to separate myself as I am now from the scared teenager that I was back then lying on the cold metal table. I begin to feel sorry for her.

What if she could have seen past the momentary fear?

What if she had known more about God and His grace?

What if she had felt like she had more than one choice?

"Tell me what you are thinking." Carole tilts her head in anticipation of my response.

My eyes shift above her head to the canvas frame on the wall. A beautiful blue butterfly is resting on top of tiny pink flowers. My eyes scan the verse printed on the picture. Ecclesiastes 3:11. One that I have now memorized and even tattooed its reference on my wrist to remind me of its promise. "'He has made everything beautiful in its time.' You know what word really sticks out to me in that Bible verse?"

The lady who has been my guide, friend, and disciplinarian all in one for the past few months gently raises the side of her mouth into a half smile. "What word would that be?"

"Its. Such a tiny little word, but it carries so much weight and lifts the burden off my shoulders. 'Its time', not my time. Not when I believe everything should be okay, but the situation's timing." I readjust in the chair and pull my leg under myself to sit a little taller.

I feel a rush of hope with this brand-new epiphany. "God will make everything beautiful in the correct time for the situation. I just need to sit back, trust God, and wait to see how He will make each situation beautiful. I understand I must be an active participant to see it, but I also know that when I learn to fight off my anxiety and respond how I know God wants me to respond, that allows Him to work all the puzzle pieces I have created for myself, or sometimes despite myself, into something beautiful."

My eyes grow wider as my future self becomes clearer, and I start covering my old self with some grace. "That's what I need to focus on. Not feeling sorry for myself. Not hating myself for my past decisions. Not hiding out in my house from reality, but putting all the things I have learned from our sessions, my pastor, my Christian friends, my Bible studies, and even just sitting and talking to God, putting all those new bits of knowledge together. I need to forgive that scared girl who walked out of that clinic with her head hung low and see what God can do with that puzzle piece. It doesn't need to be my responsibility to hold on to it anymore. That's what Pastor Alan was getting at this past Sunday when he said something about directions and sins and dust. What was that verse he used?" My eyes dart down, trying to dig the memory back up out of the back part of my brain.

"'As far as the east is from the west, so far has He removed our transgressions from us. As a father has compassion for his children, so the Lord has compassion on those who fear Him. For He knows our frame; He remembers that we are dust.' Psalm 103:12-14. One of my all-time favorites." Carole spouts out the verse like she really can see into my head.

"Yes! That's it! Remembering that He has compassion for us like a parent does a child is sort of hard for me to understand since I have no kids of my own, but I have a dog that I love so much! Sometimes when I get home from school, he has gotten into the trash, and it is everywhere. I just have to remind myself that he is a dog and does the best he can. I love him so much and would do anything for him." *Maybe I should stop and get him a special treat from the butcher shop on the way home today.*

"And what about your kids at school? From what I hear around town, your students and their parents adore you. I've heard some say that third grade was their favorite year because of you," Carole raises her eyebrows in this new connection that I feel coming on. "When your kids in your class do something that they know is outright wrong, how do you feel about that?"

Rowdy from this past school year comes to mind. Man, his parents named him appropriately. He definitely kept me on my toes day to day. I treasured the quiet days when his family was out of town for a week before Christmas break, but I sure loved that kid. I understood that his choices were determined by his mood for the day and whether or not he took his medicine in the morning.

I can relate because I've noticed lately that if I don't get my God time in the mornings to help set my mood, I don't make the best decisions that day either.

"That makes sense. Sure, my plans might be momentarily disrupted, but I take care of the issue and get right back on track. I don't dwell on it. There are too many other things to do and focus on."

"I don't think I could've said it better myself. Do you remind them about what they did every day, or do you just move on with your life?" Her eyebrows raise up again.

My head nods again, letting her know I understand the crossover of the idea. I'm not sure if it is in agreement or in defeat of accepting this new outlook. My sins were long ago forgiven when I asked Him for the first time. I need to move on with my life and stop picking them back up.

I can almost feel my puzzle pieces shifting closer together.

"I'm so proud of you, Annie. You have worked so hard these past few months. Working through forgiving your mom and dad a couple of months ago for what they were incapable of giving you what you needed when you were younger. And this breakthrough just now. I can almost see a twinkle in your eye." Carole beams at me like I never saw my mom do when I was younger. "Have you ever seen layered glass art?"

I'm taken aback a bit with this unrelated question out of left field. But I know her well enough to know there will be a meaningful connection somewhere. "No, I don't think I've ever heard of that before."

"It is some of the most beautiful art pieces that I have ever seen. They can comprise anywhere from two painted layers to hundreds of layers of plate glass. When you look at it straight on, you get the basic concept of what the picture is. However, if you were to move it from side to side while keeping your eyes on the same spot, additional details would pop into view that weren't visible before. Each layer adds to the depth and complexity of the entire picture. If you were to slide a layer out and look at it on its own, it would be flat and not hold a lot of meaning."

She tilts her head, and her eyes squint ever so slightly. "Each layer is an integral part of the picture. You can begin to really understand how the entire picture is created through its multiple layers. They are really quite fascinating."

Carole shifts in her chair, and her face contorts while she digs up some deeper thoughts. "I truly believe that layered art describes us as a human species perfectly."

"How is that? Because we break so easily, and it's hard to put us back together?" She smiles at my quick wit.

"Good one!" She quickly jumps up to retrieve a framed picture from a small easel on her desk.

"I purchased this one as a visual reminder that all of my clients that come in to visit with me have multiple layers." She hands me the framed glass picture.

It's much heavier than I expected from looking at its small size. It takes both hands to keep it from falling to the floor and crashing. Looking straight at it, I notice it is composed of wildflowers and a couple of butterflies fluttering around some petals. It makes me think of Summer and the wildflower patch.

"Slowly move the frame side to side and tilt it up and down," she instructs. I do as I'm told and notice the details put into some of the back layers of glass. Without some of those layers, one wouldn't even realize it was a butterfly. By itself, it just looks like a blob of yellow paint. The thought and planning that had to go into such a creation is amazing. How each blob comes together with another blob to create a work of art.

"Wow... This is remarkable..." I slowly continue to explore the hidden layers that add so much depth to the picture. A tilt produces a bee in the background that I hadn't noticed before. "And, just exactly how does this relate to humans in your world?"

"We are each like a layered glass art masterpiece. Some of our layers are created by our free will; some layers are created by our situations; some layers are forced upon us by others' free will. But the beautiful part of it all is how God can organize the different layers to create His unique masterpiece. He is in control of how our layers work together to create what His perfect will is for our lives if we allow Him to do so. And, in doing so, creates a one-of-a-kind testament to the rest of the world that no matter what happens in our life, no matter what good or bad choices we make or are made for us or against us, God is in control of the final outcome of all our layers." Carole moves to the edge of her seat.

"We don't come into this world as a blank slate. We come into this world with our first layer being decisions that our parents have made for us, and it starts from there. We start with layers of being loved or being seen as an inconvenience. We may have certain layers forced upon us, but it is our choice how we respond to each of them and how we incorporate them into the bigger picture of our life."

Carole sits back in her chair with a slow sigh. "We should learn how to love our layers. They are what makes us who we are today." With her last statement, she seems to relax, almost as if she has been holding that in and just waiting for the perfect time to enlighten me with her revelation.

Love my layers? Maybe she's right. My life, like so many others that I can think of, is composed of many layers. Wouldn't we all understand each other so much better if we were transparent enough to see each other's layers? We could better understand why each of us acts or reacts the way that we do. Even if some of us have similar layers, we each face crossroads to choose how to incorporate those layers differently.

Maybe I find myself at another crossroads in my life right now. Or perhaps I've just been stuck on this one layer for almost three decades. I believe it's time to take this fork in the road and add an additional layer to my life. One where I can finally lay the burden of my past decisions down at the cross of my Jesus Christ and go wherever he leads me.

I give Carole a hug, thanking her once again for helping me as I process all the layers in my life.

My old red chevy truck is my ride of choice for the day. At one point in my life, I thought this truck would take me away from here. But now I realize I've been driving in circles around this issue for my whole life.

Placing the photograph back in its original resting place on the dash, my fingers gently slide over the face of the little girl in the photo. Even though she wouldn't agree with some decisions I have made in my life, her innocent heart would understand that I did the best I could with each layer that came my way.

Without a doubt, I know my child is in heaven. In my mind, she is about four years old and dances in a wildflower patch, chasing the butterflies with all the other little ones whose lives were cut short either by someone's choice, health complications, or abuse. I know my grandfather is there with her, collecting all the wildflowers that she brings and has wide open arms for a ready hug. I am confident I will see her beautiful face one day.

My eyes seek their reflection in the rearview mirror. I can see the hurts and regrets that have shaped me into who I am today. But as I examine even closer, I also see the softness of God's mercy and grace seeping into those painful memories. If God will forgive me, then who am I to hold grudges against myself?

I slowly nod at my reflection as I realize it's time for a new layer in my life. I place the gearshift into drive, just like I used to as a little girl. What a full circle I have come to today.

I honk the horn as I pull into Liza's driveway. She wants to treat me to a burger and cherry vanilla Dr. Pepper at Rick's Drive-In like we used to when we were younger.

Memories come flooding back of the afternoon I pulled in to get her so many years ago. The choices I made that night and in the following months changed my life forever.

I was forced to grow up too fast by the outcomes of my own choices.

My choices created layers that affected me in ways I didn't understand until recently.

These layers can be healed with understanding and applying God's grace.

Liza walks down the driveway carrying a bouquet of wildflowers from her daughter's new flower shop. Her blonde bobbed hair now sports a hint of gray. She still has the same charismatic smile with the sweetest personality to match, despite all that life has thrown at her and her family through the years.

The past twenty-eight years flash through my mind. So many layers have made me who I am today. Happy layers. Painful layers. Sweet layers. Hurtful layers. Where do I choose to go from here?

Grandpa was correct. Choices can either be easy or choices can be worth it. Resenting my layers would be easy. Choosing to love my layers would be worth it.

Starting today, I choose to love my layers.

I will love them because I am worth it.

Reflection Questions

1. Which storyline was your favorite? Jasmine or Summer? Why?

2. Jasmine, Summer, and Annie each sat at a fork in the road, realizing their decisions would affect the rest of their lives. What forks in the road have you dealt with, past or present?

3. This book is not written to question our past decisions and wonder what would have been, but it is to challenge you to consider what others have been through in their life and what makes them who they are today. How can you apply this thought process in your life to make a difference to those around you?

4. Jasmine saw the world through her layer of perfect expectations that she put on everything due to how she was raised. Summer responded to her world through a layer of responsibility that she had put on herself when she was young and cared for her hurting mother. These layers affected the way they saw themselves and also the way they responded to others and what was happening around them. What layer do you see your happenings through, and what layer would you like to see them through?

5. Several times, Jasmine refers to her mom expecting perfection from everyone around her. Her mom explains her "layered" reason she acted like this in Chapter 37 through her fourth letter. Do you find you expect perfection from yourself or others around you? What caused this layer to develop in your life?

6. In the last chapter we see Annie working on forgiving herself for a past decision. At one point, Carole told her, "Don't judge yesterday's decisions by today's wisdom." Surely, we can all look back and think of some choices we made in the past that we wouldn't make with today's wisdom. Are you also able to look at others with the same grace? Not judging who they are today with decisions they made in the past?

7. On a more lighthearted level, what is a decision you made in the past that makes you shake your head at yourself today? A certain hairstyle? The sweater you wore in your seventh-grade yearbook photo? Riding that roller coaster right after lunch?

8. Summer felt like her younger brother would be alive if she had been at home instead of at college so that she could follow him to the cellar. Annie admitted to Jasmine she felt that if she had given him a duck like he wanted instead of a dog, he would still be alive. Why do we feel like we have so much control over what happens in other people's lives?

9. In Jasmine's story Pennie and Tony marry and move into her father's house. She even names the baby after her father. We don't see a reconciliation as of yet in Summer's story. Think of a time when God used someone to interact in your life to send you down a different path, or maybe a time that you felt like God used you to interact in someone else's life.

10. Several "nuggets" of wisdom were dropped throughout the story. Which one stuck with you? Is it a new layer you can apply in your life?

11. The primary message from this book is to learn how to "Love Your Layers." The layers of your life make you who you are today. Thinking back over the layers in my life, I can see how even the "bad" layers have shaped who I am and have enabled me to be more merciful and compassionate with others. None of us are perfect. We all have been through and will go through hard times in our lives. God never promised a life without trials, but He promises to be with us through them. "For I, the Lord your God, will hold your right hand, saying to you, 'Fear not, I will help you.'" Isaiah 41:13. What layers of your life have made you who you are, and how did you see God with you in each layer? How have these layers shaped who you are today?

Content Warnings

If you or anyone you know is in an **abusive relationship, please reach out to someone. There are people who want to help. *This website has the option to erase its search history of its existence.*
National Domestic Violence Hotline
https://www.thehotline.org/
1-800-799-SAFE (7233)
Text START to 88788

If you find yourself at a place with an **unexpected pregnancy, please consider your choices carefully. Resources are available at
https://unplannedpregnancy.com/
https://optionline.org/ or https://care-net.org/

If you or anyone you know is dealing with the **emotional toll and healing process of a miscarriage, there is help available. One resource available is at https://www.pregnancyloss.org/

The **emotional aftermath of an abortion years later can be hard to deal with for some. If you or anyone you know is having a hard time, there is help available. One resource available is at
https://hurtbyabortion.org/

For I am about to do something new. See, I have already begun!
Do you not see it? I will make a pathway through the
wilderness. I will create rivers in the dry wasteland.
Isaiah 43:19 NLT

Acknowledgements

Thank you above all to my Lord Jesus Christ, who embodies the definition of love, mercy, and grace.

Thank you to my husband, who endlessly encouraged me as I spent hours upon hours "still writing the book." I love you always and forever. 😊

Thank you to my girls, whose excitement and encouragement for me kept me going through those writer's block moments. The suggestions you both made for sections of this book were stupendous! 💕

Thank you to Mom and Dad, whom God blessed me with and who equipped me with so many priceless memories, even the pop-up camper. 😊

Thank you to Dr. Miller and his fabulous staff, who allow God to work through God-given talents and who saved my life. Twice. I'm enjoying my cherry-on-the-top years to the fullest!

Thank you to Rhonda Duffie for meeting with me and teaching me all about the history of Glass, Texas. I asked her to name the mascot for the school, and she instantly suggested the Panthers because of the history of the Panther Cave located in the area. Duffie Park mentioned in the book is also named after her.

Thank you to Steve T for his expertise on the airplane scene.

Thank you to Carole M for her expertise on the counseling session scene and for allowing me to name the counselor after her.

Thank you to Claire Fraise for her encouraging YouTube videos and her individual help! The video explaining your Story Plot Grid made all the difference in keeping my plots and subplots straight! @WritewithClaireFraise

Thank you to Abbie Emmons for her countless videos on writing tips. They helped tremendously! @AbbieEmmons

Thank you to my Book Club ladies for their encouraging words and belief in my vision. Thank you for not laughing me out of the club when I brought up the idea of writing a book! Your constant encouragement and interest fueled me more than you know!

A big thanks to my Alpha Readers: Cathy, Claudia, Kathy, Laurie, Lisa, and Tristyn. Thank you for taking the time to read, giving me your honest feedback, and suggesting changes to help streamline the story. They made a HUGE difference!!!

A big thanks to my Beta Readers: Amber, Becky, Caren, Cricket, Deni, Gayla, Graci, Haylee, Kay, Kendra, Lauren, Naomi, Sara, Tori, and Trendy. Your input and responses helped more than you know!

Thank you for taking so much time to help with editing! Your time and input made such a big difference! Becky, Claudia, Deni, Sara, and Trendy.

Notes About the Origin of the Story

I have never had an abortion, but I have had a miscarriage. I know what it is like to wonder what life would have been like had that baby survived and what difference he or she would have made in the world. These thoughts have intrigued me for decades.

Another thing I have always wondered about is how different my life would have been if my mom or dad had made different decisions early in my life. I feel like I grew up in a Beaver Cleaver family from Mayberry. (Ideal family from a small town for all you young ones actually reading this.) With one or two different choices, my life could have differed totally from what it was. A different hometown.... A different home environment.... These thoughts have also intrigued me for decades.

So, I combined the two ideas. What would have been if...? And the story, Layers, began to live in my head a few years ago.

The rest of the story was created from research, observations, and my imagination.

And above all, lots and lots of prayer.

Transparent Motivations
for the Story

The spiritual warfare roller coaster that I am currently on while trying to wrap up the final details of this book is crippling. I fully understand that this story ends on a very controversial topic. But as a new friend so wisely advised me today, "Everything isn't for everybody."

This book is primarily for those who find themselves with an unintended pregnancy and in a situation where they don't know what to do. As Annie's grandfather says, "Please weigh your options thoughtfully."

This book is for all the babies that weren't aborted. The lives that were spared and given a chance, no matter what the circumstances they were born under, because they were worth it.

Second, this book is for those seeking self-forgiveness and for more than abortion issues. I am so hard on myself for so many things: choices, lack of perfection, stupid decisions, procrastination, and the list could go on and on. I struggle with self-forgiveness. Some say no one needs self-forgiveness, and it is not our place to forgive ourselves. Then what do you do with the shame and guilt? Remember, if God will forgive you, then who are you to hold grudges against yourself? Lay them at the feet of our Savior and move on.

As I stated at the beginning of this book, I have long prayed for the hands holding it, the eyes reading it, and the ears listening to it. I pray this story touches you, whether it be for yourself or for your perception of someone else.

We are all on this journey of life together.
And every layer we learn to love is worth it.

About the Author

I am married to the love of my life, mother of our two beautiful daughters and their wonderful husbands, and Mimi to our special Bugs here and in heaven.

As I look back on the layers of my life, reading was always a favorite pastime. A book was in my hands at all times, whether it was while riding my bicycle on the country roads when I was younger or sitting in the back seat of my parents' car late at night using the headlights behind me to see. The endless possibilities of escaping into many worlds and situations always intrigued me. Now that I am in my retired layer, I have finally found the time to make my dreams of writing my own book come true.

I hope to write stories not just to entertain you but to change you. I pray you can add the needed layers of grace and mercy to your perception of yourself and others around you.

"Now to Him who is able to do exceedingly abundantly above all that we ask or think, according to the power that works in us."
Ephesians 3:20 NKJV

EVERY. SINGLE. TIME.

www.ingramcontent.com/pod-product-compliance
Lightning Source LLC
Chambersburg PA
CBHW051243260626
47162CB00002B/579